Muenchner Kindl

25/9/13

'papers arrived yet
Fawlty?'

Thank you

Barney

The Volga German

by

~~Colin Sloan~~

Colin Sloan

First Published in Great Britain in 2013 by
Resurgam Press
The Lock Keepers House
26 Ballyskeagh Road, Lisburn, BT27 5TE

ISBN 9780956794826

A catalogue record for this book is available from the British Library

Typeset in Adobe Garamond Pro
Cover design © Colin Sloan; layout by Iris Colour, Belfast
Back cover image © Stewart Powell

Printed in Great Britain by
A1 City Print
32 Market Square, Lisburn, BT28 1AG

In memory of Liam Dow

1

Munich
1987

Andreas Mensche carried a tray to his favoured seat with an unspoilt view overlooking the verdigris onion domes that crown the Frauenkirche. He broke the semmel bread, carved up the white sausage and then slowly poured his usual Erdinger yeast beer. It was seven a.m. and his shift as night porter was now behind him. He allowed some crumbs to fall upon the napkin on his lap while adjusting the cross keys motif on his lapel with his left hand before reaching for the tall beer glass with his right. Drinking long and slow, letting the malt assuage his thirst, liquid bread, he thought and nodded with satisfaction into himself. He had just long enough alone to appreciate the view, the intricate pointed masonry of the Gothic hall church, the muted vibrancy of the russet slates plunging ever downward against a beaten copper sunrise. He was tired now, just as everyone else was jettisoning sleep and fuelling themselves for the day ahead. He felt his age and caught his reflection in the window with the oncoming sunlight confirming it. He hadn't noticed the long trestle table fill up as he sat.

The refectory within the Bayerischer Hof Hotel at daybreak. Its denizens and toilers, street sweepers and laundry men, technicians and trainees, all mustering within the womb of the building where shifts began and finished. Breakfast chefs ladling hot dumplings from boiler engine metal urns to ruddy-faced engineers in grime-laden overalls. Moustachioed pastry-chefs rolling out more dough and twining pretzels for the dry-mouthed congregation. The stymied vapours rising to the vaulted ceiling where the sweet air mixed with sauerkraut steam while the heat lamps below radiated the Wiener Schnitzel making everybody equally hungry. It was like this every morning, Andreas could name-count the sotto voce of sleepy-headed chambermaids without once looking up to see their faces. How they gossiped and giggled over the habits and foibles of the guests on their particular floor, their hesitant choices at the breakfast counter holding up the queue while the groundsmen behind them propped themselves against fuming radiators and thawed off the trauma induced by sweeping the kerbsides free from so much overnight snow. The tables heaved with idle chat brought on by the resuscitation of a Bavarian breakfast. His reverie was crudely interrupted by a brogued accent nearby.

'Mister, can I have the salt?'

Andreas looked over to where the voice came from and saw a red-haired man with pale and languid skin reaching a palm as wide as a spade across the table. The man wore the overalls of the kitchen help, freshly starched for the trials of another working week. Andreas lifted the salt and gave it to the man in the overalls.

'Obliged to you,' he responded.

'Bitte schon,' replied Andreas.

'What's the craic with your mits, pal?'

'Wie bitte?' Andreas asked instinctively in German.

'Your hands, did ye get the tips bit off ye or what?'

Andreas was bemused, this dolt didn't even try to speak German and to make matters worse he was asking personal questions in front of everyone at the breakfast table in the refectory of the Bayerischer Hof Hotel. He folded his napkin and rose from the table. The red-haired man looked on as Andreas turned on his heel and walked off.

'Jeez I was only trying to be sociable like.'

Another voice from further down the table responded, 'Some questions shouldn't be asked, even in German'.

The foreigner shrugged and went back to dismantling his large breakfast. A short while later in the hotel foyer, Andreas handed his night keys back to the new shift on the reception desk. Lothar placed them back on the hook and bid him a good sleep. The drum brush rotation of a floor polisher guided Andreas across the pink marble floors of the Palais Montgelas and on through the panelled door at the end of the corridor discreetly marked Staff Only. Directly on his left was the bakery; the sweet smells pervaded the hallway, powdered strudel lulling him, only to be intruded upon by the sudden crashing of pots on the bakery floor. He instinctively went to investigate and was greeted by the red-haired man he had encountered earlier in the refectory.

'I should have known that it could only be you,' Andreas sighed.

'Give me a hand here pal, it's only my third day and I don't want to get the sack already.'

'Frau Radler is the head of your housekeeping department, isn't that so?'

Andreas asked politely.

'Yes, she keeps sending one of her death angels to check on my work every so often.'

'Death angel is a term you should keep to yourself, I'm sure you meant no harm by it but people might interpret it wrongly and take exception to it. You have a lot to learn and I don't just mean German.'

He helped the younger man lift the massive pots back onto the draining board. Each pot must be two-feet in diameter and caked in residual dough and cake resin. Andreas inspected the trolley parked at the end of the counter and noticed that another dozen such pots lay in wait for the big foreigner. He shrugged his shoulders and brushed the traces of baking powder from his uniform.

'Maybe you could teach me German?'

'I don't think so. I don't even know your name.'

'It's Liam, Liam Broy.'

'My name is Andreas, Andreas Mensche.'

Liam placed the Brillo pad he was using on the draining board and reached out a pruned shovel of a hand for Andreas to shake.

'You have enough to get on with here Liam, I will not detain you.'

'Sure thing, but I really didn't mean to embarrass you back then at the breakfast table by the way.'

'I know that Liam and I might tell you about it when the time is right.'

Andreas then backed out through the swing doors of the bakery as yet another trolley of dirty pots was being wheeled in for Liam to confront. The incumbent pastry-chef had a smug look in his eye as he parked the heavy load. Liam shrugged and raised his hands up for close inspection in the natural light pervading above the sink. He had long ago forsaken the gloves that only kept filling up with water, then tearing. His fingers were marbled prunes, coated with fresh callouses from repeated stays under water. The half window was steaming up with condensation but offered him some consolation in an unrestricted view of the Munich rooftops and the snow-coated alps beyond.

Andreas paced out the cobbles along Promenadeplatz, down past the Theatinerkirche and the Feldherrnhalle. Everyone else seemed to be going in the other direction, it was like this every morning, maybe he had just gotten used to it. He put a coin in the slot and lifted a morning paper. Still against the flow, he descended the steps into the U-bahn station, punched in his monthly ticket and continued on until reaching the train platform. The warm rush from the tunnel as his train efficiently approached somehow conjured fumes of drinking chocolate mixed with candyfloss as the rails began to vibrate. The U6 howled its arrival, concentrating the thoughts of everyone gathered on the platform.

Three stops from here to Münchener Freiheit and then a short walk to Virchow Strasse to the apartment he called his own. He was greeted at the doorstep by Bob, the stray cat that everyone fed. Bob was huge and given to farting in stereo. Andreas lifted his requisite litre of milk and the six bottle beer delivery crate that came every other day from the Paulaner brewery. He could just about let himself in and deter Bob's intrusion with his shoe. The curtains were still pulled and he had gotten used to that, especially in winter, when the outlook was bleak anyway. He put the milk in the fridge and placed the beer crate beside the empties, his weight crunching on the unswept linoleum. He sat down in the kitchen space and untied his shoes. His feet ached, they always did, how many miles through all those corridors had he walked? How much longer could he keep doing this? Who cares he thought, I will do this until I drop or they catch me pissing in the soup. He undid his tie and let his jacket hang over the kitchen chair as he made final preparations for the descent into bed. The bible blackness of his bedroom beckoned just beyond, where no natural light was allowed to pervade and remind him of the hour or of his singular lifestyle. Out of that darkness he could just make out the wrinkled prow of an unmade bed, at odds with the uniformity he had so carefully cultivated in the intervening years back in the hotel. He lay there, sleep no closer than his true homeland, the cares of the night closing in around him. The sheets had by now tangled with his continual turning so at last he threw them off before probing on the floor for his slippers. He wrapped on his dressing gown and made his way back into the living room.

Coffee and Brahms German Requiem, track II 'All flesh is as grass'. Yes that would do the trick. This Deutsche Grammophon vinyl long player was scratched with overuse but it was no less thrilling. It began to crackle slowly into life as the needle pursued each groove while he poured into his cup, transporting him back to the village he grew up in before the war changed everything. He sipped slowly and unwrapped a dark chocolate ginger biscuit which melted like a dam in reaction to the starkness of the coffee in his throat. His kitchen space began to resonate with the rising crescendo of choristers' voices. Strekerau had vanished long ago, it still had coordinates on the map if you knew where to look but its location was of no concern to Andreas. Strekerau was part of his makeup, its smell as formative and long-lasting as the smoke houses that once permeated the bends on his native river Volga. It was the benchmark of his own existence, an Atlantis lost in the endless cornfields of the Russian Steppe. Finally he could relent as the music subsided, subduing the caffeine within his heartbeat.

Liam Broy was learning, albeit the hard way. He didn't know the German word for obstinate yet, and never would, he wouldn't think of it as a word to describe himself, but he was in the eyes of Frau Radler at least. He was a 'gast arbeiter', but he was untypical. On his first day at the hotel Liam had managed to break three panes of glass in the windows he was meant to be washing. One may have been pure carelessness, but three! Liam's ready excuses were plausible to Radler's subordinates, who were not a little impressed with his whistling of the choruses along the corridors to many German standards such as Beethoven's Ode to Joy and Mozart's Marriage of Figaro. How they thought could this auslander be so ignorant when he could whistle the finer tunes from a seemingly endless musical repertoire. Radler came down hard on him all the same, changing his shift patterns to agitate him, allocating the most irksome roles imaginable within the hotel. This probably would have succeeded in the resignation she was striving for in a lesser man, but not Liam Broy who was only resigned to himself. His outlook, his reasoning, forever forged and tempered by his experiences in the Irish Army. Radler's petty tactics wouldn't rub off on him or take anything away from his broad north Dublin grin.

Liam was on lates; the kitchens had to be kosher for a Jewish convention booked in later that week so he was charged with cleaning the walk-in revolving ovens with acid and a scraper knife. The acid only took when the ovens were in the process of cooling down and the searing heat formed beads of sweat down Liam's back before he even began. His overalls now clung uncomfortably to his lower back chafing his arse where it met the body-length zipper. He didn't mind wearing the thick rubber gloves provided, as he could see the damage acid could do to any non-metallic surface. On contact, the hobs would spit and sizzle, emitting acrid fumes which turned his stomach as he breathed. He made jagged, stabbing figure eight patterns as he scraped the surfaces, the residue of which he discarded into a bucket. Then they had to be rinsed thoroughly using a length of hose and piping hot water, any grime being washed off the surfaces and down the drain gulleys in the middle of the kitchen floor. Once clean and dry, the ovens would be lined in silver foil to make them kosher. Lastly, the floors were then mopped clean with bleach making them pristine for the Jewish inspectors. It was while mopping the floor of the main kitchen that Liam witnessed a roasted chicken skate across the manicured surface, closely followed by a complete pair of false teeth. Liam knew that curiosity would be the death of him, so he just kept on mopping until he had completed his station. Rinsing out the bucket and stowing the mop, he then washed his hands before going back to retrieve the roast chicken.

Gustav, the head chef, was sitting on the floor nearby. Liam lifted the chicken and saw that it was a salvageable meal and he wrapped it in some of the remaining foil. He then lifted the teeth and offered them to Gustav.

'These your gnashers Da?' he enquired.

'That pastry-chef, he attacked me,' Gustav mumbled the words quietly as he took his teeth and rose to rinse them under the nearby tap.

'That pastry-chef is a wanker, he thinks that hoarding dirty pots for me to clean will get a rise out of me.'

'Then you know what he is like. He has been provoking me, going behind my back, saying things to everyone.'

'I hear nothing pal, did you come to blows then?'

' I confronted him and he smacked my face.'

'Well he is a lot bigger than you, so it wasn't a fair fight. But you stood up to him and that's the main thing, Da.'

Just then Andreas came in with a plate. 'Is everything alright? Gustav, you are a funny colour.'

'I'm fine Andreas, this dishwasher was just calming me down.'

'His name is Liam, am I right?'

'That's me, Liam Broy the Dublin boy!'

'I was looking for something to put in a sandwich, do you have anything?'

Gustav and Liam smiled at each other.

'We have some delightful roast chicken if you would care for any?' asked Liam as he winked to Gustav.

'Stimmt, I mean perfect,' said Andreas.

'Then I will make some sandwiches for us night-owls,' said Gustav as he unwrapped the foil and reached for the catering jar of mayonnaise. He walked over to the fridge and brought out an iceberg lettuce which he threw at Liam.

'I don't want this to come skating across the floor at me,' Liam cried.

Andreas looked puzzled at that remark and began to draw up chairs as Liam started to shred the lettuce while Gustav spread the mayonnaise thickly onto virgin slices of bread. Andreas brewed up some fresh coffee.

'Look at this place,' he said at length, 'Tin foil on every working surface, it's as kosher as anything.'

'You know what the Jewish inspectors are like,' said Gustav.

'Bloody overkill if you ask me,' Liam threw in.

The three men munched down on the bulky sandwiches and quenched any thirst with coffee.

'Did you think on the idea of maybe teaching me a bit of the German Andreas?' asked Liam with a husk of bread in his mouth.

'No, if I'm honest, I didn't give it another thought.'

'I meant it you know, I'd pay you the going rate,' said Liam.

'This chicken is good Gustav,' Andreas said, changing the subject.

'Fair enough, big fella, I can take a hint,' sighed Liam.
Andreas turned to Gustav and asked him in German what had occurred earlier to upset the chef. Liam shrugged at the conversation, he couldn't pick out any words that he could have understood and besides which the Bavarian dialect was as rich as his own Dublin accent. Gustav said that the pastry-chef, who was called Anton, had taken exception to Gustav's criticism of the baked centrepiece for the Jewish conference. It was a one metre high menorah rising out of a cake carved to look like the steps up to the Wailing Wall in Jerusalem. Gustav said it lacked subtlety and Anton rounded on him. Andreas listened quietly, allowing the chef time to dismantle his rage.
Liam gathered up their cups and plates and half filled a basin to wash them. He had served enough time abroad to know by their tone that they weren't discussing him. Why should they for that matter, he was a blow-in, barely a week into the job and not much longer than that if Frau Radler had anything to do with it. He looked up at the wall clock, it was eleven fifteen p.m. and he should have been working down at 'Die alte Bayern Stube', the Old Bavarian kitchen which services the hotel nightclub by now.

This was part of his rota punishment, the kitchen help in the nightclub was the loneliest post, the service staff were all German students intent on gaining the most tips and tended to be that bit more dismissive of a gangling bottle washer who spoke little if any German. Liam paid no heed as he drained half empty Coke bottles down his neck to quench the soaring heat and began to stack the steaming half-track glass conveyer that led to the washer machine. His hands were always wet and pruned with open callouses scraping against the rough hewn fibreglass crates as they emerged from the washer. He had to stack up the dirty crates at one end and feed them through, making sure each glass wasn't upright in its compartment, then rush across the slippery floor imprinting slide marks from his monkey boots to the other end where each emerging crate had to be racked in readiness.
At intervals a stuck-up waitress would push open the service door and Liam could catch a fleeting glimpse of the strobe lit glamour beyond his reach. She would proceed to fill up the champagne buckets from the ice machine that grumbled in the corner, then polish the glasses Liam had left to drain. If he managed to get a smile from one of these waitresses, then it was purely a reflection of their own self-satisfaction. He could pick out a rhythm he recognised, reverberating through paper thin walls, taking comfort in the beat from the dance floor beyond. The yells from revellers sounded the same as any language he might understand. On re-entry she always adjusted her hair in the mirror by the service door, before carrying the sweating champagne bucket on its tray and proceeding back to the bar.

As the night wore on the profusion of different glasses with jettisoned cocktail umbrellas, flat beer and stubbed cigarettes would mount up, along with the half-eaten supper plates and the discarded meal trays brought down from the room service trolleys.

Liam would twist salvageable tobacco from the butts into a plastic pouch in his overalls to roll up later. Last orders at the night club bar were at four a.m. and Liam was still feeding the conveyor washer up to five a.m. and then he had to mop the floor clean of slide marks and detritus when his shift was long over. The fatigue he felt was only trumped and muted by the sight of one of the night orderlies who was bent double in his starched uniform on the bench by the lockers, fasting for some religious festival. Liam nodded at the crumpled figure when he finally looked up. As much as Liam felt sorry for himself, he still had a few grains of solace left for him. He punched his time sheet after his first full week and left by the side entrance of the hotel. The gravitas of his position was not lost on him, certainly not at this early hour but he took comfort that he would rather wash dishes here in central Munich where a backdrop of the baroque lay thick all around him like so much icing from a cake on a satin bed sheet than be back at home with nothing. Home for now was in Dietlinden Strasse, four stops out on the tram. This was the segregated accommodation for the men working at the hotel. Liam shared a room, ten metres by seven with Sacko, a kitchen hand from Senegal. He never got to know his last name, but he did get to know some of the first names of the numerous women Sacko brought back to the room. Their beds touched end to end, so there was little imagination needed as Sacko performed a brief courting ritual followed by intense love play well within earshot of Liam. The groans often blocked out the sound of the cockroaches scuttling along the pipe that connected the sink in the middle of the room. These prostitutes often stroked Liam's arm, plying their trade as they made their way back into the hallway and the communal toilet beyond. As a remedy to this, Liam unfurled a brewhouse banner he had liberated from a beer festival tent and used it as a curtain blind between the two beds.

'Liam, plenty of good loving left in here for you,' said Sacko.

As tired as he was Liam couldn't block out the words. He froze instead.

'I treat you this once Liam, take her after me.'

This treat was called Anna and she had the appetite of a python and the face of a hydra. Liam squirmed under the sheets as he could make out a shadow moving in his direction.

'Don't be shy Irish boy, come out to play,' she said.

It was useless trying to feign sleep and Anna knew it, she sat on the edge of his bed and stroked his outline under the covers. Sacko had his arms behind his head on the adjacent bed in post-coital triumph as he then reached into his leather jacket for his cigarettes. Anna pounced on Liam, pinning him prostrate to the bed with her strong legs. He could smell her now, more than ever, second-hand sex oozing from her every pore, she dangled her tongue in Liam's direction and dropped the strap of her chemise to reveal a large suckled breast in clear view of Liam's face.

'Your move meine liebe,' she whispered dirtily in his ear.

Liam grabbed her breast instinctively and sucked on it as if life itself depended on it. Anna momentarily turned her gaze to Sacko and he nodded approvingly. She moved even closer to Liam, revealing the other breast and he grabbed onto it too for dear life. Sacko blew smoke rings, thinly vibrating ovals which hung in the speckled rays near the only open window as he listened to the moans of the ravaging Liam was receiving across the small room.

All too soon Anna was on tiptoe down the dank hallway that led to the communal toilet, leaving Liam dishevelled and light-headed. There certainly wasn't enough room for regret in that small space and as his mind cleared, he was less inclined to be hard on himself. Sacko was by now sleeping soundly across from him, Liam reached over and stole one of his cigarettes and reflected on his own innate shyness around women. Anna had taught him something today, to enjoy a woman's body when the opportunity arose and not to just wait for love to show up.

The seventh floor of this Rococo hotel was exclusive, given over as it was to pleasure with a deliberate intent to set it apart from any other. Entry to this floor required a pass key to all comers as the hallway contained original paintings of the German School. Pride of place belonged to the 'Alte Fritz' portrait in oils of Frederick the Great by Anton Graff, on loan from the Alte Pinakothek. Sunlight was muted through tinted glass to protect the canvases and the temperature in the panelled corridor was kept at a constant level. Each of the suites that lay off it were theatrically themed. The bravura began with a hot air balloon circumventing the ceiling, rope work tapering down to the basket bed topped with golden sandbags for pillows. The bed measured three metres in diameter at the centre of the suite. The balloon was a rigid crinoline frame covered in blue silk interwoven with golden threads in classical patterns sheltering the surround sound entertainment system and an elevated drinks cabinet. This was the Montgolfier suite, echoing the two brothers seminal achievement in being the first to successfully navigate a hot air balloon over Paris in 1783. This homage would have been lost on them, as difficult to decipher as the journey to the en suite which was fraught with ornamental rigging, grappling hooks and decorative sandbags with gold tassels.

Next door was the Von Richthofen suite. Club chairs studded in baronial red leather rose to the shoulder of any sitter as if to protect them from the elements as they would for any pilot. A propeller table sat squarely over a black deep pile rug shaped in a cruciform. One side of the room was taken up with a tension wired quadruple canvas wing-span that contained the mini bar, clothes press and television set. The ice box was made from an ammunition cannister which in turn sat beside a candle-stick honed from the twin barrels of a mounted machine-gun. The walls were hung with illustrations of Sopwith Camels and Fokker Dr. I triplanes, faded montages of fallen fighter aces reflected optimistically whilst stroking furry mascots before valiantly taking to the skies. Further down the corridor was the Doge's retreat. This Venetian piano nobile had an outer chamber with noteworthy statues such as Blucher and Goethe mounted on plinths with flooring of cool terrazzo. The suite within had hand-painted wainscoting and over the marble mantlepiece at its heart hung a portrait of the young pretender Charles Stewart after the artist Antonio David. The bed was fashioned from a gondola, with a gilded six pronged prow, one for each district of Venice. It was enclosed in a canopy, reputed to have been used by the Emperor Napoleon while on campaign. The wall had a fresco of the quadriga of horses which surmount the duomo in St. Mark's Square.

The last suite in the corridor was a parody of the golden age of ocean travel when the once great liners had plied the waves contesting for the prestigious Blue Riband award for the fastest time across the Atlantic. Any liner worth its salt made strenuous efforts to iron out any hint of the nautical within their ostentatious suites, opting instead for the style of the English country retreat. A fashion that was overlooked in this instance, where portholed and riven-headed bulkheads akin to a nakedly industrial installation sat awkwardly with the aquiline refinement of the art deco of the period, culminating in a bath resembling a lifeboat. A set of teak doors at the end of the corridor heralded the entrance to the hotel's very own opera. Each suite had an opera box exclusive to this floor. The hotel grew up around an existing playhouse which had been added on to and amended as fashions came and went. It was the custom to leave alternating stage lights on long after each performance so as to endear each incumbent play to the resident ghosts within the auditorium.

Andreas kept a pass key to the seventh floor and he routinely patrolled the art laden corridor late at night when the guests were safely ensconced.

He would dim the lights and display the morning papers in each doorway, taking away any shoes that might have been left there to be polished. He gathered up any discarded trays for room service and placed them into the concealed dumb waiter. Lastly he would collect the preference tags from the door knobs for the breakfast shift. Then he could allow himself to dwell on the paintings, the brushwork, their mystique as the depth of the oils on the canvas glistened under the unobtrusive lamp lights. Thirty paintings lined the walls, more than enough for him to appreciate as he finally approached the opera doors. Four a.m. and he had the auditorium to himself. He could kick off his shoes and linger in the orchestra pit as indifferent lighting muted the outline of the stage. His eyes grew accustomed to the radiant gloom, having at first played tricks with him, he could relax in a private stall of his choosing. Above his head stretched out a panoply of the arts in a triumph of trompe-l'œil. He allowed himself to muse on how his favourite Brahms German Requiem movement II would sound if played in this gilded space and began to nod in time to the gentle build-up in his head, until his pager began to vibrate in his pocket. It was Otto from room service. Andreas roused himself out of his slouch and returned to the panelled foyer to use the in-house telephone.

'What is it Otto?'

'Frau Deubler has been ringing for you,' said Otto.

'At this hour, what the hell can she want?'

'She wouldn't tell me, you know what she's like Andreas.'

He knew alright. Kirstin Deubler was the chatelaine of the Bayerischer Hof. She was the granddaughter of the hotel's founder Joachim Greiser. Kirstin had no role within the hotel other than that of a figurehead but her life was no less bound up with its fortunes. She had a private suite with a corner window and balcony on the fifth floor.

Forty-five years ago Kirstin was a model with a passable singing voice and often found herself on the same billing as the Wehrmacht sweetheart Zarah Leander entertaining wounded troops at free concerts given in the hotel opera. It was there that she met her future husband Max Deubler. Max was a U-boat Captain with a fractured collarbone and a beard that had outgrown his long stints under the waves. Kirstin had helped Max to a fire exit after one of her performances was cut short by a visit overhead by the RAF. She directed him to the nearest shelter and said that she had to stay behind to clear any incendiaries that might ignite on the hotel roof. Max was impressed and asked if he could join her even though he could be of little help because of his injury. She conceded that he might be of use as a fire watcher, a role for which he was even less suited as he was intent on only watching her. The raid eventually turned north and the other fire watchers began to drift away from the hotel roof, leaving just the two of them sitting on the lead flashings watching the flames lick over other buildings with a strange fascination.

Max had offered her his tunic and she undid his buttons carefully, mindful of his shoulder. Instinctively she found herself drinking in this man's warmth as if it was the most natural thing in the world. She was in a playful humour amidst the devastation, teasing Max about the legitimacy of his hard-earned medal ribbons such as the Iron Cross with oak leaves. Max gave as good as he got, belittling Kirstin's stature as a model in such high heels. He rolled cigarettes with one hand, on a rolling box, a new skill that quietly impressed her as she dug a diminutive heel into his boot. This was foreplay and she knew it, if love came after, then she was all too willing to find out what it felt like too. She took the cigarette and he lit it for her. They both sat in an envious silence wrapped in intrigue about one another. Smoking was just a prelude to a kiss, an unspoken truth that they had met. She led him off the roof and down the service staircase, emerging on the fifth floor and proceeded down the corridor to her suite. Kirstin opened the door without speaking, Max followed her in and she snibbed it behind her. She took off his officer's tunic and hung it up. He held her with his good arm and they kissed in the hallway. She imprinted her curves around him, her lips pulsated as they combined each others tongues in abandonment. He loosened his grip on her and she led him into the drawing room of her apartment. She smiled as she could see her lipstick on his mouth and he winced for a moment in realisation. Kirstin approached a dresser near the French doors that led onto her balcony. She reached for two glasses and poured an equal measure of Jägermeister for them both. Handing Max a glass, she let him drink and before he could swallow she started to kiss him again tonguing his mouth open to share the Jägermeister. Their two tongues suffused with fire-water, her hands made free with his groin. Max had never kissed like this before, she had engineered this moment and his excitement was all too apparent. Kirstin stroked his lips with her finger and licked any residue, then took his glass and placed it back onto the dresser. She now unfastened the hook at the back of her skirt and it dropped to the floor revealing black market stockings beneath. Max had teased her earlier and now he could taste her, her alabaster skin hemmed into silk underwear, fawny lips warm and wet with her anticipation. He didn't know where to begin, she was off the scale in terms of anything he had come to know about women. Maybe wartime did this to people, he thought, but he wasn't even allowed to dwell on that as she took his hand once more and led him to her bedroom. She caressed his aching shoulder and undressed him, fuelling his ardour for her.

They both knew that they had found love. He was the love of her life. They married in the Alte Peter Kirche in June 1942 just as the 'Happy Times' for the German submariners were about to end. Max ran the gauntlet of the echo location destroyers once too often and he and his crew of 55 men on board U 921 were lost beneath the waves south of Finisterre in September 1944.

Kirstin still sang torchlight favourites to the wounded men in a spiralling atmosphere of false hope and morbidity where Faustian shadows loomed in a harvest of the morose. She declined to take cover in the increasing number of air raids. American by day, British by night, it didn't matter to her. She would be with her Max eventually. Stoicism mixed with a steely disregard for her own safety made her cold and aged her before her time.

Kirstin came through the war unscathed physically, she drank more, alone of course most of the time. She had her press clippings from her modelling days, her pet Miniature Schnauzer 'Rex' and a dwindling number of brittle peers and acolytes who came to lunch. She still had Max's dress uniform, the coat with medals he had lent her that night on the roof. His framed photograph, signed with love sat on her bedside table. She had evolved into a routine in the intervening years and now Andreas was a player in her duel with the world, which rarely meant the one beyond the confines of the Bayerischer Hof. Kirstin would send for Andreas because she sensed a loss in him that was unspoken yet kindred to her own. Andreas's damaged fingertips could still hammer out a tune on her grand piano and give her the chance to shine by candlelight in shades of Marlene Dietrich. She was nearing eighty now and any translucence had long evaporated with elasticity draining from the corrugated channels above her thinning lips. She was a rarity, uncorrected, coated in aspic on the fifth floor. Andreas never knew what to expect when he was obliged to pay her a visit in those early hours, but he had learned to arm himself with a bottle of Jägermeister and some rolled cigarettes. She opened the door in an evening dress after the first knock.

'Play for me Andreas, play that piece by Brahms that transports you to that place again. Where was it? I can never pronounce it properly.'

'It's called Strekerau, Frau Deubler, I tell you every time I come here.'

'Play it in memory of Strekerau then. You brought me my brandy I see, thank you. Play the Brahms, Andreas.'

Considering it was a choral work, woodwind and strings, as well as being a requiem mass at that, Andreas had fashioned a version that just about passed muster on a piano that hadn't been tuned for decades. He unbuttoned his night porter's jacket and sat next to the keys. Kirstin took the bottle over to the dresser and started to sway gently in time as Andreas played the opening bars tentatively. She still had her back to him, her arms now pressed against her stomach, a trance-like look on her face that she took care to always hide from him. This lasted for about three minutes until a major key change led her to awaken and reach for one of the roll up cigarettes. Moving to the window and the small balcony beyond, her eyes adjusted as she studied the muted glow of the Munich skyline. Andreas continued, returning to the familiar opening thread of the piece, Kirstin always took this to be the signal to pour a drink for him.

'All flesh is as the grass,' she uttered just above the keys, 'Never more so now than ever,' she added.

Andreas was used to her rhetoric and paid it no heed as he was in his own world now, where the grass covered an area the size of France. Grass grew without impediment or hindrance of any kind, stretching to a distant horizon and beyond. A blade for each soul from every generation would only fill a space large enough for a man to plough in one day. Fickle soil that formed the bread basket of mother Russia. Soil that was prized from without and within, scorched and fought over since the time of Genghis Khan. Land that was promised to Andreas's forefathers, arable land and the freedom to worship how they pleased. A promise made to entice half a million Germans to uproot and resettle in the Russian Steppe. A promise made by none other than Catherine the Great. Andreas was a naturalised German, he had been taught German at school but the students were also taught to be good Russian citizens even if they weren't orthodox or later communist. They had rights and protection under the Tsars, their communities flourished because of the strong work ethic they brought with them from Germany. Strekerau was a German-sounding name within a region of the Volga delta. A map of the United States is peppered with German-sounding names, from those who settled west. The same was once so from those who came east looking for arable land to farm and religious tolerance to thrive under. Andreas's people had chosen to go east and he was to pay for the actions taken two hundred and fifty years before he was even born.

2

1987

After another fitful night's sleep courtesy of one of Sacko's nocturnal companions, Liam punched in his time card to begin a double shift on the first day of the Jewish convention. He got his daily duties from Yaffat Laminieri, Frau Radler's lap dog. Laminieri was a French Moroccan who had come to Munich with the promise of work prior to the 1972 Olympics. He had also just come off fasting for Ramadan and was in even less tolerant form than normal.

'Listen Boy, you make shit all time with your work, am I right?'

Liam was broad and spoke low and quickly so that his insults wouldn't be understood.

'It's Broy, you greasy tuareg sack o' shite.'

He had said it so fast that Yaffat actually nodded as if he thought Liam had just agreed with him.

'So Boy, today we will check all the shit you have make before the inspectors close us down eh?'

'Whatever you say you big brown-nosing bastard.'

Yaffat had a subterranean office at the end of a long corridor which was an imposition to find at the best of times. It was more of a large chicken hutch, a wire cage to enclose the expensive banqueting items such as silver candle sticks, cutlery, ornate flower-jugs and conference PA systems. He had planted a desk into this tight space and was careful to lock his cage every time he left. He wore a white doctor's coat, which he considered a badge of acceptability, into the top pocket of which he stuffed numerous pens to make him look officious. Whatever prejudices Yaffat had experienced in his formative years in Bavaria, he now repaid in spades to any foreign subordinate. If he smiled at you at all it was because he had some irksome task in mind and that was how he got his kicks. He had a clipboard and asked Liam to accompany him as he did his rounds. Yaffat fawned and reviled other managers with equal measure, cursing softly in Arabic tones as he led Liam even further downstairs to the bin room which was heaving with large container bins, the smell of which you could cut in two on what was a hot day. He wrote a brief note to himself:

'Boy, this should have been done by now, want you make all bins empty, hose them down with hot water power hose clear?'

He pointed to the three-wheeled generator that had a long hose attached in the corner.

'When finish that, you hose drains clear of all grease and shit ok?'
Liam walked over to the edge of the bin loading-bay and could see the drainage grilles that embraced the base of the hotel kitchens. They reeked in the afternoon sun, with mangled food scraps caught up at the head of the drain. Then Yaffat walked over to the large skip beyond the loading dock.
'Now get in skip and make room for more rubbish first.'
With that he reached for a large pair of industrial gloves from a shelf in the bin room. He handed them to Liam and bid him to get into the skip. Liam put on the gloves and clambered in, the drop on the other side was more than he expected and he stumbled over cardboard cartons before retrieving his balance. Now he couldn't see Yaffat, who was still yelling instructions.
'Move card, make more room for shit, Boy.'
Liam sifted through melting bin-bags and rotting card trying to get a grip with festering rubbish that had been exposed to the sun for days. As he did so, he heard a large clunk, then a shudder of automation as the space beneath his feet seemed to be grinding back slowly. He found a foothold on the side of the skip and managed to cling on and peer over the lip. Yaffat stood with a hydraulic control switch in one hand, a cigar in the other and a huge grin on his face. The teeth were grinding however slowly, with Liam inside sorting through the rubbish.
'You fuckin' towel-headed knacker!'
Yaffat couldn't make him out over the grinding sound and certainly wouldn't have understood him anyway.
'Turn that bleedin' machine off, you bollocks!'
Yaffat cocked his head for a moment and wheeled out the trade mark nasty grin.
'Boy why you shout out? You no like to work?'
Liam could straddle the skip by now and he watched the metallic teeth grind slowly together below him. It was beyond complaining about, it was all about control with this bastard. Yaffat wheeled out the steam washer and turned on the generator which rattled loudly as it powered up, killing any dialogue. He handed Liam the hose and pointed at the drains. Liam waited for him to turn his back before releasing a dose of high pressure spray in Yaffat's direction. He shrugged in mock disbelief as Yaffat cursed him in Arabic, his starched coat misted in hot detergent. Once out of sight Liam let loose with the rod of the power hose in the manner of an air guitar. He realised that the Jewish inspectors would have a field-day with the mess down here, congealed gunge and festering remains would be a deal-breaker. Still, once he got used to the smell which was dissipating fast, he quite enjoyed being outside, it was work that could be seen to be done. He knew that this was the dirtiest work, for the lowest of the low, he had bottomed out but

was this the best Frau Radler could think of to finally be rid of him? If it was then it was a piece of piss compared to what he had been up against in the Lebanon. That was a closed book when he applied for a position with the Bayerischer Hof. He turned each of the large bins on their sides after depositing all their rubbish into the revolving skip and then he rinsed each bin thoroughly. He grew in confidence with the power hose and held it one-handed as he shaded his eyes from the sun with his other hand and was able to watch the Hypo Bank office girls walk by in their lunch break. They studiously ignored him of course, picking up the pace as the livid smells from the bin room reached the raised walkway. None of this mattered today, Yaffat was preoccupied with the Jewish inspectors and Liam got to play in the sun.

Ephraim Finkelstein would conduct the kosher inspection later that morning with Yaffat Laminieri. Finkelstein & Hasselbad were a company originally formed in Munich at the fag end of Word War I. They provided standing frames, strollers and crude prosthetic limbs to veterans of that conflict at trade prices for wounded ex-servicemen. Through innovation and better biomechanical understanding the company became a leader in the field of prosthetic limb design, helped in part with financial investment by a sympathetic Weimar government. By 1933 the company had outlets in Hannover, Bremen and Hamburg as well as trade representation in the United Kingdom and the United States. Not long after that date Finkelstein & Hasselbad would be coerced to relinquish control of their German concerns and transfer the business operation to Zurich in Switzerland. The German outlets underwent an Aryan name change and were swallowed up by the Todt organisation, which was state-funded by the incumbent Nazi regime. Lost in the convoluted bureaucracy of rearmament and megalomania, the German arm of this ground-breaking company stagnated without innovation and produced inferior products which were poorly galvanized. In Zurich, Finkelstein & Hasselbad continued to pursue cutting-edge methods in prosthetic engineering, harnessing mechanical advancement, which after World War II made the company the undisputed jewel in the crown of biomechanical engineering. It was now, some fifty-three years after the Jewish pogroms began, that an official invitation came from the Freistadt of Bavaria to its erstwhile golden egg. Ephraim was the nephew of the founder, Ephraim senior, who had moved to Israel in his twilight years. Ephraim was here to test the mettle of this olive branch. His company had long since outgrown Munich, but if he could gain good media by conferencing in this prestigious hotel, then why not? It was only business, no point in harbouring bad blood and after all this was the city of his blood, his starting point, his haaretz.

'Wake up Broy, how long have you been sleeping?'

Liam stirred from a crumpled foetal curl, overalls imprinted with benchmarks, dried-in saliva staining his starched collar. He had dreamt of the Martello tower overlooking Ireland's eye in Dublin Bay. His gawky efforts not to look squeamish as he waded out from the steps into water cold enough to retract any scrotum to the consistency of a walnut shell. He had the temerity to strip off down to his Y's, a lanky torso with the pallor of a shying sturgeon. He had got it into his head that this would impress Caitlin, it had to be her of course! The girl who grew up quickest in his street, whose pneumatic development aroused the attentions of all the neighbouring boys, the cockiest of whom she would unravel behind the Farrans van docked at the top of the road. It had never been him but he could dream and he had asked her to walk with him the short distance from the Dart stop to the Martello tower. Caitlin sat mortified, sucking on a cigarette on the upper steps, a stiff sea breeze prying at her short skirt, wishing she was anywhere else but here. Liam was about to ask himself the question why when he felt the tug of an outside force wringing him from slumber.

'What time is it?' Liam asked.

'Six thirty…did you spend the night on a locker bench?' asked Andreas.

'I guess I just didn't fancy going back to the staff dormitory and I must have fallen into a deep sleep.'

'Did no one think to wake you, what time are you due on shift?'

'Christ the night, seven o'clock, Radler's rota tricks again!'

'So you have half an hour, get into the showers and then get some food into you. What is it with you Broy?'

'Have you stayed in the dormitory lately? It's a fuckin' knacker's yard of a place you know. If it's not the scurrying of the cockroaches rattling down the pipes it'll be the moans of the whores that big black fella brings back every other night.'

'Well you can't sleep on a bench in the locker room indefinitely, I will drop by Personnel and see if we can get you a better room to share.'

'It would be great coming from you, I'm sure they would listen. Thank you.'

'Leave it with me Broy, Radler comes first, get cleaned up and eat.'

Frau Radler's rigorous shift patterns meant that Liam would invariably bump into Andreas either first thing in the morning or in the dead of night after cleaning up in the hotel nightclub. Andreas chose the hours he worked, he had honed himself into this nocturnal routine. He preferred the hotel after dark, it took on a whole new persona, without the frenetic energy of so much coming and going that consumed much of the daylight hours.

Guests were just as demanding no matter what the hour, his on-call light and pager flashed throughout the night as testimony to their specific needs and requests. Room service was paired down in the late evening and by the start of his shift at eleven p.m., there was just a smattering of people at each location including himself, the night chef, bar staff, front of house and hotel security on call. By eleven the hotel opera had disgorged its patrons who by then would have the choice of reclining in the low lit neon of the Biedermeier bar in the lobby or the stunning rooftop balcony bar, weather permitting. The great and the good of Munich society would congregate up there, the unhesitatingly wealthy could digest cocktails and canapes until three a.m. as they watched intermittent shards form from the distant electrical storms that lit up an Alp-filled horizon. They could in turn choose to frequent the hotel nightclub located in the cellar, where live jazz gave way at midnight to the frenetic sounds that permeated the kitchen space beyond where Liam sweated the night away in a frenzy, feeding and retrieving from both ends of the tank-track conveyor belt dishwasher.

The hotel had a rhythm, a routine, an unflappable pattern to reflect the social calendar and in that respect outwardly dripped of opulence and taste. Andreas was comfortable in this womb-like existence, it had been this way for the last thirty-four years since his return from captivity in the Soviet Union. The Bayerischer Hof had rehabilitated him, allowed him to assimilate, develop a routine and a sense of normality, enabling him to take stock of his life within the constraints of the unsocial hours he had grown accustomed to. He considered himself fortunate, as others he had shared captivity with had long since succumbed to malnutrition, disease, and the punishing conditions of the gulag. Outwardly Andreas and Liam had nothing to relate them in any way other than the coincidence of their both working under the same roof. Neither man knew anything of the other's former life up until now and why should they? Andreas guarded his privacy well and the time served within the Bayerischer Hof had taken most of the space afforded to him on any résumé worth reading. But the two men did have something in common. They had both been soldiers once.

Liam had served with the Irish army on attachment to the United Nations peace keeping force in the Lebanon up until 1985. His first experience of combat was forever scarred by an ambush in which the Druze militia managed to kill two of his closest friends. At the end of his tour of duty, and unable to settle back into the normality of a north Dublin housing project, he drifted across Europe looking for work until reaching Munich. The army had made him parsimonious, shunning any frivolity or ostentation.

He excelled in the physicality of the role, he revelled in the anonymity that he shared within the lower ranks. It was a rigid existence, it was disciplined and left its mark on Liam, not just on his body, but in the rigours and hardships he witnessed. He formed bonds with some of the lowest types imaginable, he had to, they watched each other's backs through low intensity operations that often went unreported during the conflict. He earned enough trust to ride point, leading the men through hostile terrain to safety. He learned how to bivouac, sleep rough, sleep soundly, if perhaps intermittently, on the march. He knew how to find water in arid terrain, set traps for animals, how to track a man through desert or open country. He could strip down his weapon and assemble it again in minutes, until his firearm became an extension of himself. He was decorated twice for bravery under fire, returning to bring a wounded comrade back from a flashpoint. These were only some of the traits and foibles Liam brought with him to Germany and even though they held him in good stead they never featured on the CV he filled out in Frau Radler's office. They were integral to him, if he couldn't share these experiences at home, then he didn't hope to share them with anyone abroad.

1942

Andreas had been a soldier too. By late June 1941 the one million ethnic naturalised Germans living peaceably in the Volga delta of southern Russia for the last two hundred years were now considered a threat to Soviet stability. Minorities such as the Tartars, the Don Cossacks, the Chechens, the Belorussians, the Ukrainians and the Kazakhs were all viewed as fifth columnists by the Politburo in Moscow. Stalin was a Georgian from the Kura river in Tbilisi, ethnic by birth and veiled his hypocrisy with his own brand of paranoia about the so-called threat from within. Representatives of the People's Commissariat for Internal Affairs (NKVD) now descended on the fertile plains of the Volga delta in a witch-hunt that confiscated long established collective farmlands from the ethnic Germans. An act accelerated by the heinous invasion of Mother Russia by Germany on the 22nd of that month. Families were evicted from their farms and homesteads, businesses in Strekerau were sequestered by the Soviets, their assets confiscated for 're-distribution' to the proletariat. Andreas's family ran the buildings and loan co-operative bank in the main street of Strekerau. Four generations of the same family had built up a reputation as honest as the toil of the Volga boatmen. The trumped-up charges having been read to Andreas's father in his office, the NKVD began looting the bank safe and taking any fittings and furniture that was wasn't nailed down. As the day wore on, alcohol being taken, the functionaries got braver and decided to torch the hammerbeam church in the town square. By nightfall, a town noted as the 'Jewel of the Volga' was festooned in flames that could be seen in the mid summer sky as far away as the industrial centre of Stalingrad some thirty kilometres away. It was open season in Strekerau, looting was freehold and with it intimidation and the threat of rape and reprisals.

Amidst this atmosphere, the Mensche family gathered one last time at their home before dispersal eastwards to a new life filled with uncertainty within the camps on the eastern steppe. Patreous Mensche hugged his daughters one by one, Katja, Elena, Rosa and then came to Andreas. He took the young man to his study.

'My son, my Andreas, I have dreaded this day. I want you to listen to me. You have to be a man now. Soon they will come and take our family home, your inheritance, my legacy. We will have to cheat these hangmen, are you with me?'

Andreas nodded his head without any confidence in what he is being told.

'These red bastards want everything and not a bit of it will go to the people who need it most.'

With that remark he grabbed Andreas by the wrist and together they both knelt down onto the persian rug that navigated the floor beneath his father's desk.

'Roll this away my boy, see the herring-bone flooring beneath, follow the pattern until you can depress a finger between the wooden tiles. Quickly, we don't have much time!'

Sure enough Andreas was able to access a latch with his finger between the lathes and on doing so he heard a snap as a trapdoor opened just beneath and to the left of where he knelt.

'Take this coin and lift the latch. It should come away quite easily.'

The flooring was so intricate it belied the hidden trapdoor which now swung open invitingly with a display of dust that dazzled when exposed to sunlight. His father reached him a torch and beckoned him to proceed onto the stepladder. Andreas had played on his father's study floor for years with his Napoleonic lead soldiers and had never known of this secret room's existence.

'I have kept copies of all our family assets in a strongbox down there. Wills and probate, title deeds, share certificates and foreign bonds. The bank has gone, with it the deeds for everyone who put their trust in us. I know you can't carry all these with you but I want you to take a pouch of gold rubles and use them to make good your escape. They will be here soon to roll count us into exile somewhere hellish but you must remember this room and more importantly the combination of its strongbox so that you can reclaim these documents one day.'

Andreas shone the torch around the cramped space within which he could just about manage to stand up straight. His father climbed down to join him and knelt awkwardly to begin turning the dial with the correct combination. Andreas watched as his dapper pinstripe suit and highly polished shoes ate up much of the faltering torchlight. Patreous swung open the strongbox door and retrieved a small pouch of what must have been coins, it was too dark to make out their value. While he was kneeling he began to write the combination numbers of the strongbox on a piece of paper which he had previously folded and concealed in his trouser braces. He turned the page over and commenced writing a brief letter of introduction to whoever on Andreas's behalf but his circulation began to suffer from kneeling too long forcing him to lean against his son until the cramp abated. Only when the flow of blood allowed did he climb back up the ladder so that he could finish the note in comfort at his desk. When he was done he slipped it into the pouch of rubles and gave it to Andreas for safe keeping and then closed over the trap door before concealing it again with the persian rug.

'The girls are too young to tell and even younger to try. It has to be you. You must get out of here, take my gelding and ride west. Ride at night and trust no one until you get to the German lines. Explain to them, tell them what took place here, that we are German too. Join with them and get our land back. Grab what you need from your room, be quick, your mother has packed you some provisions for your saddle bag.'

Andreas was shaking, still reeling from the gravitas of his father's words. He looked around his room for any grains of comfort. Any formative assurances that he could hold onto, but none were forthcoming. Only the shattered delusions forming beyond his window frame where he could make out the growing column of his near neighbours, ousted from their homes now listlessly feeling their way to the railhead, soon to be engulfed by the rolling-stock heading further east. Those forlorn faces stricken with apprehension and uncertainty as the streets they left behind began to choke with unharnessed carriages, discarded luggage amidst the flotsam of their former lives.

The NKVD funnelled and goaded them along the route, leaning against picket fences with mouths full of confiscated bread and cheese, ushering children from hiding places with the threat of a rifle butt or with the jagged edge of a broken wine bottle. Once proud dwellings neatly aligned and shingled so recently occupied now fell victim to the felonies of the louts taking state control to the nadir of its meaning. Paintings were slashed open along their frames and rolled up into kitbags, silverware, trinkets and keepsakes and any other items of value were inventoried, yet many more pieces disappeared without trace. Livestock was now herded and chased from the collective farmland. How macabre the sight of enlisted men with broken-necked chickens hanging limp from the pockets of their great coats. All of this taking place in full view of the officers, systematically moving from house to house with clipboards writing down every detail. Steadily, this onslaught moved closer up the street and nearer to Andreas's home. He had to look away to steal himself before they stole everything he held dear. Without thinking he had placed objects on the bed that might be of use to him. He grabbed his school satchel and placed the torch he had used earlier, along with a penknife and a small pair of Zeiss Ikon binoculars he had often used when hunting. He then layered in a pair of trousers, two of his best cotton shirts and three pairs of fresh underwear. He had no idea what to pack, they were all just recently laundered and within easy reach. He couldn't think straight, this was his bedroom, where he felt safest but the alien sounds outside shattered any former illusions. He put on a hunting jacket with leather patches, it matched the one his father wore on their expeditions together. The brown leather brogues he wore would have to do for any terrain to come. One last look around his room before retrieving the ruble pouch from his pillow and then with no further sentiment he went downstairs where his family had assembled in the panelled hallway.

They packed only what they too could carry. The NKVD would search them as they left, so no point in trying to smuggle anything of real value. His mother gave him a loaf of dark rye bread to pack as well as some fresh cold ham and wurst she had prepared and wrapped in cloth earlier from the larder. She broke into tears hugging Andreas close. His sisters surrounded him in an unbroken chain and they stood as one in silence. He had only minutes now if he was to make good any escape. Patreous reached out his hand and Andreas knew to take it firmly in his own to give him strength for the road ahead. His hair was ruffled from the exuberant playfulness of all their touches, Andreas kissed his mother goodbye for the last time. He left through the kitchen door without looking back as he didn't want them to see his own tears. The three-year-old gelding was a piebald called Hanzie. Patreous had walked him up from the paddock earlier, fed him and checked his harnessing before saddling him up. Andreas now stroked his mane and blew softly into Hanzie's muzzle, sharing his scent before mounting him. Soon the two were quietly negotiating the boundary hedges, disembarking at intervals, marking out the back lanes within Strekerau. Andreas could do this journey blindfolded but the frisson of real danger beyond every turn was enough to keep his caution levels high. He set himself targets to reach, familiar landmarks along the way. He passed the Poplar trees he had once climbed and played in, then stealthily, fifty paces on to the outhouses he had previously relieved himself in and taken advantage of in better times. Luckily for him the terrain had been scoured earlier by the soldiers, even the fruit trees from the small family orchards had been picked bare. The men had subsequently moved indoors looking for preserves in attic crawl spaces, cider presses in the cellars, smoked fish and meat in the dry stores beyond the kitchen spaces. The rich pickings whereof now adorned the absentee family tables to be harvested by the NKVD as and when they chose. The soldiers were gluttonous in the face of such a feast, making them lackadaisical in their searches. They grew tetchy and insubordinate as the sun rose in the sky, choosing to stay close to sources of sustenance such as the prolific number of clay kegs of peach and apple schnapps to be found in the numerous cellars.

All this was to Andreas's advantage, the indiscipline due to furtive alcohol consumption was rife in the red army, it would cloak his escape and groggy men would in many cases only imagine that they saw a young figure lead a piebald horse out of the search area and on to the open countryside beyond. In one instance a shot rang out vaguely in his direction, cracking through timbers of a barn nearby but it wasn't followed up and the culprit who fired it was roundly admonished by one of the more sober NCOs. Andreas rode his luck, the back streets were his former playground, he protected Hanzie from any danger managing to rest him in the shade from the heat of the sun at a hayloft on the edge of town. He would do as his father asked and stay here until nightfall. The tension of the day had finally caught up with him and he collapsed in the corner after tying Hanzie up and seeing that he got plenty of water from the well nearby. Night came slow in mid summer, slow and short to stifle the gathering heat of the day. Andreas turned over in his mind, his mother, her kiss goodbye, the embrace of his sisters and finally his father's words to him on parting. Had the world gone mad? After all this was his home, his heartland and now he was being chased out of it, scattered to the winds, hunted and totally alone. And what of the Germans? The bogey men he had been taught to fear and resent at the state school. Would they believe his story? Would they just take his gold and string him up like any other straggler he had heard of once falling into the unforgiving arms of the Einsatzgruppen. Sleep put an end to all this speculation. Better for him that it did, a balm for the fear that had gripped him. The devil he knew had just swept away everything he counted and relied upon. It was now up to him to persuade the devil he didn't know to believe his story

3

1987

Yaffat Laminieri was still smarting from an earful from Frau Radler only minutes before giving Ephraim the conducted tour of the service areas of the hotel. Radler thought Laminieri to be intrinsically lazy, a corner cutter, the antipathy of the model of Bavarian efficiency she had tried so long to instil in her staff. She was right of course; Yaffat had got as far as he ever would within the confines of the hotel and now sat back in his caged office while others did the dirty work. Yaffat was malign, untrusting and suspicious, he was resentful of the treatment meted out to him when he first arrived in this country. He had a chip on his shoulder about many things and took these prejudices out on his underlings. For some this was too much and they often retaliated, throwing the head up under the pressure of onerously cumbersome tasks and being fired on the spot. Nothing Yaffat could throw Liam's way would crack the Dublin man's resolve. Liam accompanied Yaffat on the kosher tour. Yaffat had made sure Liam wore a freshly starched boiler suit. It made him squirm to see Yaffat fawn over Ephraim, his heavily Arabic German accent diluted with Bavarian tones. The inspection took in all the areas previously cleansed and sterilised by Liam. The awkwardness between the two men was tangible, their mutual suspicions galvanized in a cross-section of things beyond the remit of this hotel. The tour passed off soundly enough to be kosher for the conference. Each check list demand had a tick beside it, or an amendment that could be easily corrected. At the tour's close, Yaffat had tried to put his arm around Liam's shoulder as a sign of solidarity in front of Ephraim, but his reach was found to be wanting.

All of this under the watchful eye of Andreas, who true to his word had spoken to Frau Radler about Liam's dormitory situation. Andreas told her that he thought in time she would change her opinion of Liam and to prove his worth, he proposed to take him in as a lodger for a probationary period. Radler said on his head be it and that he would regret it, she couldn't see what good it would do as Liam was just trouble. Andreas asked her to cut Liam some slack with the pattern of hours on his work rota. She relented and said that she would give him a week of straight early shifts, followed by a week of lates and so on. She warned Andreas that he was responsible from now on for anything that went wrong.

Yaffat dropped any pretence as soon as Ephraim had gone, his pock-marked skin was bereft of any real cordiality but this coldness was wasted on Liam who knew he could break the man in two if he was driven to. It was this defence mechanism that often hindered Liam to any well-meant gestures from those he hardly knew. So Andreas's opening remarks came as quite a shock.

'Broy, collect your belongings from the dormitory after your shift, you can stay at my apartment for a trial period.'

'You're serious aren't you boss? You're not havin' a fuckin' laugh?'

'Yes I am, collect your things and take them to this address, I have cleared this with Frau Radler. I am sticking my neck out here Broy, don't let me down. Radler thinks I'm mad and wants this to fall down around my ears.'

'I promise I won't let you down boss, you'll hardly know I am even there.'

'Some chance of that Broy, what are you? Six foot three?'

'Exactly! Sure there is nothing fuckin' of me, thanks boss.'

Liam took the note with the address details from Andreas and a spare set of keys to the apartment. It wouldn't take long to pack what he had in the dormitory, Sacko wasn't there when he got back, he was probably on the prowl for pussy and would be ensconced in one the lesser known haunts that never make it into the Dorling Kindersley travel guides. No chance of Liam then getting the 100 Deutsche Marks he owed, a small price to pay for the prospect of uninterrupted sleep. The soundtrack to his departure was the continuous scuttling of the roaches along the heat pipe that navigated the room. He had a small case under his bed, it had time-peeled destination stickers covering it from places he had never seen. The case had been his grandmother's, she had passed ten years before, they marked out the journeys of her retirement, with her companion Mrs Martin. Two widows, best friends who ran a chippy in Ballyfermot for years, then seeking adventure before dotage at last clouded their judgements. The case snapped open reassuringly and he piled in all his belongings, which didn't take long. The room didn't even have a lock so it was just as well he had nothing of value. Sacko would have pilfered anything long since. He pulled the door behind him.

Virchow Strasse was a tributary of the grand parade that was Ludwig Strasse. It was in Münchener Freiheit an area once frequented by the aesthetic bohemians of the Weimar era, who in the early 1920s were intent in making this district called Schwabing the artistic quarter of Munich. By 1987, she was a somewhat faded lady, with her back to the Englischer Garten, her grandeur in decline, nudged on by the unremitting architectural plans of different regimes each intent on distancing itself from the previous. This architectural cocktail could be austere to the point of eastern bloc, renderings and improvements may have been unsympathetic to any era but the period after the war was not one of respect for the past, just one of building for the future. Needless to say this district was new to Liam. The U-bahn system was new to Liam. Previously he could almost have sleepwalked onto one of the many fastidious trams that frequented the old town and taken no notice of the journey to and from work. The action of the tram as it negotiated the rails became second nature to this soporific pattern and he knew every turn before reaching the hotel. The dormitory was within the overspill of the Hauptbahnhof station, where a myriad of converging streets had been obliterated during the war along with legitimate targets such as all rolling-stock, marshalling yards and rail transport sidings adjacent to the station. The area subsequently had fallen foul of hurried housing redevelopment with landlords eager to cut corners by packing as many tenants into their substandard housing stock. Low rents and confined living spaces only enticed displaced families, unscrupulous low-lifes and an influx of foreign nationals attracted by the prospect of labour in the race to rebuild a now divided Germany. These 'Gastarbeiters' were overwhelmingly Turkish, a hangover from the political and military cordiality between Imperial Germany and the embers of the Ottoman empire. A grudging accommodation had been achieved between two conservative ideologies with little, if any, assimilation of the other's culture.

Bob the cat now observed Liam as he faltered with the keys at the main entrance. It would be a while before Bob would have any notions of curling through Liam's legs. Liam was ignorant of Bob's status, being as he was the only cat in the building. He opened the main door and reached for the light switch. Bob saw his chance and sprinted up the threadbare carpet to the first floor cat flap of number five. The apartment owner had installed the cat flap to eradicate Bob's incessant scratching at the base of his door. The light went out and Liam momentarily saw nothing but the glare through time-worn door curtains. He depressed the switch on again and walked over the circulars and uncollected mail littering the floor. Sixteen pigeon-hole mail boxes sat in a row directly to his right. He could just make out the name Mensche on number twelve. It said twelve on the key fob and he deduced that it must be at least on the next level. He paced up. The walls were painted in a dark lime gloss that was wipe easy and functional. From his vantage point on the staircase he could just make out Bob peering back through the cat flap, as if to say, 'Are you still here?'

Liam's progression was greeted on the next landing by a long neglected vase of plastic flowers mounted on a small pedestal. The hall lights left him in darkness again just as he managed to turn the door key in the latch of number twelve for the first time. No Andreas, no welcoming committee, just a hermetically sealed apartment with austere parquet flooring sitting tightly against the skirting and the radiators, reminding Liam of the corridors he spent so much time in after being sent out of class for one thing or another. He dropped the case and flicked on the hall light, catching his reflection, his unkempt full head of hair, the cow's lick which was of such a length that it could be pasted behind his left ear as if his mammy had told him so. He turned his profile in the mirror, his aquiline nose, his pale skin and finally showing his teeth as if he were under scrutiny at a horse fair. There were no mirrors back in the dormitory, Liam would often shave in the locker room, cut his own hair or ask one of the porters to do it for him. He opened the frosted vestibule door and was in another man's living space. Had Andreas planned this? Was it a test? If it was then Liam was wise to it. The better angels of his nature that came from his mother's side now took a hold of him. He needed to listen to that side and just begin to trust again. Living abroad had done that to him, not just the army but the calculated coldness that flows in from some outer region, a Hebridean wind that somehow managed the trip gathering strength until it jettisoned all its hoar-frost detachment on poor Liam in Munich of all places! That was what he would blame it on if pushed. The truth was Liam had forgotten how to trust, to open, to relate. He still had his mother's voice inside, but she was struggling to be heard over the traffic flow in Liam's mind.

He approached the table that straddled the kitchen/living area. Andreas had left a welcome note. He tore the envelope open roughly.

Bray, welcome to my apartment. You will find the guest room to your left, I have left out fresh sheets and blankets for you on the mattress. You are welcome to use the wardrobe and bedside night stand. The view has a northern aspect, so you won't be troubled by the sun when you need to sleep during the day. Please treat this as your space, but also respect my property. I have rules of course, many of which I choose not to write down as they are common sense. You are here on a trial basis, it was you after all who was experiencing hardships at the dormitory. I do not expect to experience any hardships in return from you at my home. You will be responsible for your own food, toiletries and laundry. All service bills will in future be broken down and shared equally between us. The tasks such as washing, cleaning and general housekeeping duties will be shared and monitored by me. Please ask me first before operating any of the white goods within the apartment, a dry run so to speak can save a lot of confusion down the line. Speaking of lines, you are permitted to hang your washing on the balcony at any time except Sunday which is still a day of rest in Catholic Bavaria. You are permitted to have an entertainment system in your room, but I would prefer it if you used headphones, unless of course you are a fan of Mahler or Brahms, whereupon you are allowed to play as loud as you may wish. I discourage any interaction with members of the other sex in your bedroom as the walls are so thin between yours and mine as to be almost able to join in with any dialogue. Members of the other sex are permitted to the communal areas such as the kitchen and sofa. The television is of no use to me, but I request you watch with the volume at a reasonable level so that I may not be distracted from my reading. I do not permit parties or gatherings of more than three people in the apartment. The housing management fund will be shared jointly. I retain the right to give you notice, the length of notice is up to my discretion. Please refrain from smoking in my apartment. I don't permit it, even on the balcony. As you look around you will notice a lot of personal items and memorabilia that I have collected and cherished over the intervening years. I want you to respect my property and do all that you can to maintain the condition of my apartment, including the contents thereof for the duration of your stay. I hope that these conditions are satisfactory and sensible to you, I reiterate that I have taken a leap of faith in trusting you, a jump that others are only too keen to see fall short.

Please read through this agreement again and if you deem it fair and worthy of your approval, then sign below that you are willing to adhere to the terms laid out.

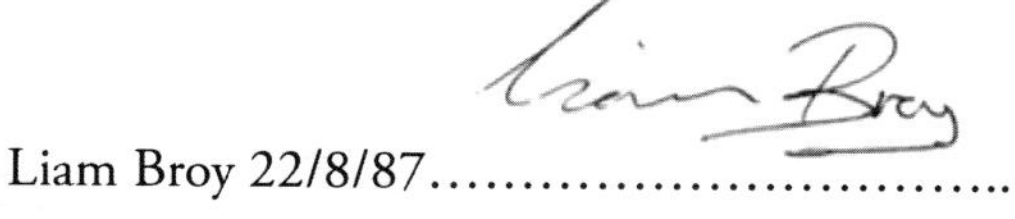

Liam Broy 22/8/87...............................

Liam left the terms on the table and took his suitcase into his new bedroom. It was as spartan and devoid of personality as himself he thought, but it was also his private space now. Having unpacked he moved back into the lounge area and studiously took in what had been Andreas's domain all those years. The mustiness of the apartment was at odds with Andreas's professional candour back at the hotel. Even Liam was tempted to throw open the blinds and let some fresh air and light fall on the post-war décor. It was at best functional, you might say, 'lived in'. Andreas's chair was unmistakeably the one with the extra flattened cushions vainly covering the protruding springs with a trail of stuffing feathers underneath. A barley twist standard lamp with a calf-skin shade was marooned in a pool of old editions of the Süddeutsch Zeitung newspaper. A tarnished brass ashtray-holder with match and cigarette dispenser rose two-feet off the ground within easy reach of the chair. To the left, a bureau with a drop down leaf that could operate as a desk. On top of the bureau, written correspondence, letters and circulars under paperweights or pinioned onto a metal spike fashioned out of a large flat cork. Liam assumed the bureau to be locked and was correct as it contained, along with many private things, the strong liquor. There was no grate where the fireplace was originally situated as Andreas had blocked up the chimney long since. He made do with a two-bar heater, the element of which produced an electrical smell akin to burnt socks. The mantlepiece survived and was festooned with lead soldiers. They were Napoleonic era by the look of things, possibly Prussian cavalry with black uniforms and a large white skull adorning their shakos. They definitely looked to be Prussian, Blucher's men who bailed out Wellington at Waterloo. Two brass spiral candlesticks with melted wax kept watch between the cavalry charge. Cobwebs surmounted the sabre thrusts of these collectable pieces. The bricked-up fireplace had numerous empty beer bottles at its base and on the other side of the chimney breast was a large teak bookcase. It was jammed with volumes, hardbacks mostly, in Russian and German. All well-thumbed and replaced in no particular way, some had migrated, forming large piles on the floor overwhelming the companion chair opposite. Liam was no reader but he could make out that most of the books appeared to be military or philosophical texts by important German or Russian thinkers. They had pieces of paper protruding from many of them where Andreas must have bookmarked them for some reason so that he could refer back to them later.

The windows were hidden behind a large black roller-blind and a patchwork throw covered the dents on a two-seater sofa pulled up tight over the threadbare hearth rug, both of which had seen better days. The ceiling light had no ornamentation, just a bulb at the end of a half metre two-core wire. Behind the sofa, a small teak cabinet matching the bookcase, upon which sat a white Fidelity record player. This had a built-in amplifier and two untidy lengths of speaker wire made their way to opposite ends of the room. The lid of the player had been detached and was now being used as a storage container for his vinyl and sat on the floor beside the cabinet. A record sat in position with the needle arm still at its centre unable to return as it had been turned off at the mains. Liam noticed that it was Brahms something something and didn't relate to it. He looked at his watch but his stomach had already told him that it was time to eat. No point in trying to cobble together anything out of Andreas's larder, it would all be labelled and listed he thought. He still had his coat on and some change rattled in his pocket so he would take himself off to the shops and scout the area while he was at it. Closing the front door he could smell the infusions of others as they prepared evening meals within on the different levels of the building. He lengthened his stride as he grew accustomed to his change of circumstance, the area was new and he was upbeat now that the dormitory was just a memory. Sure this Andreas was a sedentary bugger, but his own regimented background could deal with that. He reached a life-sized chess board that had been painted on the square that announced the shopping precinct. The pieces were in play but the protagonists had all gone home. The Spar was open and as always he tried to buy things that roughly reminded him of what he could try and cook back home. Invariably this would be spuds, bacon, baked beans, sliced white bread which resembled a loaf and milk. And beer, a six pack of the beer Andreas liked, to salute him when he arrived. It was dark when Liam put his key in the latch.

'Good you got my note then, Broy?' inquired Andreas as Liam entered.

'I did, very reasonable, fair play to you, very right and proper I signed it.'

'I think it breaks things down in such a way to set the ground rules. Better to anticipate any problems now than to run into them later. We all have to protect ourselves. You have been out shopping I see, do you like the area?'

'It's grand compared to what I have been used to. I bought some food, I thought maybe you wouldn't mind if I cooked you a meal as a way of thanking you. Nothing special like in the hotel. I got some of that beer you seem to like judging by all the empty bottles lying around here.'

'I would like that, I have been in the library all afternoon and I am very hungry,' said Andreas.

'Here, take one of these beers, I brought my own bottle opener. Well, I say my own, it's actually one that each dishwasher passes on every month, this being my month to buy the beers for the locker room card school.'

They both stood under the two-core ceiling bulb and clinked two large bottles and drained the suds from them.

'Prosit Broy!'

'Sláinte Mensche!'

Liam took off his jacket and hung it over one of the dining chairs, he proceeded to drop four large potatoes into a half full sink and then rolled up his sleeves before peeling them. Andreas flicked on the fidelity record deck and lifted its arm back from the centre so that he might wipe the vinyl with a velvet anti-static cloth. He blew on the needle before placing it into the opening grooves and the Brahms crackled into life. He then turned with the beer still in his clasp and settled into his usual chair. Liam looked over as the music slowly permeated the room, he had gathered the peelings in a sieve and dropped them into the small bin in the corner of the kitchen. Such a confined space within which to cook he pondered, although it allowed him to get familiar with the cupboards quickly and he soon found a large frying-pan. The hob was already hot to the touch so he poured a little oil into the pan and let it heat up. He chopped up the potatoes into large chips and placed them into the pan to sizzle. He opened the rashers and laid them out on tin foil wrapped around the grill pan and returned them under a low heat. He took a moment to draw down on the beer and listen to the music.

'I have never heard this before. It's very solemn, in a good way.'

'It's the German Requiem by Brahms, it reminds me of home.'

'But you're home now, do you play it every day?'

Before Andreas could answer, Liam had to return to the hob where oil was spitting at the water emitting from the chipped spuds. He raked through them with a spatula and they calmed and began to cook more evenly. The bacon was on the turn as well, getting crispier under the grill. His timing had to be just right, so he syphoned the excess juice from the baked beans using the jagged edge of the lid and dumped the rest into a small saucepan and onto a small ring at the back of the hob.

'I was going to say that Munich is my home, at least it's where I live but I was raised nearly twelve hundred kilometres away in Russia.'

'So a German piece of music reminds you of the Soviet Union?'

'It's complicated. Where I was born, everyone was German. We spoke German and Russian.'

The potatoes browned in the pan as Liam digested the thought of so many Germans living so deep inside Russia. The bacon protested under the grill before finally crinkling and again he turned over the thought in his mind of why anyone would contemplate giving up Munich for the badlands of Russia. He wanted to ask but he could see that Andreas was lost in the moment in his music and anyway this was only his first night in a new place and he didn't want to open any old sores. He turned the fat chips a few times more and then poured them out of the pan onto a length of kitchen roll to soak up the oil before transferring them onto two plates. The bacon was next and then the baked beans which he had allowed to simmer slowly on the hob.

'Here, you look like you could use a hot meal, get your nosebag into this. None of your white sausage and hot cabbage here me bucko!'

Andreas hadn't a clue what Liam had just said. His accent was too thick, his delivery too fast and Andreas's own rudimentary grasp of English was gleaned from the American forces radio he had listened to primarily for the jazz on offer. He decided to humour his new flatmate. He helped clear the table and retrieved some knives and forks from the kitchen drawer. He looked at Liam's beer and brought two fresh bottles from the crate on the floor. They both sat down at the table.

'Thank you Broy. This looks very good.'

'The last time I sat down to eat with you Mr Mensche you took insult at me for the question I asked you. The least I can do is try and make it up to you now.'

'I know you asked me about my fingers before, you didn't mean to be rude it's just your way of delivering words,' replied Andreas.

'I speak plainly and I forget that others don't necessarily speak the same way. What you see is what you get with me,' Liam replied with a mouth half-full. Andreas placed his fork back on the table and held up his hand across and in line with Liam's face.

'This is from frostbite. I lost the tips of my fingers from my time in Russia. You were the only person in over forty years to ask how these wounds came about. Most people just stare or don't ask out of politeness. It struck me that you asked out of genuine interest even if you did so at a crowded table. I realised you did it out of concern. That realisation is what led me to believe in giving you a chance to prove yourself not just to me but to those at the hotel who would rather see you fail.'

They ate while it was still hot and drained the beers as they did, Liam thanking the older man with his smiling eyes as his mouth was still too full of his pan-fried chips to utter anything coherent. Andreas watched ruefully as Liam spread butter thickly with a knife onto two slices of bread without using a side-plate. Then he liberally poured ketchup onto the butter before finally laying chips as railway sleepers onto the slices. He would then hold the bread like a corn cob up to his mouth and begin to devour. Andreas sat across from this spectacle and wondered just what had he been thinking of when he asked Liam to stay. The needle reached the end of the vinyl and the automatic arm crossed back into its cradle and the deck stopped spinning, only the high-pitched hiss from the amplifier through the speakers competed with Liam's scraping of his plate.

4

1942

My ancestors left Germany over two hundred years ago. If things had been different I might have been living in America now. They chose to move east with the promise of arable land and freedom of religious expression. This promise was kept and my people were tolerated under the Tsars and even assimilated into the new society brought about by the upheavals of the Bolshevik revolution. We always kept our German identity close and learnt German, spoke German in our homes and learnt Russian in our schools.

The region my people settled became a model for prosperity and achievement and the envy of many ethnic Russians. We brought new ideas in methods of farming and business practice which were adopted or watered down by the Soviet authorities. Our community was careful to stay out of politics, we had witnessed the widespread pogroms under the Tsars and the Soviet witch-hunts that followed the civil war. But no matter how you try, outside factors can often work against you. As I mentioned, our success was looked on with envy, we paid our taxes like any other minority which made up the Soviet Union, we contributed greatly to each and every five-year plan rolled out under Stalin. But it was the German invasion in 1941 that gave our Russian neighbours the opportunity to steal our land, take our crops and livestock and rob our banks. This was done in the name of the motherland. But greed and envy exist in any form of society and war is just the smokescreen needed to conceal their nefarious practices. How much longer would they have tolerated our success if the Germans hadn't invaded? Stalin saw fit to purge minorities at intervals throughout his tyranny, it was his own ethnic paranoia at work. We were easy prey and the label they used was that we were all fifth columnists under Hitler's sway. It may have been true that many of us listened to German radio, but so did many other nationalities anxious as to the progress of what seemed an unstoppable force throughout France and the low countries. Our treatment only drove those of us with any thoughts of reprisals and who were young enough to do anything about it into the arms of the German army. I was as reluctant to be separated from my family as anyone but my father insisted that I should join the Germans and liberate our homes from the Bolshevik thieves. I could be of use to them, the Russians didn't want us, they only wanted to force us into gulags and work camps in Siberia. I didn't realise that my own childhood died on the day I left my family and fled from Strekerau.

I travelled alone and mostly at night, which at the height of summer was late in coming. I managed four kilometres a night if I was lucky, at first through ripening fields and along unmetalled roads that stretched on forever with no boundaries to discern one from another. I took refuge in barns and wayside lofts in the first seven days until I reached the periphery of the invasion front. Once that had been crossed things got very different, the sound of shelling was just over every new horizon. At first I had been able to forage young wild rabbit but they had now all holed up somewhere deep and safe sensing a catastrophe. The barrage had frightened the birds out of the air and affected Hanzie badly too and I took time to dismount and walk him along the way to keep him calm. Worse was to follow as a result of the constant bombardment. Darkness never fell now, it was pinioned back in the sky by the explosions in my sector which terrified me to witness. Time was no longer reliable with the incursion of all this artificial daylight and without proper shelter to fall back on. It became ever more difficult to choose when to move on and even harder still to feed and protect my horse. Hanzie was losing weight as much of the grassland was now too badly scorched for him to eat. I had to make the most of the false nights avoiding the now choking roads with its exhausted scavengers seeking a respite from the marauding Luftwaffe. It was only in daylight that the ghastliness really unveiled itself at every turn. In a policy of 'scorched earth', all that could be of any use to the advancing Germans was either burnt, laid waste or put out of commission. Water soon became a commodity worth more than gold as the retreating Russians began to poison the wells in all the villages, torching every thatched roof on any habitable dwelling, even the cow sheds. And all the while the relentless procession of the displaced people taking what they could carry or pull on a cart behind them. How pitiful the few sticks of wood that they took for furniture and the pointless sentiment placed in useless heirlooms roped up in mattresses that must have meant so much at the time to have been worth the burden. How absurd and out of place some of their most precious family possessions now looked wrapped in potato-sacks in this startlingly transient environment. Their time-mottled photographs with fragile frames now trampled and soiled under nervous livestock within the cramped confines of their farm carts. Their common decency was now being tested under duress, their privacy defiled and their future very much in doubt.

It was just as well I travelled in the false night because I was going in the other direction. My route through was choked with their jettison, the retreat of a panicking population. The daylight temperatures soared with no tree-lined canopy for shade along parched country tracks that threw up great panoplies of dust when traversed in such great numbers. This dust was quick to dry any tears that fell into in the mouths of babies in a land now devoid of pity. The press of such a number of people was not without casualties and during the night I often heard cries for help from the surrounding fields, of those left behind in the melée. Their pleas grew fainter as I moved on and through them, unable to be of any assistance, as my own survival was still in question. I was reminded of tales of ancient Sparta whose hardened doctrine of leaving those who were too weak on the hillsides to be consumed by the wolves was cold and abhorrent to me when read from a textbook but now so relevant to what was happening around me. I too was eaten up by so much doubt, why was I not following them? I was walking into oblivion alone. The columns of displaced people began to thin out as I progressed further west.

I was now well within firing-range of the advancing German artillery, scavenging root crops in a pock-marked vegetable patch on an abandoned collective farm. Digging in the dirt, sifting for anything but I wasn't the first to have scraped about here judging by the shallow hollows in the pigmented soil where anything might have previously been. The farmhouse had suffered a direct hit from a shell, being as it was too much of a prime target on such a prominently exposed position for any artillerist to pass up. All the windows had been blown out and a trail of personal items had obviously been looted, sifted through and then discarded by passing opportunists. The roof had gone completely; the rafters turned in on themselves forming charred piano keys scratching at the splintered floorboards. The shell of the building held for now but I had taken a risk borne out of starvation coming up to this vulnerable spot. Hanzie was constantly agitated and my comforting him only belied my own fear and nervous exhaustion. At the back of the farmhouse was a log store, still intact but empty and adjacent to that, the shed where the farmer must have kept his tools at one time. The shed was no more that five metres by five across with a single pitched roof covered in tar. It had no windows but plenty of eyes in the knots of the weathered planks afforded air to pass through. I led Hanzie in and tied him to one of the wooden slats that must have held saws or hammers at one time. I watched him begin to transfer his weight by balancing on hooves alternately and this led me to believe that he was more settled within this temporary shelter. I stroked him in my own exhaustion and stretched my arms over his back before loosening his saddle. The shallow gully running along the middle of the floor at one time must have acted as a drain but was now congealed with diesel oil and dirt preventing me from lying on it. I took one of the few remaining tools - a rusty scythe hanging from a long nail and went back outside. The ripening crop left standing in the fields never to be harvested, could be cut in places and used as fodder and bedding. I set to work, summoning the last of my energy flailing the stalks that stood taller than me in places. I carried armfuls back in relays, offering a large pile to Hanzie and also insulating the floor where I would try and rest. I lay down and tried not to listen to my stomach complaining as it retracted with hunger until sleep came suddenly and I was out.

I don't quite know how long I slept but my horse's anxious movements woke me with a start. I could feel the ground vibrating, tremoring, pulsing, causing Hanzie to rear back against his tethering and to kick out at the wooden lathes that lined the shed. The cacophony engulfed the very ground I was lying on. I was paralysed with fear which dissipated my hunger pangs exacerbating the dryness in my throat and parching my lips. I gripped the straw on the floor and hid my head underneath to try and dull the sound as I was about to be engulfed. The mechanical whirring grew louder until it sounded like the whistle of a boiling kettle on a giant traction engine. A team of traction engines towing steam rollers bearing down on my location. Then a loud explosion to my right, followed by the whirr of metal rainfall on dry wood. The traction engines seemed to be right on top of my location now, ready to crush me where I lay. Once again I heard short bursts of metallic rainfall this time pounding against the surrounding structure, adding pain to Hanzie's panic and I was too terrified to react. The door of the shed was flung open and the dust in the space I occupied rose to greet a figure whose form couldn't yet discern as my eyes hadn't adjusted to the shock of the light. Hanzie was sweating uncontrollably at the confusion outside, pulling at his tether and snorting heavily. The figure in the doorway mustn't have noticed me on the floor at first as he relaxed his stance and lowered his weapon on seeing how fractious my horse was. He walked over my hand and I flinched, pain stabbing through me as his studded heels momentarily scraped into the back of my hand. He raised his arms slowly and spoke softly to Hanzie in a strange dialect of a language I understood from my home town. I lay prostrate as he slung his automatic weapon back over his shoulder, slowly, as if to show the horse that he meant no harm. Outside I could hear hurried orders and shouts for backup and calls for more searches. Just then another figure appeared in the doorway requesting orders and the soldier still standing on my hand gestured for the other to leave him be. I was numb with pain and then he moved closer to inspect Hanzie depressing his weight from me at last and I almost screamed with the sudden release. I lay just inches below him in the loose straw that I had used to line the floor of the shed. He now had Hanzie by the harness and was examining him studiously along his girth until he drew back his hand suddenly and I could see that it was covered in blood. Even in the straw-mottled half-light I could make out the dark smearing on Hanzie's piebald coat. I could hear the soldier talking in Hanzie's ear, stroking him again, reassuring him. He stood back a few paces before unbuckling a pistol very slowly from a leather holster. He pointed its thin matt black barrel directly in line with Hanzie's head and fired one shot.

The words had left me before the realisation set in. I don't even remember what I screamed. I do remember that I lunged at him despairingly as he in turn spun rapier-like on his heel and hit me a blow to my forehead with the flat side of his pistol and I was thrust into darkness.

When I woke he was sitting waiting. He could see me trying to focus again until the pain from his strike returned and felled me completely back down onto the straw. I lay on my side unable to turn away from the sight of my dead companion, my last link with home now irretrievably lost.

'The only reason you are alive right now is that you shouted at me in German,' he said quietly.

I still was unable to turn and face his voice, I think he knew that so he got up and walked between me and my dead horse, his muddy boots now in my line of blurred vision.

'Believe me I would never have shot him if I didn't have to. He was a pure bred, the best I have seen in this forsaken place. What the hell was he doing here? All the good livestock has been chased off long before we arrived. Was he really yours, Boris? You seem to have an attachment with him. You should have hidden him better. My men strafed the place and this is the result.'

I wept for myself as much as Hanzie and with the action of doing so I was able to move my head again slowly and try to sit up.

'I searched you while you were out cold and found no identity papers on you Boris, but I did find this peculiar letter of introduction written on your behalf in German with some scrawled numbers on the reverse side of the envelope. I found this letter and a quantity of rubles in the saddle bag. Can you explain any of this in such a way as to make it believable?'

The hand he had stood on now bled openly onto the straw and I was still light-headed but my own hurt had turned bitter again at the sight of what he had done.

'What have we got here? What am I supposed to assume? A Boris who speaks German? Say something else Boris!'

'My name isn't Boris.'

'Is it Ivan then? Or Dimitry?

'It's Andreas.'

'Is that so? A fucking German farm-boy out here in the middle of the Russian steppe? Twelve hundred kilometres from home?'

He prodded me with the muzzle of his pistol as if to see whether or not I was actually real. I was dishevelled and reeked of the byre, but I was real enough. The soldier now had company, two others had arrived and they formed a huddle talking about me as I stood stretching both arms and legs. I couldn't make out their discussion, but I could tell from his expression that he had reached a decision. He was the one they answered to and after issuing some orders he rejoined me.

'My men wanted me to just shoot you and take your rubles. But I am interested to hear your story before I do anything.'

One of them, a Gefreiter, stared at me and made a pistol-shape from his fingers and pointed it at me mockingly before joining the others securing the perimeter. I was shaking from hunger in the position I was trying to hold and the officer could see that and told me to lie down again.

'This is Russia, the great distances here begin to gnaw at you, the men act differently, go a little crazy so don't pay any heed to his provocation. Everyone is just tired all the time.'

'Could I have some water?' I asked.

He produced a small flask and I drank it down, spluttering as I did.

'Careful. Too much too quick does more harm than good. Drink slow.'

I handed him back the flask and he motioned for me to get up if I could.

'We can dress that hand for you but first you need to tell me everything. Why you are here, what you know and who sent you.'

'I know enough for you to keep me alive, enough for it to be of help to you. I was sent here by my father.'

'I can't help but credit whoever sent you as you speak flawless German.'

'I am ethnic German. You have to believe that.'

'It's not up to me to decide what you are, the Einsatzgruppen who follow in our wake will be the judge of that. You will have to convince them of your usefulness or else they will hang you as a spy.'

This was my predicament, the Russians didn't want me and the Germans didn't trust me. He told me his name was Oberleutnant Werner and that I was now a 'guest' of an advanced column of the 168th infantry division attached to the 4th Panzer Army. Oberleutnant Werner led me to a stalled panzer III tank, its crew were hastily digging a slit trench to drive the tank over so that they could sleep under it later. He climbed up as I watched and disappeared inside the turret. I could hear muffled shouts down what must have been some radio transmitter. He appeared quite animated moments later and one of the tankists offered him a tin cup of coffee to pacify him.

'Verdammt, I'm stuck with you my German farm-boy. For a day or two at least. We are too far ahead of the main group for me to have an escort bring you to them.'

He took a drink and then winced at the crew member as to its freshness. It was passable given the conditions. The heat of the day made the surface of the tank too hot to sit on comfortably, so he reached his cup down to me and then jumped down from the tank. I drank from it without a second thought, the heat from the chicory set my pulse racing as I had never tasted anything so strong.

'If you want to live through the next few days then stick close by me. I don't have any intelligence officer with me so I will have to debrief you myself. You say that you have come all this way to the invasion front to help us?'

I nodded, clutching the cup to my mouth in case he would ask for it back.

'What's up ahead? What can we expect? Did you encounter any Russian units? What was their strength? Did they have any artillery? What was the morale of the local inhabitants you came across?'

All questions fired at me with the rapidity of his automatic weapon. He led me back to the remnants of the farmhouse which was now enfiladed by three panzer tanks and where a clutch of pioneer battalion sappers were now stretching tarpaulin and tying ropes against the side of the structure to secure it for an overnight bivouac. One emerged from the ruin clutching some rafter shards, he was stripped to the waist, unflatteringly wearing field grey braces to keep his trousers up and he began throwing the shards into a shallow hole he had dug earlier. He was the cook apparently and he was setting up the rudiments of the fire oven for later that day. He saluted the Oberleutnant slovenly as we passed, Werner returned the salute and grimaced before beckoning me to sit with him on two tea chests in the shade of the tarpaulins.

I told him what I knew, what I had witnessed. I said that I hadn't encountered any Russian military along the route as it was congested with innocent civilians who would have overwhelmed any military vehicle. I told him that his planes were the only ones I had seen in the sky, flying low and east looking for rich targets such as the railheads or minor towns. I knew they were his planes because they had a singularly terrifying siren that sounded as they began their dive, strafing the congested dust tracks. The country that stretched out before them was now a featureless wasteland where the inhabitants had torched what they couldn't carry. They could expect poisoned wells at villages and crude efforts of sabotage to hinder their path. He listened intently and then spoke:

'I'm taking a risk trusting you, but I do believe you. From tomorrow you will direct the point of my column. You will be the eyes of this company. You know what's over the horizon and you can lead us safely through this country. You have seen the calibre of my men; if you help us, then you have my promise that I will do all that I can for you. Tomorrow morning, just before we leave, I want you to take some of our gasoline and pour it in the shed where I found you. Set a match to it and we will take you east.'

I gulped at the prospect, but this is what my father had wanted me to do. Oberleutnant Werner was summoned once again by the radio operator and raced over to one of the tanks. The fire from the shallow trench had been lit for some time without me noticing and an A frame had been erected over it with three large cooking pots hanging from it. The shirtless cook was stirring sausages in one of the cooking pots, wiping the smoke from his eyes at the same time as the wind changed direction every few minutes. I felt confident enough to join him.

'What's in the other pots?' I asked.

'Well not your lovely dead horse yet my young 'un.'

The shock of what he just said hung in the air along with his bad breath and his crude laughter. This was his other stock-in-trade, dishing out scathing remarks along with the liver noodle soup and dumplings. He could see how hungry I was and he grudgingly said that I could have some of the food if I brought more wood for the fire and also looked for anything to sit on that could be salvaged from the ruin. The other men began to congregate without being summoned, their stomachs had told them to. They all looked field-hardened, weary, dust-coated and dishevelled. Any outward traits of exuberance had long since been swapped for hardship with the realization that this vast country was swallowing them up with every step east. They left three men to guard the perimeter and then deposited their weapons on the ground before retrieving their mess tins from their heavy backpacks. The cook gave me a ladle and I dunked it into one of the simmering kettle drums and following his instructions I began to fill each mess tin that was held out in front of me. At first I was sloppy with nerves and shook as I served and the Gefreiter who had goaded me earlier was joking at my expense in the queue. The cook told me to ignore him so I glanced down at his dusty jackboots as I served him. He mocked me to my face, besmirching my origins, my paternal line and took delight in doing so. Some around him smirked at my vulnerability to try and curry favour with him. I ladled just enough boiling stew into his mess tin and then scalded his wrist with some residue, seeing him flinch and drop the mess tin, lose face and cry out. This revenge was enough for me but I had made an enemy and I would have to watch my back. The others were subdued by my actions, I had stood up to the Gefreiter and they now shuffled past in silence as I served on. The cook took over from me and told me to get a tin and to serve myself. I sat down in his chair as near to the fire as I could as the evening chill was drawing in. Everyone else was now too preoccupied with eating to take any heed of me, except the Gefreiter I had previously scalded and his silent glare pierced through the fire light and into me. I was later permitted to stretch out under the tarpaulin that was secured along the last supporting wall of the ruined farmhouse. Many of the enlisted men sat out in the open throwing shards and poking embers to keep the cooks oven fire burning. They shared jokes, telling each other reassuring stories of the carbolicky-smelling nurses with starched tight uniforms safely behind their lines who would look after them should they get winged buy a Russki. Some held letters open towards the firelight reciting inwardly the plaintive messages from families or lovers. These men, most of whom were only a few years older than me all had fatigue etched faces which aged them. One produced a harmonica as another started to sing folk songs in a rusticated dialect of German, he could hold a tune and caused a tear to well in some of the most hardened veterans. The songs were traditional rather than nationalistic. Some were familiar to me as they had often drifted over the crackling airwaves back home when we tuned into Deutscher Rundfunk. So I began to hum and in doing so I drew attention to myself and presently the cook took it upon himself to ask me to sing for the company. I was cajoled and then stood up, the only thing that came to mind in my nervousness was a Russian folk song called the 'Volga Boatmen'. I croaked drily then began the slow reverie that builds up in the verse of the song. Behind me a young lancer had produced a mandolin and was frantically trying to play the key I was singing in and so catch up with me. Soon after that I could hear the soft accompaniment of a harmonica which further helped the men get the gist of the background rhythm and gave me enough confidence to plough on. Here on the starlit steppe the enemy of my enemy was singing in unison one of the staples from the Soviet musical repertoire. My lyrics were convoluted and I repeated myself more often than not, but the captive audience were caught up in the exoticism of singing an enemy song so far from home. I stood down to whistles and the release of much pent-up anxiety, it was as if I had humanized this alien place a little for them. For I think that many had forgotten the reasons why they were actually here. I slept better that night, more from total exhaustion than any other in the weeks previous.

My morning task confronted me after breakfast with these men with whom even the most hardbitten had begun to accept that I was no spy or enemy agent. To some I had even become a kind of regimental mascot and as such was to be held up as a totem or lucky charm. Earlier as I washed with them, a quarter master offered me a camouflaged smock to wear and so mark me out as one of them. It swamped me so I wore my belt tight around it and took it to mean some kind of acceptance. I helped the cook wash up after serving and then retrieved the requisite amount of gasoline to torch the shed. I looked inside one last time and then lit a taper and set fire to the rickety structure. It was soon ablaze and could be seen from a great distance in this flat treeless landscape.

The tanks had by now lined up in a wide column just forward of our location, soon to fan out ever eastward, their engines revving, their commanders dusting off their black tunics with headphones slung over their jaunty forage caps intently scanning the horizon through their binoculars. Behind them a throng of panzer grenadiers had hitched a ride like so many pilot fish on a shark. A little further back waited the convoy of trucks with their axles wrought low over the potholes, straining with each heavy load. Their exteriors were overhung with Jerry cans and spare tyres, their windscreens blinded and caked with dust, their drivers side cab windows fully extended to try and ventilate the searing heat that was already accumulating. The canvas interior of one was festooned with oil drums and dozens of rows of roped up bicycles. Another held the field-kitchen, baking-oven and cooking equipment, my disingenuous cook now occupying the front passenger seat and smoking copiously. Another truck carried the field medical unit with the wounded strapped on board. Yet another stored the pontoon bridge, shoring wood, rope and materials with rubber dinghies for breaching any river where the bridge was blown to hinder our progress. The larder of smoked sausage wurst and dried goods, barrels of maize, grain, malt barley, the chicken mesh cages of sequestered livestock and barrels of fresh drinking water had two trucks of their own. The field tents, stoves, weapons including flame-throwers, mortars, mines, shells and ammunition supplies, spare tank parts and extra lengths of tank-track took up another two trucks. The last link in the chain held the ranks of infantry as well as communication equipment and towed anti-aircraft artillery pieces. Everything that could that be thought of to keep an army moving and supplied was now primed and ready and following in the rear. Lastly, followed the men on horseback the Panzer Kavallerie, the eyes and ears of the regiment who would soon spread out into the distance to search for any enemy activity.

Oberleutnant Werner had seconded a BMW motorcycle with sidecar and was gesturing to the tanks to move forward as he folded a map into his camouflaged jacket. He saw me watching the flames plume out from the shed and called me over.

'Boris, it's time to leave! You can take these spare goggles and ride behind my driver. But hold on tight, you hear? Florien is a mad driver and you will have to grab on to his belt buckle as we don't have time to stop and go back for you if you fall off, understand? and Boris, I still have your rubles! You will have to earn them back from me, do you hear?'

'It's Andreas, Oberleutnant Werner. See, I remember your name and I will earn them all back as I have counted them.'

'Very good Boris,' he shouted over the moving tank engines.

The pall of dust created by such activity would have blinded Andreas's eyes had he not put the goggles on in time. Overhead could now be seen the blanketing fuselages of so many German aircraft covering our approach giving the enemy notice of our intent. The dust-cloud we created meant there was no looking back and we made good progress over the swathes of abandoned farmland, meeting no opposition or minefields. The Russians had just melted away leaving the hurried detritus as symbols of former habitation. I clung to Florien's leather coat buckles, he did ride like a mad man, but this was to avoid craters in our path and also to try and keep pace with the tanks. I never felt more alive in my life, I was sure that I was retracing my steps and by doing so in the process taking back what was my own.

I had been used to moving guardedly under cover of darkness, but I was now in the vanguard of a military machine rolling east so aggressively, churning up everything in its path. An hour passed so quickly and some time later I could make out the gold painted latticed onion domes of an orthodox church rising up through a black pall of smoke on the far bank of a river to our left. The tanks wheeled round to infiltrate the outskirts of the town which had grown up around the church and had now been set ablaze by the locals as they fled. I hadn't dared get this close to Belgorod previously as it was choked with refugees and I was forced to sleep under the arches of a bridge that led there until nightfall ten days ago. That bridge had subsequently been blown up and now forward units of the 168th division were pouring steady fire on the remaining defenders on the other side of the river bank so that our pioneer sappers could begin to construct a temporary pontoon bridgehead for the tanks to cross.

The Russians had dug in at the only crossing point and were going to make a fist of it using the natural defences of a large salient in the river with a steep ridge to their back, thus making it hard for them to be outflanked or encircled. Oberleutnant Werner gave the coordinates to the wireless operator to call in an air strike from the Luftwaffe to soften the Russians' resolve. He knew that this would not be quick in coming so he ordered six tanks to concentrate their fire on the far bank of the river. He wanted the town taken before nightfall with or without air support. It was around this time that I saw first hand the real face of war as the casualties on our side began to mount up. The pioneer sappers were cut down by enfilading rapid fire as they waded through the river. Some lay face down already turning the rock pools red from where I watched. Their companions tried in vain under withering fire to secure ropes to the remnants of the bridge and the only thing that they could achieve was the retrieval of the wounded. They began to pour into a dressing station set up in one of the trucks within the convoy. Two sappers approached carrying another casualty with a stomach wound that bled profusely, so much so that a third sapper had to keep his hand on the wound to stem the flow. They laid him out on a stretcher and he was lifted up into the back of the lorry. His wounds were so bad that all they could do was give him morphine to numb his agony. He was the first man I ever saw die in front of me. He kept calling for someone called Hannelore, his wife or his mother, then his eyes fixed on a point beyond us all and he died.

The explosions and gunfire going off all around gave me little time to ponder. I could see Oberleutnant Werner arguing with a tank commander ahead of me, so I decided to stay close by him. The tanks shelled the far bank as Werner watched through his binoculars, they began to find their range and I could see a number of Russian soldiers being thrown into the air such was the force of the shelling. These were the snipers whose precision shooting had decimated our pioneers in the river. They fell like stones from attic roofs and concealed window balconies as buildings disintegrated from beneath them. The result was that the Russians began to pull back through the town and the Oberleutnant felt confident enough to order another bridging party to try again. Ten men went into the water under a covering barrage from our tanks. They carried ropes and shoring wood above their heads in rapid waist-high water. Two pioneers reached the central pillar of the damaged bridge without incident at the mid point in the river. They began tying the ropes to secure the pontoon to the central pillar. The others began attaching pontoon rafts to the hook eye loops on the rope and another two pioneers on the river bank took up the slack and eventually the pontoon ropes were tied and staked securely. Yet more pontoon rafts were now floated out into the river and attached to the hook eyes to further strengthen the floating bridge. While this was happening six sappers were nailing planks to what now resembled a floating barge stretching halfway across the river. These planks gave the bridge rigidity and the strength to potentially take the weight of our tanks. With no enemy snipers firing from the far bank, the hammering of planks went on into the evening and this noise was soon drowned out by the Luftwaffe raid on the town which caused further havoc and panic to our advantage. By dusk the bridge was finished and a detachment of infantry was to be sent over with small arms and mortars to ascertain the enemies strength and capture an enemy 'mouth' so we might know what their plans were. This detachment was led by the Gefreiter I had crossed the day before.

His name was Hauser and he had cultivated a singular reputation of being hard as nails and appeared to relish hand-to-hand combat with the Soviets. Hauser gathered a clique of men around him, all heady with a whiff of national socialism, unlike most of Werner's company. Hauser saw this fight as a crusade against the scourge of bolshevism. I wondered why he hadn't tried for the Waffen SS instead of the Wehrmacht, but I think he had some dubious traits and something shady in his background which even they baulked at when assessing recruits. The Waffen SS prided itself on taking only the elite, not just the fanatical, so Hauser threw in his lot with the 168th. To my surprise he requested Oberleutnant Werner to give permission for me to accompany them on this mission considering that I was the only one who could speak Russian fluently. Werner knew that a history was developing between me and Hauser, but he agreed to the request to keep face. I was given a steel helmet but wasn't to be given a weapon, they didn't trust me enough yet and certainly weren't aware of my background of hunting with firearms back home. We set out in the summer twilight, our target already unnaturally illuminated by the incendiary fires taking hold across the river. I reached the pontoon bridge drawing up the rear carrying extra ammunition boxes. The river glistened between the planks below our feet and flowed fiercely around the pontoon barges that were fastened tight to the bridge.

Gefreiter Hauser was in front all the time making animated gestures and signals to those close enough to understand them. He had a number of stick grenades poking from his jacket and one in each jackboot. He wore a bandolier of ammunition across his back and carried both a Mauser pistol and an MP-38 machine gun. We made it to the far bank unmolested, where even in the half light the devastation caused from our tanks was manifestly obvious. Russian gun emplacements were scorched and mangled with flesh immolated in the fireball that must have terrified and overwhelmed the occupants. Hauser signalled that we fan out through the narrow street that led ultimately to the shingle-domed church at the top of an incline. Each one of them in turn chose a building to search, clear and make safe before moving on. A slow progress began until we were sure no hidden traps were in store for us. Some were eager to show Hauser their mettle and took unnecessary risks jumping from shattered windows in the gaps from house to house. One named Zeigler landed with such force he fell through the smouldering floor of an upstairs bedroom and was stuck fast with so much kit strapped around him. His luck had run out as the room below was occupied by one of the last concealed Russian snipers. Zeigler's screams for help only drew enemy fire from up the street and were soon muffled, then extinguished, as the sniper despatched him with a knife across his throat. The Russian then tried to double back, only to get caught in the crossfire and was torn apart. I think he was cut down by his own side and he fell just metres from where I was hiding, prostrate with fear behind an upturned Soviet staff car. Hauser shouted for more ammunition and then he sprinted through the withering dissonance to where the dead Russian lay and retrieved his sniper rifle. He spotted me and dived for cover alongside me cradling the telescopic scope of the sniper rifle as he fell.

'I could kill you right here Boris, who would know? I could snap your neck and who would care? Oberleutnant Werner is across the river, he won't hear your screams. Give me more ammunition you Russian half-breed. Follow me now or I swear I will make you dance for the Russki snipers!'

He tightened his grip around the collar of my camouflage smock and his glare will live long in my memory. He slapped my face hard then dragged me up, cursing at the weight on his back. He then zig-zagged across the street back to one of the burning houses. I knew I had to follow, I was a target if I stayed, both for him and the Russians. Bullets chipped the cobblestones between my strides as I ran.

Hauser was waiting and I threw myself past him, our presence no longer a secret and we began to draw down heavy enemy fire from the direction of the church. Hauser sprayed bullets through party walls and interconnecting doorways along the narrow hallway on the ground floor indiscriminately. Outside again, we traced our path over rickety backyard fences and low dividing walls until finally we reached the last house before the church. Hauser kicked in the back door and signalled our arrival by lobbing in a stick grenade. We waited for the five second delay to pass and then heard a dull thud coming from within. The dust cloud had yet to dissipate when Hauser entered. We breathed in the cordite smoke and plaster dust, our eyes began to sting in the pitch blackness. Hauser clumsily tripped over two dead Russians as he felt his way for the staircase which was now missing any support rail. I could barely make him out propped against the shredded wallpaper avoiding holes in the staircase, vainly hauling himself up, arms stretched wide for balance and not succeeding. For a curious moment his pose reminded me of the rough-hewn Cossack dancers, part of the circus that would visit with us each summer back in Strekerau. Amidst all the chaos I was conjuring with clowns until Hauser's eyes caught sight of me in the gloom.

'Catch this rifle Boris, it's weighing me down. Don't drop it or I will tan your hide.'

I stepped forward after lowering the ammunition box and he threw the weapon at me. I caught it and confidently checked the safety catch, which must have unsettled him as I saw him feel for his Mauser pistol. I hadn't held such a bespoke rifle before with its intricate barrelling but I knew how to handle it and I think Hauser took note. I followed him up and he tentatively opened the door of the upstairs bedroom which he was certain had a clear view overlooking the church. The room had been decimated of any semblance of domesticity thanks to the Luftwaffe raid. Hauser crawled on his belly, hugging the splintered floorboards to the shell hole in the opposite wall that once held the window frame. He sat on the floor with his back to the wall, staring over and yet right through me. He seemed to be counting in his head. The machine gun barrage outside could be measured and he was timing the gaps between bursts. A five second gap between fifteen second bursts, repeated three bursts a minute until the magazine was empty. After two minutes focusing in his mind he jumped up and leaned out the window and shouted 'Kommt' at the top of his voice. Within seconds I could hear the others negotiating the staircase. He was within touching distance of the twisted onion spires whose ornate fragility appeared to offer no vantage points for enemy snipers. They hauled the Panzerfaust-30 and a supply of shells up the staircase with great difficulty. Hauser motioned at them to hurry and in doing so one of them caught a ricochet bullet straight through the heart as he tried to carry the Panzerfaust into position and was dead before he hit the floor. Another took his place and both he and Hauser lay flat under the shell hole. It would only have taken a well thrown grenade to kill us all. Hauser again counted the magazine rounds while he held onto the Panzerfaust. It ceased firing when he had anticipated and he was already up and aiming through the sight finder of the cumbersome weapon at the roof shingles of the church. The other Grenadier fed in a shell and the firing action recoiled into Hauser's shoulder. It left the chamber immediately with a loud thud and tore into the timber structure of the church at very close range setting it alight as if it were kindling.

The startled Russians scrambled out the front porch of the church firing wildly in all directions. Hauser stepped back from the opening whilst gripping his shoulder in obvious discomfort and two others proceeded to concentrate their fire from above as the defenders began to clump in a pile like dead wood. The man to Hauser's right, I think he was called Fiebig, jerked forward suddenly dropping his MP-38 and fell to the floorboards. He was shot expertly through the forehead at the helmet line with a high velocity bullet that exited the back of his neck and embedded in the skirting board to my right. Hauser grabbed Fiebig's MP-38 and stood over his body firing in a rage until the magazine was empty. Only one Russian remained alive and that only because he had hidden under his comrades. As soon as the firing ceased he chose to scamper under the crawl space of the burning church. He began pitifully to shriek 'nicht schiessen' in broken German. Hauser paused and hid behind the wall facing us, breathing heavily, his MP-38 still smoking hot. He whispered coldly at me to stay down as he was convinced there was a sniper somewhere out there. He and the others crawled past me and crept back down the stairs intent on somehow confronting and capturing the Russian hiding under the burning church.

I still had the SVT-40 semi-automatic sniping rifle with 3.5 x SVT PU scope so I snaked slowly over to the shattered window frame which was now illuminated by the burning church, my heart thumping through my chest. I pulled out the magazine clip and checked how many bullets were left. Fiebig's coagulated blood spread around me, dripping darkly through the gaps in the floorboards and I had to use all my strength to turn his head away from me. His fixated stare and that of his companion asking silent questions as to the reason for our being here in the first instance. My size might have helped me to hide better and I was eventually able to train the sniper rifle muzzle through a small air block ventilation opening at floor level. The 3.5 x SVT PU scope on my captured Russian sniper rifle magnified everything dramatically. I wished that I had such a thing when wild boar hunting with my father. I took my eye away from the gun sight for a moment as I heard Hauser's faltering dialect trying to coax the Russian to come out. I instinctively trained the scope on the natural vantage points overlooking the square and a sudden reflective flash caught my attention. I looked above the lens as if the sudden shock could have made me imagine what I saw. I now adjusted the focus and true enough I could make out another gun sight over a hundred metres away on the second floor of a workers' residential building. My heart was in my mouth as I slowly retracted the rifle from the air block and released the safety catch. I kissed the weapon, something I always did on my hunting trips. Then I stretched back into position, my stomach hugging the floorboards, my legs spread open for balance. He was still there, I could just make out the netting he had used to try and stop any glare as he lay between two sandbags. His glass scope couldn't help but shimmer in the fire haze just for a moment betraying him, as I'm sure it now betrayed me. I had no time to ask Hauser. I would only give my position away. I only had seconds. He was waiting for someone to move in the square. The discipline that my father had instilled in me when handling a hunting rifle now came to my aid. I squeezed the trigger as calmly as I could but the action of this strange new weapon dislodged my whole body. Hauser and his men heard the repeat of this single shot echo around the ravaged shop fronts confirming the presence of a sniper. I unscrewed the scope from the body of the rifle and held it to the gap in the air brick. The shape had moved, the sandbag had toppled, his rifle now pointing into the air. My God the elation, the adrenalin rush! I looked out over the window recess and Hauser was still crouching, frozen behind a garden wall at street level.

'I got him,' I shouted.

'You got the shooter?' cried Hauser disbelievingly.

'Yes he's dead.'

'Do you fucking believe it, he just shot one of his own.'

'He is different from them,' one of them whispered.

'I don't know what to think,' shrugged Hauser.

'Give the kid a chance, he could easily have shot us from up there with that sniper rifle. He had plenty of time to line us up if he wanted to.'

'It goes against anything we were brought up to believe.'

'Hauser, the kid thinks he's German. Let it go, he saved our skin.'

He got to his feet and ran over to the crawl space under the burning church. The Russian had succumbed to smoke inhalation from above and Hauser called for help to drag him out. They carried him back to my position as I scanned the square for any movement. I could hear them take the prisoner through to the back room. Hauser shouted up to me to take the dog tags off the two fallen men beside me. This grim task wasn't easy, even in the stark light from the church fire I still fumbled with their tunic buttons nervously, shaking as I tried to snap the tag chains from their bloodstained bodies. I knew that this was a test and even though I had killed a sniper, Hauser was still trying to get to me. But it wasn't him this time that did, how often is it that the little things can set you off rather than the bigger ones. I noticed something gleam from Fiebig's tunic pocket. A harmonica fell to the floor, pristine silver encasing the mouthpiece now soaking up his blood. Fiebig must have been the one who had accompanied me as I sang in what seems a different lifetime and now he lay in a crumpled heap on a dusty floor lifeless and forlorn. I was too focused on just trying to hold a tune to take in who was playing the harmonica. I picked it up and wiped it down and put it in my pocket along with other personal items from the two dead men. I took a moment as the flames began to lick at the crumpled windows and then collected up all the weapons I could and made my way back downstairs.

The Russian was still coming round when I entered the room. They hadn't beaten him yet as he wasn't coherent enough to make any sense. He sat limply on a chair, his thick head of hair hanging low over the kitchen table. He wore a mottled green uniform with no insignia and no belt, singed and dirty from where he had hidden. His face, from what I could make out, was blackened and his eyes were bloodshot and he began to stare wildly at everyone in the room. Hauser had removed the man's boots and tied his wrists together behind his back and now offered him some water from his flask. Hauser held the flask at the man's mouth tilting just enough over his parched lips.

'Boris talk to him, make him see sense,' whispered Hauser in my ear.

I took a chair and sat opposite the prisoner. He still slouched with his head bowed, but I could tell he was definitely taking stock of everyone in the room. I was handed a note with some questions hastily scribbled onto it, similar to those asked to me previously by Oberleutnant Werner. The prisoner looked up when I began speaking, knowing my accent was regional Russian not just faltering Russian. I told him that we would see that he got fair treatment if he cooperated with us, to which he shrugged his shoulders but still remained silent. Hauser gave me a grubby pencil and something to write on which turned out to be the underside of his army pay book. I began by asking him about the strength and formation of his unit. He didn't respond so I tried to lighten my approach by asking him where he was from. Nothing. I then tried another tack, I told him what to expect if he didn't help us, that the men I was with were only too ready to avenge their fallen comrades. He looked up at me for a moment and then asked me my age. I told him, he then asked me what the hell I was doing with these enemies of the motherland. It stopped me in my tracks and then I regained my composure and told him that I had already lost everything to the NKVD. He spat at me which just missed and hit the table and said I would hang either way. This really affected me and I could see that Hauser was about to intervene. I shook my head at Hauser and tried again. I quietly asked for him to give me something to tell these men, anything, even just the number of his unit, anything so that they wouldn't have to beat it out of him. He called me a bastard and said that I was neither one thing nor the other, a misfit. I got up from the table, my anger seething through my eyes and I pulled his head back by his hair. It was as if all the pent up emotions had rallied inside me for this one moment. I looked into his face and spat directly into it, which grabbed everyone's attention. I was shaking from doing such a thing as it was totally out of character. I was shaking but I think he couldn't tell because he began to speak again as my spit dripped down his face. He said that I was lucky his hands were tied as he would roll me over and make me beg for my life. I held my nerve along with the table edge and I slowly told him that his life was now in my hands and I only had to say the word to end it. He was right though and it had sunk in to me, I was damned if I did and damned if I didn't and this realisation had worked on him too, he knew I had nothing to lose. I asked him his name again and this time he told me. Sergei Ivanov. His unit was the 220th rifle division, its strength all but wiped out, its commander was Col. Yakov Vronskiy.

I wrote down what he told me on the reverse side of the pay book and handed it to Hauser. His rifle division had been covering the retreat through the town when it had come under heavy bombardment from our tanks. They had been decimated and had fallen back on the church and had lost all contact with their division. They had no tanks and couldn't offer any resistance to our artillery. I offered Sergei some more water and he grudgingly let me pour it into his mouth. He knew that his usefulness to us was all but used up, that even his own side would have him shot for revealing any more than he had. His whole countenance had changed from rage and aggression to one of submission. He asked me what would happen now. I wasn't sure myself, but I tried to convince him that he wouldn't be shot out of hand. If he cooperated further he would get fair treatment from Oberleutnant Werner. Hauser told me to untie him and they watched his every move as I gave him back his boots. I asked him if he was strong enough to walk and he nodded. He was to be my responsibility until we got back across the river.

5

1987

Liam slept in the following morning, a strange bed with an unworn mattress, fresh sheets and soft pillows in a new setting had all played their part. Andreas's story had grown in intensity, drowning out the small hours along with the alcohol. He was able to get accustomed to his new surroundings as fresh sunlight mixed with dust particles through the chinks in his curtain covering the half open window. Beyond the street noises below he could distinctly hear children cackle like so many geese in a nearby school playground. He listened to the unfamiliar creaks and gurgling pipes, muffled yawns and hurried footsteps around him on different floor levels as others prepared themselves for the working day ahead.

He had a week of lates to look forward to thanks to Frau Radler. It was a lot to take in. He had listened to Andreas that first evening out of politeness and then with an interest that consumed him as his story unfolded. Here was a man stripped of his childhood through no fault of his own, caught up in a maelstrom that had torn him from the things he loved and had propelled him roughly into adulthood hanging tightly to the coat-tails of an invading army. A sixteen-year-old boy who had up until now only ever killed a young wild boar and that had been from a distance in his father's woods, who now had taken a human life and witnessed death at close quarters. Liam was a pragmatist but even he had misgivings about Andreas throwing his lot in with one of the darkest regimes that had ever roamed this planet. He was only sixteen; he couldn't have known the hideous truth and anyway he was only doing what his father had told him. He felt sure that Andreas had ruminated often over his actions in the intervening years, but Liam wanted to hear more. Let him speak of it when he wants to, he thought, as he began to make his bed. Liam couldn't push this, it was obvious that Andreas wanted to get something off his chest and that he was the conduit after all this time. He had the apartment to himself as Andreas had risen earlier to accompany one of the hotel residents to a funeral service at the Alter Nordfriedhof cemetery.

Kirstin Deubler answered Andreas's knock at 10 a.m. It struck him how unusual it was to see her during the day. Her rivened features somehow seemed softer in the middle of the night when she would normally send for him. By that late hour the Jägermeister would have worked its magic and transported her back to 1942. She pretended to kiss him on both cheeks and led him through the faded grandeur of her Biedermeier suite solemnly dressed in a black Loden Frey outfit with a jet necklace. Passing her curtain-call array of framed photographs and press clippings and on into the main reception room where he had played for her so many times before on her Bechstein B-208 piano dating from the 1920s. How he loved stroking every key, its resonance and tone sourced from the finest wood and ivory and now a rarity since the factory was destroyed in Berlin by the night raids during the war. He doubted that Kirstin held it in such high esteem as she couldn't play, but overcame this stuffy reserve by knowing she always had it tuned regularly and that he was the only one ever allowed to play it for her.

He wasn't the only visitor that morning. A valkyrie of a woman now sat bolt upright across from him, also creped in black, holding a steaming Dresden china cup and saucer on her lap. She, like Kirstin, was from another age, one that they both clung onto virulently and Andreas was expected to pay court to them considering her patronage of him. Andreas had dressed appropriately for this ritual, dusting off his great coat and wearing a freshly starched shirt and black tie. He may not have been of the same caste as these two chatelaines but he was cultivated enough to look the part when needed.

'Frau Hesslering, I would like to introduce you to Andreas Mensche, my trusted comforter and a long-standing servant of this hotel. He has agreed to accompany us both to Teddy's funeral at the Asam Kirche in Sendlinger Strasse and later to the interment at the Alter Nordfriedhof.'

Andreas tried to absorb just what a 'trusted comforter' meant. He motioned to shake Frau Hesslering's hand, but all she would offer was a nod in his direction. The two ladies somehow occupied most of the space on the two-seater chairs and Andreas was inclined to stand on ceremony.

'Teddy will be missed, we will not see his like again,' said Frau Hesslering.

'Indeed, Teddy was an echt mann, a true gentleman,' agreed Kirstin.

Andreas wasn't here just to make up the numbers as he knew Teddy too. Teddy Fernsehn had been the artistic director of the Kleine Komoedie theatre within the Bayerischer Hof for the last forty years. He had been a firm proponent of Kirstin's singing talents, even if these tended towards bias as it cemented his position with her parents who owned the hotel. Teddy was exempted from military service on account of his employers' influence and intervention. His finest role was in playing down his sexuality in public at least and the theatre was seldom under scrutiny from the Nazis as it continually gave gratis morale-boosting performances for recuperating troops on a regular basis. Teddy had free reign to engage a polyglot cast from all the European countries now under German control. The longevity of the shows that were often state subsidized, unwittingly kept some of the more politically outspoken performers out of the concentration camps. Teddy's artistic empathy knew no bounds and many talented Jewish actors and musicians found sanctuary within the tight knit group of players at the Kleine Komoedie. A network had been established within the theatre group, a tight cell of committed individuals sworn to secrecy. That first link in the chain leading to other links which stretched tenuously across southern Germany down to Bodensee on Lake Constance and on to the shared border with Switzerland. Provision was made for the close families of the Jewish performers to stay short-term under the stage of the theatre until an escape route was verified and false papers could be obtained on the black market. These vulnerable individuals were secreted and fed under the very noses of the Nazi authorities who nightly monopolized the best stalls in the theatre. This escape network operated sporadically with no routine and no pattern, successfully within the heart of Munich for the duration of the war. It ultimately led to an overwhelmingly agreed motion within the Israeli Kennesit in 1971 to offer Teddy Fernsehn the title of a Righteous Gentile. Many of the veteran performers and their relatives had now returned to repay the numerous unselfish acts of kindness along with their respects today at Teddy's funeral.

It was Teddy who had first noticed Andreas begging, dressed in rags along the street near his favourite restaurant Osteria Bavaria back in June 1953. Teddy was close to the Italian owners and out of pity he ushered Andreas in through the delivery entrance and ensured he was fed properly. The owners in turn gave Andreas odd jobs to do in the restaurant kitchen, until he had put some meat back on his own bones. They never questioned Andreas's background, they could tell he had been incarcerated, starved and maltreated. Andreas was allowed to sleep in the cellar, which in his eyes was quite an improvement to the impoverished conditions of the Begavat gulag where he had languished for the last ten years. In four years he graduated to become a front of house waiter, always conscious of his frostbitten and scarred fingers, he wore white gloves when pouring and serving. Teddy was a frequent patron as he did much business at table and when not conducting business he would feel confident enough to bring a budding protégé. He always asked for Andreas to serve him at his favourite table. Apparently it was the same table where Unity Mitford used to wait on the off chance Hitler might come in for a vegetarian meal. This irony wasn't lost on Teddy who in his small way had subverted the Nazi cause by freeing up so many actors and musicians who would otherwise have rotted in Sachsenhausen or Mauthausen concentration camps. Teddy thought that Andreas was ready to apply for the vacancy that had risen in the Bayerischer Hof for the position of trainee wine waiter. He encouraged him, saying that he would provide a reference. Andreas was flattered, but stressed that he would prefer a less prominent role because of his hands primarily and also because of the spotlight it might put him under. Teddy knew not to press the topic and then when the opportunity arose, he guided Andreas to the position he had now occupied for over twenty years, that of night porter.

Andreas escorted the two ladies out of the suite to the lift, on through the pink-marbled lobby and out to the waiting taxi. He paid the driver on reaching Sendlinger Strasse, holding the car door open adjacent to the bottom steps of the imposing frontage of the Asam Kirche. They were just in time to take one of the few remaining seats and were each given a black serrated order of service card with the details etched in gold script. How like Teddy it was to have chosen this venue. He wasn't religious by any means but had stored the memory of this sacred space like a playing-card to trump any of his theatre productions into a cocked hat. Teddy's black silk with gold trim pall now took centre stage emblazoned by a huge bouquet of the white roses he loved to buttonhole. The incense fused with charcoal smoke and rose upwards from the thurible to the cupola in the painted ceiling creating the dry ice anticipation of a live performance. Golden cherubs appeared to trumpet news of the fallen impresario from niches throughout the gilded interior and the red lantern light on the altar heralded the presence of the host and the beginning of the funeral mass. The congregation was restricted to close family, former colleagues and associates. It was all done as Teddy had requested, in Latin. Andreas was sensitive to the fact that Kirstin was getting tearful, so he offered her his handkerchief for which she was grateful.

It was hard to imagine someone who had been such a constant to everyone, not just Andreas, with so much vitality and joie de vivre being cut down and laid waste within that plain pine box for corrupt worms to one day feed from. Teddy hadn't had enough of life despite the years. The wrangling fears that tend to haunt our middle age never caught up with his shadow, at least not in public. But life had, it seemed, finally had enough of him. When those are fortunate to do what they love to do most, they have tendency to lose track of time. The strain of taking on too much within the theatre had irrevocably taken its toll on him. Teddy simply couldn't or wouldn't relinquish the torch. The hours he had put in had tested the best of his many relationships, leaving no one to look after him and only really left him with his one true love…the theatre. The burning fits and meteors of love had died out and had been replaced by fevers that went undiagnosed for too long to be healed. He had anticipated, planned and choreographed a trap for us, an emotional delectation worthy of any stage, played out for one performance only. The moment of high drama was reserved for the climax when from the choir stalls rose the haunting melancholia of Mozart's Requiem K626 in D minor, the Introitus complete with Soprano singer, The Kyrie Eleison sung by the choir. It was truly beautiful to behold within the echoing confines of that Baroque space. Four of his former lovers then carried his coffin draped pall down the candlelit aisle and out into the light. Everyone was affected in some way not only by his passing, but by the detail he had put into his final journey with them.

There was a gathering for him after the interment in the Alter Nordfriedhof. Where else but in the Kleine Komoedie theatre in the heart of the Bayerischer Hof. People came from any strand past or present connected with the hotel and rippling out through every strata of Munich society. Teddy had arranged this too and had made provision for a free bar all afternoon and into the early evening. The Sekt flowed and the steins clinked as the hubbub grew louder exorcizing the solemness expressed earlier and Teddy would have approved. His 'children of the theatre' spontaneously took it in turns to perform medleys of the finest curtain-calls during his tenure as everyone else took their drinks to the stalls and boxes. Kirstin was invited to sing and refused politely at first, relenting only if she could be accompanied by Andreas on the piano. This was to be his first and only live performance, the spotlight was on Kirstin, but he was a bag of nerves to begin with. She turned the pages of his sheet music as he adjusted the seat at the grand piano. What was she in the mood for? What would they appreciate? Something relatively recent, a torch song with an old-fashioned twist and she settled for 'Maybe this time' from Cabaret. Andreas started the slow build up accompanied by Florian Bruchner on clarinet. It was mesmeric from start to finish, Kirstin defied the critics of her later years and sang for Teddy, sang powerfully and straight from the heart. She was roundly applauded and Andreas, along with Florian, bowed with her to the chants of more. What more could she give? She looked at Andreas and he shrugged. It could only be 'Lili Marlene'. People began to stamp their feet in time to the beat as Andreas hammered out the marching tune and Kirstin took up the silky hook lines of the lyrics that propelled such a wonderful song along. She wove some magic with her timing; the way she carried herself in the spotlight, her true emotion, her voice had a resonance which bathed in the comfort of singing again in her favourite space after all those years. It reached a crescendo and again the three of them soaked up the applause. Kirstin shaded her eyes from the glare with one hand while accepting a rose bouquet with the other and then turning for a moment she thought she caught a glimpse of Teddy standing in the wings blowing her a kiss. Alongside him her only love Max and the rest of his drowned U-boat crew now resplendent in their dress uniforms, medals and ribbons, waving magnums of Veuve Clicquot, fine cigars and whistling for her to come with them. She took one last bow and kissed Andreas goodbye for what she knew was the last time and left the stage. Kirstin Deubler, chatelaine of the Bayerischer Hof passed peacefully in her sleep later that same evening. The clocks in all formal and function rooms, bars and even the hotel reception were veiled in black as a mark of respect until after her burial and one light was left on above the stage of the Kleine Komoedie to appease her ghost. The line ended with her, she couldn't have left this life on a better high, she had made every provision for the hotel's future and left Andreas her Bechstein piano and a bottle of Jägermeister.

Traudl Radler was in her office when Liam punched in early for his shift which began at 7 p.m. She had occupied the position of Haus Damen with the hotel for thirty-two years. She was now fifty-five and wore her hair in a severe bun, within which she could secrete pencils as she wrote up the weekly shift rotas for her department. Traudl's family background was shrouded in mystery and daring, as her parents had fled Dresden with whatever belongings they could muster after the devastation wrought there in early 1945. Whatever grievances she had against any English speaking person were formulated within the inferno which took her younger sister's life when that city was carbonized by the RAF. Dresden was then the scorched amber in Saxony's crown now deep inside the German Democratic Republic, a puppet state heavily censured by the Soviets. Her contact with the wider family circle that remained in the east was negligible. The upheaval, the loss and the sense of injustice were traits that on occasion percolated through the icy veneer of this woman's demeanour, especially when confronted by what she took to be arrogance.

Liam had completely forgotten that his three month probationary interview was with Frau Radler that same evening. He had nothing else on his mind other than winning back some hard earned Deutsch Marks at a card school he had joined, held in the men's locker room between shifts. His concentration was spoilt when he got word that he was expected in her office first thing. He showed his hand and opted out of the game, his losing streak still intact. Liam looked at himself in the mirror of his locker door before slamming it shut, he would pass muster he thought nonchalantly. 'Good enough for this heathen bitch', he mumbled while the game went on around him. He flicked back the large lock of hair over his left eye and behind his huge Irish earlobe. He was a big man in a tight-fitting, newly starched boiler suit, slightly ungainly looking as the trouser bottoms rose up over his monkey boots showing off his thick ankles. He sighed and made his way to Frau Radler's office.

She made him wait of course. Her prerogative, the austere ante-room with nothing to read and no view, just two chairs in a glorified corridor to concentrate the mind. The minutes went by and as they did Liam's mind began to wander, it didn't take much. Underlings in her image tapped and announced their arrival at her door and then entered politely. He really didn't mind, after all he was still on the clock. As the last one left her office she said that he could enter. Liam nodded in his gauche way as she turned on her heel and was gone before she could see him look her up and down. He righted himself, adjusted the pouch of Drum rolling tobacco and the lighter in his tight back pocket and knocked her door.

'Herein,' she called out.

Liam walked in, closing the door behind him. She sat at a desk in front of the only window, triple glazed overlooking a small courtyard. A large radiator was behind her chair, economically half on. Her desk was small and very tidy with little to personalize it. The walls were adorned with pictures of the hotel from different time periods, nothing here to distract from the role that had taken over her life. She continued to write on a ledger as Liam made a move for the chair in front of her desk.

'I don't remember inviting you to sit down, Broy!' she erupted.

Liam froze mid stance reaching out for the chair, the boiler suit uncomfortably riding up his bum.

'You want to interview me standing up?' he asked.

'I don't remember inviting you to comment either,' she barked.

'Christ the night,' he muttered quietly, whilst poised awkwardly.

'I don't want to interview you either, you are not an actor or a musician, or a politician are you?' she enquired sarcastically.

'Can I change position Frau Radler? I'm in considerable discomfort standing here with my legs akimbo.'

She looked up from her ledger and down her horn rimmed glasses at him. She finally gave him permission to sit down and he flopped onto the chair.

'I am obliged to have this discussion with you as the probationary period has elapsed. I want you to know that I am as uncomfortable as you were just now, by your even being in my office. There is something about you Broy, I can't put my finger on it, but it just doesn't fit.'

'Are you talking about me boiler suit cos it rides up me arse?'

'That was a perfect example of what I'm trying to get at here. You don't fit in here Broy and no amount of testimonials from long-standing colleagues is going to change my point of view.'

'I'm house-trained I swear! Jeez, you have been riding me since the day and hour I started here. What have I ever done to you?'

Frau Radler rose from her desk and approached the large filing cabinet in the other corner of the room, still smarting from his cheek. Liam's file was near the front, of course, and she opened it at her desk. She found a checklist questionnaire which she started to fill in with ticks. She didn't ask him a single question as she did so. She shook her head as she thought about some of the questions and then reluctantly put a tick in the box. After five minutes of further head shaking and sighing she reached the last question.

'I have to fill this in in front of you. No point in my trying to translate it for you to fill in. You have to score above seventy per cent to pass this questionnaire and keep your position with us. You are sitting on sixty per cent which I feel is generous of me. The last question is therefore vital. It reads, "In what way do you feel you have proved to be an asset to the hotel?"'

Radler read the question to Liam slowly in her coldly detached English accent and smiled inwardly knowing that he surely couldn't give her a valid answer and pass the test. Liam sat knees splayed open with his hands on them as if he was the captain in a team photograph. The past three months now played back through his mind, the lonesome shifts, the hideous chores, the disparaging looks, the uselessly attritional days off, the discriminating attitudes. What had he to show for putting up with it?

'I covered your asses when we had that bunch of Yids here.'

'What is that supposed to mean exactly?' she enquired.

'The Jewish fellas. I made sure the dirty work was done for that gob-shite Yaffat. It was me who got the place kosher for the Jewish convention. Yaffat did fuck all as usual, the lazy towel-headed knacker.'

Traudl was incredulous, she had never heard anything quite like it before. She picked out words she half understood coming from such a thick brogued accent. She took them in and focused on what he had said before finally commenting:

'In your inimitable way Broy you are trying to tell me that you showed teamwork and diligence when that was required recently with the convention. Am I right? Proper terminology? Your language is exotic but straightforward all the same.' Traudl knew Liam was grasping at anything to hold onto his position and despite her misgivings she realized that he was also a valuable enemy of her own enemy Yaffat Laminieri, the back stabbing Moroccan termite whom she detested only marginally more than Liam.

'That answer gives you the extra ten per cent you need to stay. I am watching you Broy. One foot wrong, one more pane of glass smashed while cleaning and you are out. Understood?'

Liam got up and put out his hand. Traudl thought about it for a moment, but couldn't bring herself to shake it.

Later that same evening Liam was rota'd to cover at 'Die alte Bayern Stube' on the dead-man shift. He was the solitary kitchen hand even though it was packed for a late night testimonial party for Dieter Hoeness the striker with Bayern Munich. The opposition that evening for the friendly match at the Olympiastadion was Liverpool FC and both sets of players, wives and girlfriends partied hard at the nightclub afterwards. Liam wasn't a fan of either club, but hearing so many accents he understood filtering through to the kitchen caused him to go autograph-hunting for his football-mad nephew during a lull in the rinse cycle. The big man with squelching monkey boots cut a strange figure as he plucked a pen from an incredulous waitress. He stooped awkwardly around the dance floor, the strobe lighting bouncing off his overalls in time to the music, much to the chagrin of the student waiters.

He didn't even follow football so he would draw near to a familiar accent and then grab a beer mat from a table and tear one side off it before asking the startled incumbent to sign it. This was hit-or-miss as his first conquest shrugged and asked for a pen. He turned out to be the charter coach driver for the Liverpool squad and he split himself with laughter at the table as Liam moved on. Liam did just about recognise Kenny Dalglish who was at another table near the back animatedly chatting with Ronnie Moran a veteran of the boot room staff. Liam cast a shadow over the pair, eclipsing their banter before producing his beer-mat and a pen. Dalglish obliged and passed the beer-mat to Ronnie who shouted over the music as to whether Liam wanted any dedication. On hearing Liam's thick Dublin accent Kenny gestured to a waitress who hovered instantly at their table. Before Dalglish could speak, the waitress asked if the kitchen hand was bothering either of them. Kenny told her that Liam was their guest and asked him to sit with them and what he preferred to drink. Liam opted for a Helles beer and smiled ironically at the waitress when she returned with a tray full of drinks.

This was perfect, now he couldn't be touched and he knew it. Let the dishes pile up in that sweatshop beyond the dance floor for a while, he would only have to stay on late anyhow. Radler had given him the all-clear earlier and he was now an invited guest of some very important hotel residents. He sat between Dalglish and Moran silently as they chatted on about injuries and forthcoming friendlies. He drank slow and long and proceeded to roll a cigarette as the smarting waitress looked daggers at him from the service door. Dalglish commented on the size of Liam's hands as he gripped his stein, wishing his own goalkeeper Bruce Grobbelaar had such a pair and that the only other shot-stopper with such a pair of shovels was Pat Jennings. Liam knew Jennings was from Newry and had played Gaelic and that he had even scored a goal once while between the sticks at Tottenham. Soon he gathered more signatures as important names such as John Barnes, Alan Hanson and Steve McMahon appeared at the manager's table. He stood and drained his glass, burped quietly and thanked Kenny, his back pocket bulging with signed beer-mats. He walked straight across the packed dance floor without a second thought and on beyond through the swing doors to the tropical climes of the deep bed conveyor washer which had been turned off in his absence. Four large trolleys of dirty plates, glasses and trays awaited him.

He was late finishing and too early to get the first U-bahn. The dripping crates of highball, wine and cocktail glasses were stacked neatly in tall rows along one wall of the Alte Bayern Stube kitchen. Plate racks were full and cutlery and crockery were stored neatly where they belonged. The conveyor washing machine was cooling down and the room began to clear of steam. He had just enough hot water to mop down the floor space and turn off the lights behind him. In the men's locker-room he peeled off his musty overalls and languidly stepped into the changing room showers. The pulsating water soothed his aching muscles, pummelling his neck, back and shoulders. He faced into the shower head and opened his mouth to the pressure beating at his face. He was lost for a few minutes, enchanted by the heat and the refuge it gave his tired body. Opening his eyes only as he reached for the shower gel, he lathered away the tensions of the inhospitable shift that had so often been his lot.

Andreas was the only one in the hotel refectory before 7 a.m. He had his usual yeast beer and white sausage in front of him. He had taken just one sip as Liam joined him with his breakfast tray. Liam couldn't get his head round the whole beer at breakfast time thing and shook his head disparagingly at Andreas. It was a cultural nuance, but back home you had to be up all night to be drinking a beer at this time in the morning. Liam's plate was stacked high as if there was no tomorrow and he ate as if he had a taxi waiting downstairs. Andreas conversely cut up his sausage neatly and tore his semmel bread tidily, pausing to wipe his mouth with a napkin and take sparing sips of weissbier. Liam was diametrically opposite to anything he held in high regard but he could see something in him that he trusted and he was genuinely pleased that Liam had got through Radler's probationary measures. It was as if Andreas was passing on the mantle of trust that others like Teddy had at one time placed in him. If nothing else he would hopefully learn some English from Liam but he guessed that there was more to this Irishman than he let on. Liam told Andreas about the night before, waxing that he was guest of honour at 'King Kenny's' table, how it had pissed off the service staff and how they had tried to break his spirit by stockpiling shit loads of dirty stuff for him to wash. His bravado was a defence mechanism to deflect his own insecurities, Andreas could read this because he had seen it before. It's what people do to protect themselves in unfamiliar circumstances, something takes over, it either gets them through or it can drag them down. Something told him that Liam was trustworthy and that he could confide in him, a stranger and a foreign one at that.

After breakfast Liam escorted Andreas to the U-bahn station near the Salvatore Kirche and sat with him not saying much until they reached Münchener Freiheit. Liam was ready for sleep as he turned his key in the latch, but Andreas seemed restless, excited even and Liam was too tired to ask why. Maybe he should have because he didn't get much rest that morning. Andreas was playing his vinyl collection next door just loud enough to keep him from any prospect of a deep slumber. He was animated, moving furniture, clattering into things, cleaning up discarded magazines, lifting crates and rattling their empty beer bottles. He drew the curtains for the first time in living memory, bathing what was actually quite a large space in fresh sunlight. He began to studiously measure the frames of the large sliding windows with a tailor's tape. It was too much to let go unnoticed and Liam eventually got up and wrapped on his dressing gown before reaching for his slippers.

'What the fuck Andreas? Can you not sleep or what? My body clock is all over the place now.'

Liam had a knack of making the most hostile quip sound strangely phlegmatic and unthreatening, rendering humour to it with a disarmingly celtic aside. Anyway Andreas was so preoccupied that he probably didn't pay any heed and just hummed to himself, moving the tape measure along the glass, having temporarily forgotten that Liam was now a resident here too.

He stockpiled his erstwhile disarray of books into boxes in the hallway. He had moved all the furniture back against one wall and yet more boxes sat on top of the furniture. The record player was now unplugged and sitting on the kitchen table along with the ashtray stand and different beer steins collected from all over the floor. Liam could now make out a rug that had always been there but that he hadn't noticed before, covering the middle of the room. The thick curtains and roller blind had been dismantled and taken down revealing the large glass sliding doors which led out onto a generous balcony with two rickety chairs in need of a coat of paint.

'I'm going to wash these windows before the men come and remove the glass panes,'said Andreas

'I can do that for you, I do it every day in life,' replied Liam, 'Why are they removing the glass panes by the way?'

'I wonder how they are going to negotiate it over the balcony?'

'Negotiate what exactly? asked Liam.

'They know what they're doing I suppose, they do this all the time. Why should my place be any different?'

'Are you going to share with me Andreas, I live here too!'

'My piano of course! My Bechstein is coming later today.'

It was too much for Liam to take in and he just shrugged as he filled a bucket with warm water and just a little detergent. He found a sponge in the cupboard under the sink and then walked over to the large window and proceeded to wash it down. He asked Andreas for some old newspaper and used it to buff up the glass as it began to dry. His reach was extensive and soon both sides shimmered in the late morning sun.

The crane arrived at 2 p.m., the removal men had been parked in the street for the last hour in readiness having had their lunch in the cab of the lorry. Four men, two of which had by now made it up to Andreas's apartment. They wore navy overalls similarly as unbecoming as Liam's. They were both thickset Bavarians who muttered amongst themselves as Liam ate toast in the kitchen. They debated the space, the clearance, the snags, even the wind direction, all the practicalities and incidentals before deciding that it was going to work. The window frame came away quite easily and was removed in an efficiently German fashion on castors and now resided along the only other uncluttered wall. They deliberated over the balcony wall clearance space for an age, quibbling in a clipped local dialect that had Andreas joining in. Liam moved over to the balcony's edge. He could see the removal lorry three floors below and the other two men struggling to get the mothballed piano into a position so it could be harnessed by the crane. This was a delicate procedure as the crane's tank tracks imprinted their way along Virchow Strasse alerting a throng of interested passers-by. Liam removed the balcony chairs and Andreas lifted the parched Yucca plants.

A sling had been fashioned from four ropes around the piano with a large ring bonded where the ropes joined at one end held up by one of the men. The crane now straddled the insulated piano and it lowered its chain so that its hook could be attached to the ring securely. It began to rain lightly as the wipers on the crane began to turn, the driver alternating levers professionally. The hook met the eye and was fastened securely. The crane extended its length before taking up the slack. The piano began to levitate and as it did so it began to spin slightly but still managed to avoid the tree line and boundary fences. This was expected and soon it righted itself as it rose above the street lighting and on toward the apartment building and up and in line with the other two removal men. One of them leaned precariously over the balcony and managed to tie a rope around one of the piano legs and that way he guided it over and into the confined balcony space. The crane edged the piano in so slowly to compensate for the wind that had picked up along with the rain.

A series of fractious hand movements followed that could be interpreted from the ground and the Bechstein piano was finally ensconced on Andrea's balcony with its nose jutting in to the apartment. The other two removal men lost no time in climbing up to the third floor. Once again they fitted castors to the feet of the piano helping it to negotiate the journey to the living room.

It had taken less than an hour and only another forty minutes to reinstate the balcony window. The last thing delivered by the removal men was the piano-stool and Liam took it in after signing their job sheet. Andreas was in rapture, it had all gone relatively smoothly and now he had Kirstin's legacy here in place for him to play as soon as the piano tuner had done his work.

6

1942

Belgorod was now in German hands. Bringing a hollow euphoria with empty plaudits to the the 168th Infantry Division. Certainty had long since evaporated along with the morning mists that permeated the reed beds within the Don basin, the last natural barrier before the Volga and the Ural mountains. The looming prospect of a second winter was the only tangible horizon they could see and still no prospect of a Russian submission to show for it. The Soviets had just melted away. Somehow this Slavic under race that they had been taught to think of as primordial, had managed to dismantle all their heavy industry workshops and factories along the invasion front onto their rolling stock and relocate them together with their workforce a further thousand miles east beyond German reach. It was unthinkable, incomprehensible and it was just as well that the German propaganda machine never got wind of it as it would have been impossible to have spun it to their own advantage.

Nothing had been learnt from history. The Russians, they had been led to believe, had no stomach for a fight. Indeed at first the Germans had been welcomed as liberators, marching into Kiev with flowers down their gun barrels and a Mädchen on each arm, brimming with bread and salt, tributes from a thankful multitude. But these people weren't Russians, they were Belo-Russian, Ukrainian and Chechen ethnic groups who had nothing to thank Stalin for. And instead of cultivating their support, the mop up work was done in the wake of the frontline troops by the Einsatzgruppen who singled out the Jews, the commissars, the non-conformists and any other innocent who didn't fit in or just got in the way. A bullet through the back of the head was their remedy. One bullet for efficiency, fired into the skulls of three men whilst they stood in single file over grave pit of their own making.

Again nothing had been learnt from history. Russia was always more than the sum of its parts, it was polyglot, vast and diverse but it also had a cohesion that a foreigner could never hope to understand. Russia was the embodiment of a mother, a figurehead to its people and intrinsically intertwined with the Christian faith. Even an iconoclast like Stalin recognised this when he had tried in vain to subjugate the influence of the orthodox church by way of desecration. He learnt quickly that if the Russian people's staunch faith could be harnessed in the ideal of nationhood then he might be able to defeat the invader and install radical communism by another means long-term. Mother Russia had always prevailed against the invader, be it 'La Patrie' under Napoleon or the 'Fatherland' under Hitler. The thread of faith written in Cyrillic that bonded her people in times of great peril had once again awoken the sleeping giant that was Russia.

It was a bitter pill to take, but Blitzkrieg simply didn't work out here. The unremitting steppe landscape stared back at you blankly for hundreds of miles in every direction, stretching resources, thinning out resolve and lengthening tenuous supply lifelines. An advancing army was left vulnerable by the sheer hubris of its protagonists. Panzer tanks ate up territory and in doing so more often than not left their infantry support far behind in their haste. Both swallowed up gasoline to the detriment of their supply lines which were threadbare at best and vulnerable to partisan attack from the rear. The serried ranks of these partisans now overflowed with the very people whose 'hearts and minds' could once have been won over by the Germans if treated properly. These highly motivated fighters opened up what was ostensibly a new front by using the swathes of ancient forests for cover, training and organisation behind the German lines. They caused mayhem by blowing up bridges, ambushing vulnerable patrols and tearing up stretches of valuable rail links.

It was already proving to be a logistical nightmare as the railway gauges in the Soviet Union and even in Poland where supplies often originated, differed from the gauges used in Germany. So any train that serviced the advancing Wehrmacht had to wait until the railway lines were altered. A prolonged winter campaign hadn't been anticipated and the ethos of Blitzkrieg made no provision for it, so lives began to be lost needlessly for want of thermal clothing, affecting morale as the weather closed in. The chain of supply was stretched to breaking point and then froze completely as the German onslaught stalled in temperatures as low as minus forty degrees near Khimki metro station only twelve kilometres from the gleaming spires of the Kremlin in the centre of Moscow that first December. This was to be the high watermark on the assault for the Russian capital, although the arrogance of many made them too snow-blind to see that the writing was already on the wall. In scenes not dissimilar to those recollected by their fathers during the Great War, stagnation prevailed as trenches were dug and fires were lit for the first time under lorry axles in the forlorn hope that it might help to start their engines. The heady days of mass encirclements were now a distant memory. How could any army, let alone the Soviet army sustain losses of over six hundred thousand men at one engagement and still manage to field another composed of similar strength only days later without a struggle? The

Siberian ski troops held in reserve expecting a Japanese attack in the far east were now railed in to relieve the capital. These fresh replacements tore into the unwitting Germans like so many stags from a thicket. The beleaguered defenders in many cases just ran in shock from their slit trenches into the drifting snow and froze to death forming contorted shapes until covered by fresh drifts for a season. It was in danger of turning into a rout and gave the Soviets proof that the Germans were by no means the invincible force they had so often been portrayed. The stark realisation began to creep in with the slow build up of morning frosts in what was to be the second winter of this campaign, that this struggle was different and unconventional. It wasn't just a clash of ideologies now - it was a fight to the death without quarter on either side.

My charge, my prisoner Sergei must have sensed that his time was up and even before I could secure his interrogation with Oberleutnant Werner, he had used the confusion of our crossing at the congested bridgehead to his own advantage by making good his escape. He even had the temerity to smile at me knowingly before he leapt into the furious torrent below the pontoons. Gefreiter Hauser watched powerlessly and cursed me loudly from the far riverbank as this unfolded for not reacting sooner so as to shoot Sergei before he disappeared under the water. I levelled my rifle on the surface of the river and trained it on the far bank, but nothing but froth and foam flowed through my gun sight. I secretly wanted Sergei to get away so I fired off a few shots aimlessly before Hauser caught up with me and then he marched me up to the Oberleutnant and declared my incompetence to be noted along with the lesser known truth that I had taken out the sniper in the town centre. I was surprised that Hauser mentioned the sniper incident as I was certain he wanted me in bad odour with everyone. Oberleutnant Werner weighed up all he had said and then ventured to guess that we had probably got as much information as possible out of Sergei anyway. Hauser was a bastard but he was turning out to be a fair-minded one after all.

The pontoon bridgehead held long enough for all the tanks and supply trucks to cross into the town and units from the division secured the perimeter while others foraged what they could from the devastation. We stayed long enough to replenish water from the river and to bury and commemorate our dead. I presented the dog tags of the fallen to the Oberleutnant who insisted on writing to each individual's family. The church in the town square was by now a charred ruin and its once brilliant onion domes had sadly succumbed to the flames and had fallen in on themselves. To the rear of the ruined church was the burial ground where we laid to rest our fallen in one freshly dug grave with a simple carved cross and our comrades' helmets spread on the compacted soil at its base. A volley was fired over them by our volunteer unit, now including myself. The inhabitants had taken what they could and followed the Soviet withdrawal. Strategically, Belgorod was just another place on the map that stretched further eastward, sweeping downward ever nearer the Volga. It was vital that it was taken, but now that it was there was nothing left in the town to even celebrate its value. The hand-picked unit, including myself, were given extra rations by the cook that evening, which we shared together and even Hauser grudgingly let me sit with his men as they unwound and shared what schnapps they had. I was now accepted by them without question, no longer just a mascot, or a Hiwi, a Freiwillig or a Russian called 'Boris' who had turned. I had proved my worth and shown my mettle and they would close ranks to defend me when the time came. It came sooner than I thought when the main body of 4th Panzer Army under Oberstgeneral Hermann Hoth caught up with our division and consolidated our position.

There was a tendency for foreign volunteers to be grouped together and form pioneer or labour detachments doing dangerous manual tasks such as minefield clearing for the regular army. When we came under inspection by Hoth's staff officers I caused quite a stir as it was obvious by my age and appearance that I wasn't a German soldier. Hauser was promoted to Obergefreiter as we stood rigidly to attention for his leadership in taking Belgorod. When given the opportunity to speak he showed a hitherto absent line in modesty which belied the cold exterior I had previously witnessed. He praised the tight camaraderie of our group and stressed that even though I was a dishevelled teenager, I was of more value to the 168th as a field scout and interpreter than a labourer on some arduous task. His words struck home and the order was given for me to take the oath and that I receive an appropriate uniform and that I was also to be allowed to keep my sniper rifle. Hoth's adjutant looked at me in a new light and asked me where I was originally from. I spoke without an accent which intrigued him, but my voice began to falter as it had been so long since I had said the name of my town. Tears now welled in my eyes and one dropped down my face, to my disappointment, as I looked down and uttered the word Strekerau. He told me not to mind, that this hard campaign would make a man of me and that I would soon see Strekerau again as it was well within the remit of the 4th Panzer Army to pass through there.

I knew the terrain we were now covering so well; this was the great sweep of land between the two great rivers, the Don and the Volga. I could see the next obvious target in my mind long before the campaign maps had been unfolded on the trestle table at Hoth's makeshift headquarters. Voronezh sat on the Don river, it was an arterial communications centre which Hitler had wanted taken quickly, so he devoted his elite Grossdeutschland division and the newly formed 24th mechanised Panzer Division to its capture. He had stressed his desire for all other component parts of the 4th Panzer Army to encircle the town and cut it off from any hope of relief as quickly as possible so as to concentrate all efforts in the push southward towards a city on the Volga that shared Stalin's name. In doing so he weakened the grip on Voronezh, which led to fierce and attritional street fighting, an overture of what to expect at Stalingrad. Our division was now swallowed up by the 4th Panzer Army and formed a powerful pincer that was designed to support General Paulus's 6th Army in its subjugation of the Caucasus region and the exploitation of the rich oil supplies that lay just beyond our reach.

It was at this time that Stalin decided to transfer his most ruthlessly capable general, Georgy Zhukov, from the now relatively quiet Moscow front to defend Stalingrad. Zhukov was Stalin's 'fireman', he had quashed successfully the attack on Moscow at great cost to the Russians in men and material. These were the two inexhaustible supplies that would secure our own ultimate downfall, along with the Russian climate. Stalin resented Zhukov's leadership skills, but his own had proved disastrous in the previous months, leading to spiralling losses and devastating troop encirclements. But the men just kept coming to defend the Motherland from the fascist invader. As Peoples Commissar for defence, Stalin issued order no. 227 'Ni shagu nazad!' 'Not a step back!'. This was a line in the sand. There were to be no more withdrawals, routs or retreats. Behind every Soviet corps or division there would be a well-armed blocking division consisting of two hundred men who would shoot anyone who gave up territory and turned their backs on the enemy. It was a calculated risk, too much land had been given up already, too much grain and lend-lease armaments had fallen into German hands, something had to be done to shore up the defence of Russia.

Much propaganda was made when we finally reached the banks of the river Volga. It was navigable from the Baltic in ancient times as far as the Caspian Sea. The Vikings had somehow managed to steer their longships this far, first for plunder and later for trade and settlement. The Norsemen had eventually assimilated into the region and later settlers, such as the ethnic Germans, in the eighteenth century made this rich and fertile river basin their new homeland. If the Ukraine to the west was the bread basket of Russia, then the Volga was the artery from which trade flowed from the dark ages until the new dark age that we presently inhabited. Stalingrad straddled the river, it was a model of the Soviet industrial town, aspiring to be a major city but still an easily negotiable town none the less. Stalingrad was at the foot of the Ural mountains and also acted as the gateway to the rich oilfields that Hitler needed so badly to replenish his armies. The city was laid out in an austere grid-like pattern with different industrial areas and no defined town centre. It had major factories like the Red October tractor works which had been converted to tank production following the German invasion. The closer Hitler's troops got to this unprepossessing city, the more myopically it was viewed as a prize to be offered up by his generals. It never held strategic importance until they were almost on top of it and by then it was too late. The city that bore his name would stand and fight or fall and die with the river at their backs. It was a slowly closing coffin lid that would seal all our fates leaving an indelible scar on its protagonists; both those that lived and those that still fertilize its Volga shoreline.

I had let my own excitement of being so near Strekerau get the better of me. I was supposed to be the 'eyes' of our division but I hadn't noticed the dismounted riders who had been stalking us along the horizon for some time. The dust in our wake made us an easy target to follow and more often than not it blinded us from our immediate surroundings. I still had the goggles that Oberleutnant Werner had issued me with but I was more intent on the traffic that flowed in the opposite direction to us. We had shadowed a train line for the past forty kilometres and during that length of time I saw twenty-two train carriages pass behind our lines with pristine Studebaker trucks and machinery, all lend-leased to the Soviets from America and now in our possession. I counted ten more carriages of dejected Russian prisoners heading behind our lines. It was heartening, but nothing like the numbers Hauser had boasted of capturing in that first invasion summer. If this was the calibre of armaments being sent across the Atlantic, combined with the growing number of homegrown T-34 tanks being hurriedly produced, then God help us.

It began to rain in the afternoon and I and a clutch of my comrades hid under the oilskin covers that protected the ever dwindling supply of gasoline barrels in the trucks. It rained for five and a half days, leaving the unmetalled tracks that we drove along, a claggy sodden mess. This respite from the elements only lasted a short while as we were often called upon to help push any stricken vehicles out of the ever deepening mud flats. Our horses suffered tremendously from the conditions as they struggled to cope with already heavy burdens in the perilous sucking mud. Some just gave up the fight and had to be shot in harness where they lay and were soon crushed by the oncoming traffic, forming unintended plugs in the puddled craters that passed for roads in these parts.

It was as if the elements were now conspiring against us as late summer with its dust storms and sweltering nights gave way to severe rain storms and early morning frosts. The weather, unlike the terrain, was closing in, inviting us to make mistakes, funnelling men and material down the Volga corridor to a place that the Soviet Stavka had begun to see as the trap that would destroy an entire German army and turn out to be the starting point in a reversal of fortunes. It was hubris that had blinded us, not the dust storms or the rain, but the hubris of others intent on redrawing maps, no matter what the cost in men.

The riders whom I had been oblivious to had remounted and moved from the relative cover of a sporadic tree line and emboldened by the rain, now rode in the open, making good progress on the soft turf about five hundred metres to our left. They made a splendid sight even in such a downpour, with long waterproof capes which stretched well over their strong grey charges. I counted thirty of them, all expertly handling fit horses over the waterlogged turf and confidently getting closer to our convoy. I could make out their black Astrakhan fur hats, emblazoned with a silver badge of the 5th Don Cossack regiment at the centre, the curved sweep of their sabre sheaths dancing in the rain. They cut such a striking image, a throwback to another age. They were the Don Cossacks I had been told of back in my classroom in Strekerau. These fiercely independent horsemen whose lineage and loyalty were so often at odds with the Stalinist regime, had somehow kept their traits and customs intact and who now threw in their lot with us as quickly as their native territory was being liberated.

Our convoy was impeded by torrential rain bringing flash-floods onto already disintegrating roads. We were subjected to biting winds that lashed at pillions and outriders on motorbikes and forced many to jump for cover from the tanks they had hitched a ride on. The Cossacks seemed impervious to the elements as they dismounted on the slick grass, leaving their horses with five of their number before travelling up to the head of our convoy and ingratiating themselves with our senior command. We were obliged to camp here tonight along the sunken road taking whatever shelter we could from the weather and perhaps I would get a better look at these exotic horsemen.

I was supposed to be keeping my eyes peeled on the leaden sky for any stray Sturmovik ground attack aircraft but my binocular lens just welled with rain water each time I pointed them upwards. Visibility was abject at best and the only aircraft I had seen in the past few days was our own. I pointed my binoculars at our intriguing visitors who had by now sought cover under the hastily erected tarpaulin tent which acted as Hoth's command post. It was ringed by three half tracks, manned and armed with anti-aircraft guns, but even so, it would still have made a ripe target for any ambitious pilot, allowing for the atrocious weather conditions. I could see the Cossack cavalrymen hanging up their waterproof smocks, revealing their distinctive ethnic paramilitary garb. How at ease with themselves they looked in comparison to the awkwardly autocratic Prussian staff officers Oberstgeneral Hoth surrounded himself with. They centred in on the wood burning stove, getting close enough to singe their copious beards, taking off their Astrakhan hats and shaking the rain off their bodies like wolfhounds. One began breaking up a chair, smashing it to pieces under his boots and fed it into the stove. Generaloberst Hoth was incandescent and pointed out that they had a plentiful supply of wood already and that the chair had been one of his favourites. Much laughter followed as the Cossacks drew up yet more chairs and pretended to smash them up before relaxing in them. This seemed to break the ice and Hoth ordered refreshments along with cold meat, bread and steaming bratwurst to be served and the Cossacks took full advantage of his hospitality. They drank from the bottle and passed it on among themselves. The battered trestle table had been placed in front of them and before long a large campaign map was held in place upon it by four freshly emptied vodka bottles. They were only getting warmed up, but General Hoth wanted as much detail about what lay ahead as they could offer before the alcohol clouded their judgement. They told him that they had seen two whole Soviet armies, the 64th and the 62nd under General Chuickov strategically falling back in the direction of Stalingrad. These armies were to merge and make a stand, being supplied and reinforced from the ferry landings that meandered along both banks of the river Volga. Hoth's original orders within the remit of Operation Case Blue were to encircle Stalingrad quickly with his panzer tanks, cut it off from any hope of relief and act as a foil to allow the Sixth Army under Paulus to proceed on to the oil-rich territories beyond. Hitler had again changed his mind and Hoth knew that an opportunity had now been lost. The Cossacks spoke of the defensive measures now being thrown up around the city. They had observed Katyusha rocket launchers being ominously dug into the slopes and riverbanks. These 'Stalin organs' were terrifying to hear, never mind the damage they wreaked. From their vantage points along the grassy bluffs that stretched out from the city, the horsemen witnessed strong points being improvised out of a ring of factories and grain elevators that could be fortified and defended so as to slow down any onslaught. Many of the civilian population had chosen to stay, emboldened by Soviet rhetoric and had begun building tank traps and digging defensive trenches. It was a bleak prospect and no amount of vodka could dilute the bad tidings.

Later that evening I was summoned to the command tent as it turned out that Hoth's chief interpreter had succumbed to too much alcohol and was by now a gibbering fool making no sense in either language. I was taken forward by Hauser, who was revelling in his new role as Obergefreiter, taking salutes and shooting the breeze with the rank and file that oiled the wheels of this great army until we at last got out of the rain and he had to revert to a subordinate again. He bent my ear before we entered the tent.

'Don't let me down in here Mensche. This is your chance to shine out. Listen carefully to the General and even more carefully to that rabble. They are all pissed, I can smell the fumes from here, so just take your time and I will wait outside with the other NCOs, okay?'

I nodded, he had called me by my surname for the first time which was a little unnerving and I then remembered to salute and Hauser offered the faintest of smiles and saluted back at me. I had no time to dwell on it as the drapes were held open by one of the sentries and I approached the reclining group of figures circled around a large temporary stove in the middle of the tent. Perhaps I was too diminutive to notice, but some of them did turn in the direction of the draught from the open tent flap and then focused on my approach. I got to within two metres of the General who was standing in shirt sleeves and braces, offering his back when his adjutant challenged me. I thought later that had I been so minded, then maybe I could have got a round or two off if I was an assassin. I saluted and waited to be addressed. Presently, General Hoth drained his glass and turned to meet the commotion on my arrival. This was 'Papa' Hermann Hoth, Generaloberst of the 4th Panzer Army. He was wiry, diminutive, angular and had sinuous fingers. He looked campaign-worn and bore the aspect of a man who tried to hide his emotions behind a gambler's eyes. He reminded me of a parched textbook drawing of a Roman senator, but I wasn't allowed to dwell on my image making as he was eager for me to listen to the group of ribald cossacks that he held sway over.

'What do they call you?' he asked. I told him my name. 'What is the number of your division?' he enquired. I gave him the details. 'You speak Russian fluently?'

I told him that I did and he led me by the shoulder and in among the throng of swaying horsemen who were heating up nicely to the extent that they were mutually flea-grooming their beards. One of them playfully tried to trip me up with an outstretched riding boot as I walked past him. I regained my balance and cursed him in Russian. The others roused themselves somewhat on hearing my accent. Some pulled on their long beards, wondering as to my dialect and began tapping their clay pipes on the side of their chairs in approval at me standing up to their leader. I had no idea who he was, they all looked the same to me, slouching with their sword scabbards brushing the floor. Because one had made me stumble, embarrassing me in front of the General, then in my eyes they all had all lost some of their former heroic stature.

General Hoth stepped in, sensing my annoyance and told me not to pay any heed to their antics. They were a pagan lot and to them I was just a boy. He then looked at me again and said that I was in actual fact just a boy. He asked me where I was from and how I managed to end up in a German uniform. I gave him the abridged version of events as I could see time was of the essence and that the Cossacks would soon be so drunk as to be of no use whatsoever. When I mentioned Strekerau however, their leader perked up and questioned me over the name of my village. How did I know of such a place? I told them. How did I manage to escape from the clutches of the NKVD? He mixed his enquiry with expletives and mumbled curses, more frustrated with himself for not being able to ask me more and converse with me properly. It transpired that the Cossack leader whose name I have forgotten had formerly been with the circus troupe that performed annually in my home town. This brought on pangs of nostalgia within me that I tried to suppress by recounting the hardships of my journey west and my experiences with the 168th Division.

General Hoth listened intently to my German dialect in translation and the answers I gave in Russian to his Cossack guests. Hoth hadn't heard of the Volga Germans until now and was shaking his head in fascination and asked me to point out the location of my town on his campaign map. It was small, but it was just visible written in Cyrillic and German. The General poured over the map, noting the proximity of Strekerau to Stalingrad, the rail links and arterial routes that fed from such a small town that might be of any strategic value. He asked me if I could ride a horse. I told him that I had been born in a town where horses outnumbered people and that they were all thoroughbreds and that Oberleutnant Werner could testify to that. He had appeared to have already formulated a plan in his mind when he finally spoke.

'Would you like to see your town again?'

I welled at the words that emerged from his mouth.

'Shall I take that as a yes? Private?'

'Mensche, sir.'

'Very well, that settles it. Tomorrow morning, maybe late morning judging by the heads these boys will have, I want you to join with them and proceed to Strekerau. Is that understood?' I saluted and tried to make myself look bigger in the process, 'What did your people do there?' he asked.

I said that my father was in banking and that the town was run like a cooperative and that each family had a stake in every prospective venture taken by the bank. Every farm, every new tractor, every barn raised, every crop successfully brought in, was paid for by the cooperative and the profit was shared equally and reinvested in times of good harvests and bad by the inhabitants. The town elders decided not to form a council, so that no one person could become mayor and exploit their position. Instead all new measures, investments and improvements from street lighting, sanitation, rail network improvement to the provision for an extension to the burial ground for the dead, had to be proposed and open to a public ballot. This postal ballot was in the form of a multiple choice questionnaire that was filled in by everyone eligible and became the responsibility of the head of each household. This system had been adequate long before collective farming had been made compulsory by the Soviets and it worked so well in our town that the Russian officials had, until 1941, turned a blind eye to it. Everyone got enough of what they needed and the profits all were poured back into the cooperative.

The General looked up from the map again and asked me if the name of my town should not have been changed to 'Utopia', but then he smiled and said that it would have to go to a postal ballot first. On a more serious note he assumed that the NKVD would have confiscated all the savings and all the proceeds, title deeds and legal documents held at my father's bank. I assumed he wanted me to reply, so I told him that my father was a very cautious man and that he had made copies of all title deeds and binding legal documents. I ventured further to say that he had hidden all the original copies in a safe within a secret room under our own house, a room I was certain the NKVD wouldn't locate because I had never known of its existence until the day I was forced to flee Strekerau.

I could see that this was a lot for him to take in. Momentarily, he had lit on the idea of the propaganda it would generate for the German cause. Vulnerable, peaceable ex-patriot Germans ushered off their land and robbed by the villainous Soviet state. But the hypocrite in him spoke too of the fact that it was the German invasion that had destroyed the Strekerau idyll forever.

It was not in the interests of the army or in the character of its commander to personalize a target or stray from an objective. His judgement had been honed from hard campaigns fighting in two world wars allowing little room for sentiment. He was not now about to be sidetracked by ordering a mercy mission to a German enclave that had previously been overrun by the NKVD. Nor was he made of stone either and the boy's story had registered a hit when soothed with vodka. His people were without a doubt now dead, the journey east was a death sentence in itself. But the boy needed to know for sure. Strekerau was just on the periphery of his area of influence. His army was soon to right-wheel down the Volga delta and provide much needed support on the flanks before Stalingrad. He could afford for an errant bunch of Cossack irregulars to act as a scouting party in what was bound to be by now a venture to nothing more than a ghost town.

The Cossacks by this time were beyond consulting. They had shared the last bottle and offered me the dregs to swig from. I took it to mean some sort of acceptance, so I smiled at the General, who in turn nodded, I took the bottle and drank. It shot down my throat like a liquid fireball and took my voice with it for a few seconds. I regained my composure and the General was sensitive to the fact that it was I who was now being questioned over a matter that I was still coming to terms with in my own head. He had the wit and the patience to let me talk about a place just over the near horizon, not his home, but my home and he understood that proximity asks questions of the heart that common sense can't explain. He had got what he wanted to know and more besides from me and I had tried to do as he asked but the horsemen were now too far gone and began to wax about their own experiences in such a way as to be of no use to anybody. I masked my frustrations with them sufficiently to be able to keep up with their conversation, which often had me guessing just what it was they were describing. A lot of the time they just argued amongst themselves, old rivalries coming to the fore within such a tightly-knit group. At length the General dismissed me and told me to get some rest for a journey in the morning to Strekerau with the horsemen.

7

1987

The Bechstein piano now took up much of the living room. Andreas couldn't help but lift the lid and touch a key every time he passed by as if to convince himself that it was really there. It was a connection that even Liam couldn't help but notice, but wasn't sure if it was his place to ask. He was sure that sentiment had a lot to do with it and maybe Andreas would share that in due course along with his unravelling war story. Liam understood that the piano was good for Andreas and that maybe his being there too seemed to lift the man's spirits. He didn't need to ask, he just had to listen to the music that poured from Andreas to know that this was some kind of therapy. He played what he knew, from the large bale of sheet music, tinted ochre with age and wrapped in twine under his piano stool. Soon the building began to resonate with Andreas's renditions of some of the most beautiful music. Before long pieces of paper would be pushed under their front door with handwritten requests from other residents. Liam would often sift through the growing collection of sheet music to try and find the appropriate piece.

'Andreas, I don't have the ear for all this classical stuff, but you are not bad.'

Andreas nodded and turned the page as he continued with Beethoven's Nocturne in D Major for piano, requested by Alois Kaltenbrunner from down the hall at number fourteen. Liam soon learnt not to try and converse with Andreas whilst he played for want of a reaction. It would often take a moment or two after finishing for Andreas to emerge from what could only be described as a trance.

'I liked that one,' said Liam.

'It's an old friend,' replied Andreas. 'Probably the wrong time of day to play it, but I think the Kaltenbrunners appreciated it. I must get in touch with the piano tuner as she needs tweaking.'

'She?' asked Liam.

'Yes. All beautiful things with sleek lines and curves are feminine, wouldn't you agree?'

'I never gave it much thought, but come to think of it, yes.'

Liam got up and asked Andreas if he wanted a coffee. The afternoon rays danced off the Bechstein, momentarily blinding Liam as he walked into the kitchen and filled the kettle.

'Do you like music Liam?'

'I like some. Probably stuff you have never heard of. Traditional stuff, do you know what I mean?'

'Tell me more,' asked Andreas.

'I like Planxty and Moving Hearts, ever heard of them?'

Andreas shook his head. Liam let the kettle begin to sing and went into his room for a rummage through his case. He emerged with a tin whistle with a green mouthpiece.

'I can play one of these, but only from memory, I can't read music or anything. I used to listen to a lot of folk music and picked it up along the way.'

Liam poured hot water into the percolater unleashing freshly ground aromas.

Andreas got up from the piano stool and walked over to look at the tin whistle.

'Can you play something for me?'

'Let's drink our coffee first and then I will try okay?'

'Where do you go to in your mind when you play, Andreas?' The words hung in the air for a little longer with no accompaniment.

'Strekerau of course and my family. Remembering my mother playing piano for us on Sunday evenings. It was her that taught me how to play.'

Liam felt emboldened enough to ask, 'So playing transports you back to when you were all together?'

'I belonged to a big family in a rambling house, but yes we did come together on a Sunday evening to listen to her play the classics I try to have now.'

'You do her proud, Andreas.'

'Thank you Liam, I want to know what you are going to play for me?'

Liam drained his cup and took up the tin whistle.

'This is a ballad with a bit of tin whistle brought in by yours truly in the chorus. Now I'm going to have to sing so prepare yourself for a shock okay?'

Andreas smiled not knowing what to expect but just thought it polite to do so.

'This is called "True love knows no season."

Billy Gray rode into Gantry way back in '83
There he first met with young Sarah Maclean
The wild rose of morning had faded with the dawning
Heralding springtime in Billy's eyes that day.'

Liam's voice gathered in confidence as he remembered long digested lyrics. He had his eyes closed so he couldn't see how Andreas was reacting to his rendition. He was beginning to relax when the chorus prompted him to put the whistle to his lips. He was rusty, but regained his balance and kept the tune alive. A second verse and then the whistle again coming in with the chorus, he was more certain of himself.

'True love knows no season
No rhyme or no reason
Justice is as cold as the grange of County Clare.'

One last verse and then a final chorus on the tin whistle until Liam let it fade with his breath before finishing. Andreas hadn't stopped him yet and was still in the room as far as he could tell. Liam hadn't thought of that tune in years and found himself transported like Andreas had been earlier on the piano. He opened his eyes.

'That was wonderful Liam.'

'You think?'

'Of course. It was unlike anything I have ever heard. I didn't know you could sing.'

'I used to sing for pints in the army.'

'You were in the army?' asked Andreas.

'Yes. The Irish Army.'

Andreas took both their empty mugs over to the sink and began to rinse them with hot water, 'You sit and listen to me talking about the war in the east and all this time you were a soldier as well?' he asked.

'It's your house, your rules, you lead the conversations. Besides it would have come up eventually,' replied Liam.

'You served. You know what it is like then. The things I described to you. You know what it means to be caught up in something like that.'

'I know a little. I know about the intensity. I learnt that even in the maelstrom of a fire fight there are isolated pockets of calm where everything catches up with you. Breathing spaces where the real decisions are made and your heart stops beating through a parched throat and you can finally hear yourself think.'

'Then you know as well that it does you no good to keep things like that bottled up forever,' said Andreas.

'Who can you tell? The men you shared with? Risked your life for? Some of whom you might have got close to. No, they relive it at some unexpectedly dark moment of every day and don't need reminded. There is no support group yet to help them through what they are thinking. This is the fallout you never trained for, you just try to box it off in your head and give it a label marked 'readjustment'. So when that time comes where you have a glass of something strong pressed into your hand by a civilian and they think that by that gesture they can ask you anything about what you did and if you took a life, then think of that label and make a 'readjustment.' It's what I do to avoid the thousand yard stare when I recount some tale or other. As for your family…I'm sorry Andreas, I meant my family…they are all too wrapped up in their own tawdry lives back in the mad scramble that is Dublin to care. Who can you tell? So far the only person who has listened to what I have gone through was doing so because I paid them for their time to do so. A prostitute and an old soldier. It's like one of those reproduction engravings by Hogarth on a pub wall, a montage of things spiralling out of control within a cautionary tale.'

'My piano is where I 'box things off', Liam. I associate it with the positive things in my life. It is my therapy, I can release the ghosts that persist and that you can recognise in your own experience. The German Requiem is my lament for Strekerau. I play it to remind me of my roots, the hazy summers and harsh winters of my childhood. I play it in tribute to my brothers and sisters who I never saw again. I play it for my mother who taught me each key to play and for my father who taught me how to fend for myself. The piano is a balm for my loss, for as long as I play there is a flicker of a chance a member of my family might hear it and return to me.'

'I have only found that as time moves on it raises more questions than answers,' said Liam.

'Go on,' invited Andreas.

'That luxury item that no one ever requests on a desert island discs?'

Andreas looked puzzled.

'Back on the armed forces radio network we got to listen to a programme from the BBC World Service called Desert Island Discs. The interviewer would invite a guest to choose a number of records and personal items to see them through a stay on a fictional desert island. We eagerly tuned into this every Sunday before going out on patrol with the peace-keeping force in Beirut. Some of the records were highbrow stuff - the kind of things you might play Andreas. Some of the personal items chosen were naff and sentimental and wouldn't have helped your survival. I mean, we were soldiers, we were trained to be pragmatic and to deal with any situation so we had a head start compared to those invited onto that radio programme. But the one thing that no one ever asked for was the benefit of hindsight. Wisdom is not a commodity, it's not a life preserver or an essential oil, you can't attract low flying aircraft with it and it won't enable you to judge the tide and swim out over the breakers into the open sea and escape the island. But wisdom is hindsight and I have learnt to try and harness it to get me out of some tight spots. Hindsight helped me deal with an incident that occurred during my time on routine patrol in the Lebanon.

I had joined up with two others I had grown up with from my housing estate in Ballyfermot. Lar Hennessy and Ger Couples. They were just as impoverished as me so the army seemed to be a way out from all the shite we had to wade through back home. I'm over six foot so I had no trouble being accepted, Lar was a bit short-sighted and Ger had flat feet, but all three of us managed to get in. I don't think that I would have continued if they hadn't been with me. We joined the Irish army not thinking that we would actually see any active service. Christ the night, Ireland is a neutral country but even it has to do its bit with the United Nations. The Lebanon to me was just a song by that femme looking fella in the Human League. I knew fuck all about the people, the history or the cultural reasons as to why it was in such a turmoil. To me it was just an insurmountable mess, a melting-pot of differing factions that we as peace-keepers were given the task of keeping apart. There was no agreement on any side, the Israelis, the PLO, the Druze, Hezbollah and Amal militia, the Americans and all other colours in between. All I knew was that we were literally caught in the crossfire and we paid for it.

We were given the task of manning a chain of strategically defensive positions on Mount Lebanon overlooking the Beqaa Valley. We were welcomed by many of the local population who were Christian and had long-held grudges against the muslim Druze militia. We had Christian guides who helped us thread our way to the most strategic vantage points over the valley. This way we were able to fortify and command the major routes in and out of Beirut. We provided covering support for the roadblocks at army checkpoints that had been set up in the Beqaa Valley to try and curtail the growing number of suicide bombings that had begun to cause havoc in the region. My unit operated from eight dispersed machine-gun nests, three men in each and, to be honest, I had begun to think that our position up in the mountains was impregnable. The cedar tree line on this snow-capped mountain mixed with the friendly welcome caused us to drop our guard. It was this complacency that got the better of me when we were attacked by the Druze militia late one evening. We were betrayed of course. How could you ever hope to have the hearts and minds of everyone you were sent to protect?

They came in slow in the dark without making a sound. They knew every detail of our routine, down to the habits of our regulated existence. They sneaked up on each emplacement on a moonless night and overpowered us. Expertly they cupped one hand over a mouth, leaving the other hand free to make a deep incision into the necks of my mates so as not to give themselves away. When they finally got to my machine-gun nest, we didn't even have the chance to get off a round. I had just answered the call of nature and was returning to my post when I heard a muffled scream from my position. I could see Lar was dead when I jumped back in. A single puncture wound from a thin blade had ruptured his carotid artery; I doubt whether he actually saw his adversary. It was clean and he almost looked like he was asleep despite the blood loss. I didn't have time to dwell on my friend as Ger was missing too. Ger had put up a fight though and I could make out the trail marks from the struggle he must have made leading beyond the gun emplacement. My blood was up and without thinking I lit a flare and grabbed the machine-gun. The vicinity was now brightly illuminated and I could make out some of their stragglers heading for the cover of the tree line in the pink haze generated by the flare. I aimed at them and fired. I must have dropped ten of them, but I kept up my fire until the belt ran out. My hand froze to the weapon as I spun it on its axis looking for more targets. The flare had dwindled and I grabbed my rifle from the floor of the emplacement and went hunting. I soon caught up with Gerry. He was slumped against a sapling, his eyes fixed and dilated with one hand still clutching at the dagger embedded in his neck. He must have fought bravely to have made it this far. It made me livid and acting on impulse I went down to the tree line to see if I could dispatch any more of them. When I got there, some were still twitching so I pressed my boots into their wounds so as not to let them go easy. I could hear the moans of them and I think I was so angry that I relished it. Bullets are too good for them I thought and I waited for them to die.'

This was the first time Liam had been able to talk about it openly and for some reason it seemed much easier to confide in a stranger. He had always been the quiet one of the three, shy even, but way too strong to be picked on except by the two friends he had now lost. This grief he had buried deep and in doing so it had lined his skin, prematurely ageing him, making him stoop somewhat in deference to the burden he was carrying. It had hardened his opinions on what really mattered, making him manifestly defensive. He was still one of them though, a knacker from Ballyfermot but he didn't wear or choose to share this inner loss with anyone. Certainly not with Lar and Ger's extended families when he returned on leave to attend both funerals back in Dublin. His commanding officer had prepared the ground by writing articulate, even if inaccurate accounts which would still be sensitive to the needs of the bereaved families in the manner of their deaths. No matter how much drink Liam was plied with at both wakes he wouldn't stray from the official version. His frame was large enough to drink anyone, who insisted on hearing what really happened, under the table and the families took comfort from his being with their loved ones when it came to the crunch. He was a resplendent reminder in his dress uniform of what the three of them had set out to do. He complied, played a supporting role to those grieving, of which he was one and tried for a while to fit in at home. He was being everything to those around him, without ever being himself. He had the discipline to keep up this performance until the end of his leave period. His mother who knew him better than he knew himself, could see right through his act but had decided to let him talk about it on his terms and only when he wanted to. She would have to wait as Liam had too many battles in his head still to win as well as a return tour of duty to the Lebanon to contend with. He found an interim remedy of a sort in the form of the luxuriant black Lebanese resin which he bought openly from the shanty town souks on the outskirts of Beirut. It relaxed him when off duty, took away the constant stress of watchfulness and worry. He smoked it or inhaled it through a smashed bottle covering two knives pressed tightly over some of the resin and then heated up on an open fire. The calm it brought may have been a temporary release but it led his mind to inquire more about the history of the conflict he was so embroiled in, the culture of the people he had fought and the value of his being there at all.

'We had paid the price for complacency. I can see that now. Without knowing it we had taken sides in a conflict that we were meant to be impartial to. We were the fools on the hill breathing in the rarified air, thinking that we were above the petty squabbles of these ancient adversaries. We didn't know or care why we were there in the first place. I knew it was complicated but it was never properly explained to me and now that I had just lost the only two friends who mattered to me, I was too angry to even try to understand. Anger scarred my thoughts, Andreas. I had killed ten men that night and it still wasn't enough. I wanted to scalp them, make trophies of their hides but that wouldn't have healed the pain I felt for the loss of my mates. To me they had died for nothing, miles from home on a hillside too arid even for their own burial. From this distance in time I now understand that we were like deaf men who had stumbled into someone else's private argument and who started trading insults to try and distract them. An ancient feud that we had intruded upon, that we couldn't hope to resolve, only add to its complexity.'

'Hindsight taught you something Liam. We were both caught up in events beyond our control. You couldn't help but avenge your feelings and I know how that feels too. There is no mention of vengeance in the army training manual so you deal with it at the time in the only way you know. You lost two close friends in succession, two people you had grown up with. How else were you supposed to react? You may even have felt a bit guilty that you had survived and they hadn't, again part of the kaleidoscope of emotions that confronted you. You took those lives out of anger and vengeance and it was justified at that moment. It was what you had been trained to do and you have nothing to reproach yourself over about your methods or your state of mind. It's the fallout from the questions raised in your head at the time and how you deal with them later that matters. It's because up until now it has been you alone asking those questions, leading to arguments in your head. The inner turmoil that eats away at so many battle-fatigued soldiers when they finally rejoin the so-called real world. Civilians and family back home may have your interests at heart, but they haven't experienced it first hand. Some shy away from asking about the things that haunt you most, some pry awkwardly into things that have yet to heal and some are supportive enough to wait until you first bring up the subject. I have been recounting my own experiences to you, the things I have witnessed and you have listened patiently and now you have confided in me and I think that it has helped us both.'

'I saw things differently after the Lebanon. Previously I had put a value on things that turned out to be crap before going out there, things that localised my life or so I thought. I was naïve enough to try and take these safe opinions abroad with me so as to live in this kind of protective bubble. I know now that you can't do that. You rely too much on others for your own survival and they rely just as much on you to step up to the mark. But this is the first time that I have talked about it with someone who has actually experienced what I have gone through. I owe Lar and Ger this much to keep their memory alive.'

Andreas put a hand on Liam's shoulder in a moment of mutual understanding that spoke for them both. He knew that Liam had a story to tell and it turned out that it was just as intricate as his own. He had spoken up for Liam against the judgements of others back at the hotel and given him a chance to prove himself, which he had. He also realized that he had more in common with Liam than just about anyone else he knew. His colleagues knew nothing of his past and here was this 'auslander', this dour big Irishman to whom he had recounted his innermost struggles.

'Nothing we can do can bring them back, we can only drink to their memory. I have a bottle of Jägermeister hidden somewhere for just such a moment. It was gifted to me by Kirstin Deubler.' Andreas produced some keys from his waistcoat and proceeded over to the tantalus which adorned the dresser along the wall. He unlocked the decanter and wiped down two glasses that were adjacent with a drying cloth. He poured two large measures of Jägermeister and offered one glass to Liam.

'Absent friends,' Andreas said.

'Absent friends,' replied Liam as their glasses collided.

Andreas took his drink back over to the piano and perched on the piano stool.

'Tastes good, it has a bit of central heating in it,' said Liam.
'Not as good as your Irish whiskey though, I'm sure you are thinking?
'That would depend. If you mean Catholic whiskey or Protestant whiskey.'
'Surely you people over there don't quibble over the origins of the malt?'
'Well, being a good Catholic boy I am partial to Powers Three Swallows. The swallows are actually the number of sips you should take to quaff a measure. Powers is smoother than their great rival across the river Liffey, Jamesons.'
'And what if I was a Protestant whiskey drinker?' inquired Andreas.
'In that case you would be sipping at that Bushmills,' sighed Liam.
'Well as I am from Lutheran stock then it would have to be Bushmills.'
'Suit yourself, but I'm sticking to the Powers Three Swallows. But here as we are drinking Jägermeister in Munich, then this can be our very own Munich agreement.'
Liam downed his glass and Andreas held out the bottle to pour him another measure.
'Now that's the finer points of Irish Whiskey sorted out, Scotch is in a league of its own too, but I heard somewhere that you actually make a whiskey in Germany. Is that true at all or what? Sure that would be like us making Schnapps and that would be so very wrong!'
Andreas poured himself another measure and settled back behind the piano.

8

1942

Obergefreiter Hauser shook Andreas awake earlier than usual. How he had managed to get any sleep was a miracle considering his blanket roll was completely saturated by rainwater dripping down the guy ropes which secured the tarpaulins to the trucks. It had been raining constantly for five days and the division was now stuck fast in the mud.
'Mensche, you had better get cleaned up and then fall in for some breakfast. After which I want to do a kit inspection with you and also I want you to strip down your weapon, clean it thoroughly and then only after I have inspected it can you join the Cossacks.' This was Hauser at his most pedantic. He clung to his level of authority, envious at having heard that Andreas had mixed so successfully at Papa Hoth's campaign table. To be

fair, his attitude to Andreas had changed markedly since Belgorod. Andreas was no longer a 'Boris', he was a comrade and had proved his worth to the division. He could see that the kid prized the rifle that had once belonged to the Russian sniper, that he slept with it in his arms and protected the lens and scope in his kit bag. He could break the rifle apart in minutes and it was in pristine condition as he slung it over his shoulder after his kit inspection.

'You are going home Mensche. How do you feel about that?' asked Hauser.

'Numb and nervous. I think I'm scared of what I will find there.'

'You have seen a lot more than one should at your age already. This journey will answer all the questions you have been asking yourself. I was wrong about you, Mensche. I saw steel in your resolve when you interrogated the prisoner even though he escaped and since then I haven't worried about how you would get on. The big Cossack, their leader is called Fyodor Solntsev. He cheats at cards and drinks abundantly but I think you will be alright with him. You speak their language for a start and you saw how they behave already so you know your own mind. But be careful. They fall out over the slightest thing and take offence easily, so learn to be thick-skinned and hold your tongue. Watch them, how they ride, how they interact together, learn from them and you just might make it back to the division in one piece.'

This was as close to parental advice as Andreas could ever expect with Hauser. It was just past seven a.m. and the others he had served with had gathered in various states of dishevelment in the pouring rain to wish him well. They stood to attention when Oberleutnant Werner approached. Andreas saluted him and the Oberleutnant took him to one side.

'Mensche do you want your rubles? Do you want all or just some for now? You might not see me again and I wouldn't like you to think me a thief!'

'I trusted you completely with my money Oberleutnant. I would like you to keep half and share it amongst the men and I will use the other half to keep these Cossacks sweet. Is that okay?'

The Oberleutnant nodded and Andreas smiled as he saluted him for what might have been the last time and began to make his way over to the command tent were the Cossacks were preparing their mounts.

They had slung their waterproof smocks over their bandoliers which criss-crossed their chests. Their smocks stretched far enough to keep their fur-lined saddles dry and protect the carbines strapped on either side from the rain. They looked brave and formidable despite the hangovers they must be feeling. Each one of them wore the prized Astrakhan hat emblazoned with the crossed swords badge that signified the 5th Don Cossack regiment. As I approached them their leader Fyodor signalled for a fresh horse to be prepared for me. He appeared remarkably composed and looked more comfortable to be back in the saddle, free from the constraints of the convoy.

'Now young 'un, we will see if you can keep up with us. I have been informed that you are capable with a horse. I want you to get familiar with this one.'

I could see it was a mare, about three years old and judging by her chestnut coat she was from the Don region.

'What do they call you?' I whispered as I held her tentatively.

'She is called Freyja. From the Norse mythology. Do you like her?' asked Fyodor.

I nodded in appreciation. Freyja was statuesque even in a rainstorm. I calmly closed in on her muzzle and let her get used to my scent before trying anything.

A couple of the Cossack outriders nodded their approval as I looked like I actually knew what I was doing. It had worked before with Hanzie, why not now? Fyodor told me to check her harnessing and to buckle my rifle through a loop hanging down from the saddle. I was able to take my ammunition cannister off my backpack and tie it to the other side of the saddle along with my sleeping blanket. I lifted myself up into her stirrups and mounted Freyja and sat for a moment waiting for her to react. Nothing. They offered up my backpack and gave me a smock to wear. I think I might have just about passed for one of them from a distance despite my Einheitsmütze field cap. I was ready and I think Freyja was too as she seemed to resent standing for long periods in the pouring rain judging by the snorting she was doing.

Fyodor saluted Generaloberst Hoth who was standing in from the rain by the tent flap and then turned in his saddle to give the order for us to advance. It was a relief to finally be moving and even in the pelting downpour we made a dignified progression riding parallel to the convoy. Fyodor was out in front flanked by two outriders carrying the 5th Cossack guidons which fluttered limply from their long staffs. We followed behind in pairs and I did my best to keep the pace beside a man whose name I never learnt on a strange horse over very boggy terrain in a rainstorm. I was grateful for having previous experience with Hanzie as this would not have been possible without him. Freyja was fresh and keen, but she responded well to my bedding in on her. We took an age to pass by the massed ranks of the 4th Panzer army, I had forgotten how vast our strength was when I had insulated all my thoughts into fitting in with the 168th. We passed this formidable line-up and were cheered as we went until all I had begun to take for granted receded into the bleakness of the waterlogged steppe.

I was roughly retracing my steps through a deluge that cast unfamiliar shadows over the landscape filling me with a deep foreboding on every new horizon. It has often been said that the return journey passes more quickly and ordinarily that would have been of some comfort to me, but not now. I began to relate to some of the landmarks that confronted us. I recognized crossroads where small settlements and farmsteads once thrived, whose inhabitants had done business with my father. The tenantry of these collective farms had previously pulled together and the cooperative system worked as a result. I knew these places from trips out in the buggy with my father in better times. I was glad that he didn't live to see their condition now. Flooded field strips with rotting maize still trying to make a stand but leaning heavily, their stalks nodding downward and giving in on one side of the lane. On the other, over ripened corn with saturated seed heads stretching over a bedraggled scarecrow with the aspect of a drowning man. He appeared to be pointing the way, funnelling us precariously down a lane that I barely recognized. The only harvest that had passed this way had been human for I saw no sign of any people.

If my memory served me this was once land owned by the Kottinger family. I had gone to school with their two youngest children, Ernst and Gesela. I last saw them from my bedroom window being barracked and herded into the goods trains at the railhead by the NKVD. Sure enough through the sheet rain we approached their farmstead or what was left of it. Rafters exposed to the elements, every window blown out and the door frame missing at the front. Fyodor raised his right glove and we came to a halt in the farmyard. I was given the task of stabling the horses in the Kottinger barn. It still had enough of a corrugated roof to provide shelter for all thirty of them. They formed a steaming huddle tied to the rail that ran the length of the barn, instinctively they searched in the empty troughs for some kind of feed and found only rainwater. There was nobody left to gather in the crops, so no fodder was set aside for any of the farm animals. All livestock had either been driven off or eaten by wild animals.

The man whose name I never learnt approached me and said that we should try and gather some of the stalks of hay that had ripened and become top heavy, falling beneath the wide brim of the barn roof as it might still be without mould in places and therefore edible. If we didn't do it soon then the horses would start to eat the fresh grass and that might cause colic. We walked through the the barn and found that the stalks had indeed ripened under the roof lip, the guttering of which had channelled the rainwater away. The outer sheaths, although saturated, had protected the inner core which was salvageable. He produced a ball of twine from one pocket and threw it to me. He asked if I had a knife and I shook my head. He then gave me his and told me to cut the twine into metre lengths. He unsheathed his sword and began threshing the stalks nearest to him. I followed nervously behind and sorted the dry sheaths from the rotten, gathering them up into bundles. It wasn't long before I had ten metre length bales of straw tied up. He had worked up quite a sweat which the rain did its best to disguise until he eventually looked round at my efforts and said that it was enough. He asked for his knife back and we took the bundles into the barn and scattered them roughly in the feeding troughs.

Fyodor was pleased with himself. He had liberated some of the Kottinger schnapps that somehow must have been previously overlooked by other looters. The man whose name I never learnt and I joined the rest in the only room on the ground floor of the farmhouse that was still relatively dry. This was once the front parlour in which the Kottingers would have entertained guests and it looked familiar to me. Fyodor must have noticed my reaction as he handed the bottle of schnapps to all in the room and he came over to me. He asked me did I know where I was. I told him that this farm was only three kilometres from Strekerau. He said that was just as well as we would have to press on as there was no prospect of any food here. I was glad he had said that as some of his men were beginning to get a little too comfortable and I didn't fancy spending the night in a house that brought back a lot of memories.

The rain was the only constant, the one surety that nature still had a role in all this madness and that perhaps, given time, even it could wash away the sins being enacted upon her innocent earth. My mood constantly fluctuated, striking every notch along the scale between depression and euphoria. I knew I had to summon the strength to cope with what to expect when we reached my home town. The Cossacks didn't care what I was feeling, they were too busy living in the moment to be concerned about my grief. They had orders to take me to the town I had been brought up in and they didn't care either way if it turned out well for me. There might even be something in it for them. They were too free-spirited to be resentful of the task as this was well within their region. Some of them I began to realise had formed the circus troupe that had year on year pitched their tent in Strekerau. They knew that the inhabitants of my town had always been receptive, but now that the circumstances had altered dramatically their overriding instincts led them here to see what if anything they could get for themselves. This was a discipline I wasn't used to. Fyodor had an almost tribal sway over the rest, keeping them in line. He had harnessed their spirit, giving them in the process a fierce reputation in battle. But something always bubbled underneath, an underlying resentment that my well honed Germanic sensibilities couldn't decipher. Their loyalties ran deeper than the remits of this conflict.

We reached the outskirts of my town after five o'clock. I had approached it from every direction in the past, but never with such a heavy heart as now.

Slowly the memory map of thickets, barns and outhouses, plain fences and cherry orchards dissolved into my collective consciousness to be overridden by scarred and charred earthly remains. I knew I was home and I could do this route blindfolded, but the obstacles that now paved the way would soon engulf me. The rain had long since put out the fires that had been lit under the neatly shingled dwellings that once nestled here. I perched on Freyja, in truth I clung to her atop the bluff that overlooked the town. Fyodor gave orders for his men to spread out and approach from every angle so that we wouldn't leave ourselves vulnerable to a surprise attack. Was I really home? I could never call it that again but I did grow up there. Did I feel so safe back then so as to have been lulled into a smug complacency and as punishment I was to live to see the other side of all that carnage? Was I meant to be the only former inhabitant to return and witness this? Perhaps to give an account at a later date so that it might be believed. Who would listen anyway? After all, the truth in any history is usually written by the victor. My people's people were just another ethnic group whose fate was sealed on entering the stagnant carriages that sped away from the railhead to the far east, another statistic in the great Soviet experiment. It really was that simple.

Fyodor rode ahead of me and we progressed down a narrow ravine that led from the bluff, which in happier times had acted as a slide in the snow for our bin lid toboggans. Freyja kept a foothold as I kept clutching at memories and we progressed on through the scattered outskirts. We passed the burnt out dwellings of families I could name count stretching back three generations. The town was laid out in a grid system and the streets were named after prominent people, German names that were tolerated by the Soviet authorities until very recently. The street signs were gone and with them any semblance of normality. A methodical deconstruction had been unleashed here. After the state police had conducted their headcount and rounded up all the locals, the NKVD had done its best to obliterate any trace of a settlement. How quiet it was, it seemed even the jackdaws preferred to dine elsewhere, leaving us to approach the main street with a dust cloud forming at our backs. Brick chimney-stacks stood sentinel above the charcoal remains of former houses. Even the linden trees which had been pleached and trained to create shade along each street were now carbonated.

We teamed up with the others in what must have been the town square although it was unrecognisable to me by now. Where the bank, courthouse, church, post office, school and cooperative store should have stood, now only combusted outlines remained. These centred around a scorched water fountain within a fractured flowerbed. There was no longer a clock tower to set your watch by, no landmarks throwing shade, leaving nothing to refer to. You could still discern the charred floor plans of these former buildings, leading to parched back yards behind with barren views. This was hard to take in and even Fyodor could sense my heartbreak. His words were of no comfort though, they washed over me and I can't remember them, such was the harshness of my embitterment. I could make out where the bank had once stood as it had a reinforced cellar that took the weight of the vault. Every adjacent building had caved in on itself forming powdery mounds of fallen masonry. The vault contained a walk-in safe which was fire retardant. The safe stood defiantly open, its contents long since pillaged and the scattered safe deposit trays had turned white in the sequential fire-storm. The tile floor of the bank was intact in places and I could discern the border where my father's office must once have been. Now was not the time for nostalgia but I could not help thinking of him dressed as Father Christmas as he sat behind his desk on the last working day before the holidays. How affable he was with his staff and how diligently he loaned and invested on behalf of the workers' cooperative. He told me on that last day we spoke that he had made copies of all the shares and deeds our family owned. Would there be any trace of them after all this destruction? Was the secret room under his study floor still intact?

In my time we had moved house only twice. My father, unlike other ambitious bank officials, had chosen to remain with the Strekerau savings bank which dealt solely with the workers co-op. In doing so he would have to wait until any promotional prospects arose internally as the co-op only had one branch. As his talent and responsibilities grew steadily, soon more children came along and the need for a larger dwelling became a priority. Finally we were able to move to Landauer Strasse which was in the heart of the more bourgeois district of the town. The gaps between houses grew and we now had a front and back lawn big enough to keep Hanzie, my piebald, in an enclosed paddock.

I could pace out my steps from the ruins of the bank in the direction of our old house. It must have been the best part of a kilometre. So I dismounted Freyja and without any landmarks to help me I led her in what I thought was the right direction. Fyodor sent the man whose name I had never learnt, to cover my back from a discreet distance. I began to wish I had kept my eyes shut as my route was strewn with burnt-out vehicles and abandoned carts. Everything coated in a thin layer of dust that you couldn't avoid breathing in. Again I counted the blackened chimney-stacks until I reached what was once a crossroads and I knew that I was on the right track. From here it was just three houses down Landauer Strasse to my own home. I paced out the charred plot outlines until I stood where our gate must have once been. The path was still there, paving intact but no porch, no sturdy front door, no reliable edifice. Just the tangled debris left in the wake of something violent unleashed on everything I once held dear. My shadow watcher had perched on the street corner pavement at a polite distance giving me leave to explore. Without thinking I began to climb into the wreckage of my former existence. The surface pile soon gave way beneath my feet and I was sent tumbling through shards of carbonated planking until I landed on a secure structure. My face was covered in brick dust and my eyelids stung from the lime mortar residue. I stretched my limbs and knew that I hadn't broken any bones. I had landed on the trapdoor above the secret room my father had previously shown me. My fall had inadvertently revealed it again and I thanked God for helping me. I wiped away the thin layer of dust that I had disturbed and soon located the latch hidden within the herringbone pattern which was made from cedar which I knew to be a hardwood that doesn't burn very well. I sprung to my knees invigorated and tried to turn it. Nothing. I spat on it to try and lubricate it. Still nothing. I got up and jumped over the debris mound and made my way over to Freyja. The shadow watcher approached me as I unfastened my rifle from the saddle. He got very animated with me doing this so I told him to follow and watch. We both jumped down onto the cedar trapdoor. He tried to open it and it still wouldn't budge. I gestured for him to move back and then I levelled my rifle with the latch, took aim and fired.

The bolt on the underside must have buckled or broke as I was able to lift the latch with relative ease and the trap door in the floor swung open once more. I asked the man whose name I never learnt for his box of matches. I struck one and cupped it over the edge before climbing down the step ladder to be consumed by the pitch darkness below. He threw me the box of matches when he saw that I had reached the bottom step. Without doubt this room hadn't been discovered by the NKVD. It did seem smaller, but then perhaps I had done a lot of growing up in the interim. I lit another match and I could make out the strongbox in the corner. Then I remembered that my father had written down the combination numbers on the back of my letter of introduction. Oberleutnant Werner had kept this letter safe inside my pouch of rubles and it was now in Freyja's saddle-bag. The match burnt my finger and went out as I climbed back up the ladder. I retrieved my rifle and secured it back on Frejya before searching her saddle-bag for my father's note. The man whose name I never learnt asked me what I was doing. I found the crumpled note and read it again, taking comfort from my father's handwriting before turning it over to see the combination numbers. I told him that he was about to become a rich man and he took off his hat and scratched his head. I climbed down again and lit another match and paced out the room shedding light onto every corner. There was nothing else of any interest other than the strongbox. Again I burnt my finger and promptly lit another match. I spun the dial for a complete revolution so as to clear the combination. Then I turned it left four times until settling over 9, then right three times before stopping over 4. I turned it left two times before stopping over 2 and finally I turned it right once until I paused over the 7. I could feel a tightness in the dial as I began to turn it left for the last time until it caught fast. I pulled the handle which gave way and the strongbox opened.

The man whose name I never learnt had climbed down. He had a canvas sack slung over his shoulder and he was craning to see what was in the strongbox, excitement written all over his face. I lit yet another match to get a better look and I could make out four shelves within. Two contained pouches of rubles and the other two were taken up by scrolls of paper which I took to be title deeds and share certificates. Every family had been a stakeholder in the cooperative so they all had lost something. There must have been over three hundred share certificates and title deeds rolled up in there. My father must have kept copies made from the originals which had subsequently been looted and burned back in the bank vault. They had all thrown in their lot with the Strekerau Savings and Loan Bank and unravelling just one scroll hammered home what each family in Strekerau had lost. This was what set my father apart, he had made provision for it. He didn't see this day coming but he had made allowance for the fact that it might. It didn't take much to realise that I had to share some, if not all, the rubles with my Cossack hosts. They had lost everything too, so some kind of bargain would have to be struck. I didn't take them for bandits, they had a code of honour which bonded them to Fyodor and he was many things but not a thief. I counted ten pouches of rubles, of which I gave seven to the man whose name I never learnt, keeping three for myself. I took the certificates that were pertinent to my own family and then we both climbed up the ladder and back out into the daylight.

Fyodor seemed happy, although it was hard to tell any expression given that he had so much facial hair. I'm sure he hadn't seen so much money for quite a long time. They divided it out equally and what they wouldn't spend on drink they would send back to their families. It was difficult to see just what they could spend it on in such harsh conditions where every settlement we came across was immolated to the consistency of a wafer. We were the richest men in hell, with nowhere to even hang our hats. He didn't see the point of our staying in Strekerau a moment longer and I was with him on that as there was nothing left that could have been any comfort to me. But for the rolled up papers in that strongbox, my people might as well have never existed. I checked that the pouches and title deeds were secured safely within my saddle-bag and then mounted up with the rest of them.

I was very much in favour as we left the precincts of my childhood behind and rode out into the open steppe once more to retrace our route back to the Fourth Panzer Army. We were in a column of two as before with me and my shadow watcher towards the rear. We had travelled perhaps only six kilometres out of Strekerau when we were strafed by a lone Ilushin IL2 ground attack aircraft which had been flying low in the poor conditions to try and observe any German troop movements. He had used the incessant rain as a cloak to sweep down upon the head of our column and only then did his engine give him away when almost right on top of us and he was able to pour down concentrated fire unhindered. The leading horses and their mounts including Fyodor had been slaughtered by the machine cannon which couldn't help but rip through flesh and sinew with every burst. Freyja now froze as the line ahead of us collapsed, falling haphazardly, being sucked into the mire, every pothole of which soon filled with the blood of the fallen. I managed to somehow fall free of her and narrowly avoid my pelvis being crushed, landing on her flank as she too fell into the morass. Above me I could hear the aircraft bank up into the sky, her faltering engine noise at high altitude as she prepared to swoop low for another attack on such an irresistible target. Its machine cannon ripped into us and all I could do was listen to the thud as every other bullet hit home and those that didn't stirred up the syrupy mud that surrounded me. I had used Freyja as a shield and soon I could sense her chest begin to heave slowly from the pounding until she could no longer sustain a breath nor flare her nostrils, her reins loosened and her long neck and mane slid gently into the enveloping morass.

I lay there for the longest time with matted hair blinding me, my face congealed in Freyja's blood until long after the engine had ceased and had flown back to report our position, no doubt soaking up praise for a worthy kill. It was now dark and my senses were closing in, heightening any sound, making my heart thump out of my chest. At length I grew accustomed to the gloom and I began to distinguish between the objects and outlines in my field of vision amid the carnage. The man whose name I had never learnt, who had ridden for so long beside me, now stared up into the heavens through unblinking eyes and was missing the better part of his cranium. He was slumped in a kneeling position near his fallen horse with a rifle in his hands. He must have tried to fire off a round only to be riddled for his pains. The sullen air was now heavy with steam emitting from the laboured breathing of both men and horses. I hadn't noticed that it had actually stopped raining and had now been replaced by a torpid mist that was almost tangible. My boots were full of dirty water and that combined with the weight of the mud on my clothing made it difficult for me to move, never mind stand. My eardrums must have been caked in mud because I could not now hear the moans of those too far gone to be helped. I would have been of no assistance to them as I was wrapped in numbed shock. I waded through mangled bodies, bloody gristle and butchered horseflesh. I tripped in the newly-formed gullies that now rippled and divided both dead horse and rider. I strayed onto the horrifically frozen expressions on the faces of men who had just moments earlier been singing in unison, whose pockets were bulging with rubles. I reached the fractured remnants of the front column and the broken body of Fyodor splayed on top of two outriders. He hadn't been able to react, the shock of what had transpired still written large in his horrified expression. I knelt and closed his eyes. It was no fair fight but he had died leading his men and if I kept repeating to myself that as I rifled through his pockets, then maybe I could just about live with myself. I had to do something practical to try and survive. Fyodor had always kept a hip flask in his coat pocket and I had seen him swig from it often as I followed from behind.

This was about as low as I could get, but I was shaking and beginning to feel what others might term as the onset of hypothermia. I found the flask, it had been recently topped with schnapps from the Kottinger farm. I unscrewed the lid and raised it to my lips.

'My Lord God please forgive me for leading these poor souls to their deaths,' was all I could think of to say as some kind of eulogy.

I drank the schnapps. It warmed my throat and fuelled my senses again warming up my body even if only superficially. One of the ruble pouches and a pocket compass had dislodged from Fyodor's waterproof smock. I retrieved them without thinking, he would have done the same, you have to do what you can to survive. I stood over him and raised the flask to my mouth again. I could feel it instantly saving me, giving me the ability to stand apart from the carnage, allowing me to gather some kind of courage to go on. I had to find something to eat and keep it for later as the schnapps wouldn't quell my appetite for long. I remembered that Alexei was in charge of victuals and that he rode about six horses behind Fyodor. Squinting down through the line of devastation I counted back and made out the position roughly where Alexei should have been riding. His horse was older than the others and needed to be much stronger as he often weighed it down with wild turkey, dried fish and rabbits he had shot and tied up on his saddle to dry along our route. I took a bandolier from Fyodor's body and placed it around my shoulder and retraced my faltering steps towards where I thought Alexei might have been. I was correct, his large horse was easier to find and poor Alexei was lying nearby, face down. With no room for any other feelings than my own, I tore the dead wildfowl from his saddle and in doing so his pouch of rubles fell into my possession. How could I be so transfixed by gain at this lowest ebb? Simple answer was that I might buy or bribe my way out of this chaos and a steely resolve prompted me to search for more pouches of coins from the fallen. A little while later I broke away from the trail of the dead and hastened forward to the path we had formerly been riding on. If I had stayed and tried to give them a decent burial then I would have soon fallen from exhaustion. I was on foot, but I had food, something to drink, money and a compass to help give me directions. I had my rifle and plenty of ammunition. I also knew the terrain. If I could find some shelter very quickly I might just make it.

I tried to remember each one of their Cossack faces as I walked. I did this to keep my mind from wandering and partly as a kind of tribute to their sacrifice. In the short time I had come to know them, their strong personalties had come to influence and develop my own, imprinting on me their many quirks and traits. Fyodor had not instilled the rigid discipline I had come to expect in the German army. Every member of his maverick group had a role and each one trusted the other like a brother only closer. They were different from any other group in that they all came from the same region and were more loyal to it than to any country. Now they had fallen as one, thirty men lay dead on the rise behind me where the crows had now begun to gather in numbers and I had somehow got up and walked away. Was I spared so I could tell of their bravery? These horsemen from another age were just grist to the mill of a modern war.

9

1987

Yaffat Laminieri was in a good mood. Liam always had cause for concern when this was the case as it usually involved some kind of arduous chore that he would only be half equipped to carry out. Liam wasn't interested as to the reasons why but he was watchful for the downside of Yaffat's levity. The signs were readily apparent. Today of all days, he wore a freshly starched white doctor's coat with a name tag pinned and crudely Dymo'd across it. His hurriedly bought combination of hotel lobby gift shop hair and body gel made him smell like a prairie vine which was overpowering. His extensive display of gold and black fountain pens collected over the years from lost property jutted riotously from his top coat pocket. Yes, he was definitely in some kind of peacock mode but who was the lucky peahen? Liam took note of this distraction and thought that maybe he could just use it to his own advantage to get one back on Yaffat. After all Yaffat was married but he never took as much time over himself before now. It made Liam squirm to see the balding coot preen what was left of his curls with so much gel as would saturate and stain any pillow case.

Each and every high summer without fail and just as the social calendar demanded, the great and the good of Munich society withdrew from the city to take possession of their resplendent lake, shore and alpine retreats nestling along the Austrian border but still conveniently close to the autobahn for any unscheduled trips back to the Bavarian capital. Ordinarily this would have dented the turnover at the many society watering-holes and eateries within the classier hotels of Munich. However with their departure came a new arrival to keep the coffers of municipal trade well stocked. This was the yearly migration for the summer months of the wealthy arab oil barons and their extended families. Apartment buildings and whole floors in some of the most prestigious hotels were booked up months in advance at eye-watering prices that defied logic but were deemed as reasonable amounts by Arab families with some of the deepest pockets in the world. They took advantage of the best medical care available and came to Munich ostensibly to get better but also to spend some of that wealth. Prices in the nearby retail outlets and convenience stores rocketed and peaked for two months during their stay in the city. It was a bonanza and the character of the numerous kerb side cafes, restaurants and hotels that clamourously fought to cater for this clientele changed markedly. They hurriedly typed up new menus providing a distinctly eastern flavour and the nuanced aromas of Machboos Arabic rice so favoured in Saudi Arabia would hang in the air in the many residential squares and meeting places. The Arab men dressed traditionally and would stroll in groups, rarely if ever to be seen in public with their wives. The women were impossible to distinguish, mother or daughter as they were clad head to toe in black abayas, wearing hijabs. They gathered together like a murder of crows on the municipal benches to watch their children at play during this time which began after Ramadan and ended in late September before the commencement of the larger beer festivals.

Immediately outside the Bayerischer Hof is a small oval-shaped public park encircled by tramlines. This leafy artery was a favoured space for the well off and the sartorial whose perambulations often with their well-groomed pets could be pure theatre to watch. It was a respite at lunch-time for smartly-dressed employees to dispose of a quick sandwich on one of the many park benches. At its heart was an equestrian statue whose symbolism had long since been hijacked by its conversion to a rock shrine for dead musicians. The latest addition being that of reggae luminary Peter Tosh. His candle, glass holder and photograph would soon fade in the elements along with the many others including of course John Lennon, Elvis, Jimi Hendrix, Janice Joplin, Brian Jones, Keith Moon, John Bonham, Bob Marley, Bon Scott, Jim Morrison, Patsy Cline and Buddy Holly. The shrine was allowed to blossom as it was considered a sign of outward toleration by an otherwise conservative city council. However the musical connection adjacent to the hotel wasn't just random, the Kleine Komoedie theatre had always been a purveyor of musicals and many famous musicians, conductors and bands had stayed at the Bayerischer Hof. Perhaps the most famous being that of The Beatles and the more recent stay of Michael Jackson during the first leg of his sellout 'Bad' tour, for which he had taken up a whole floor of the exclusive Palais Montgelas within the hotel.

Across the park but still in Promenadeplatz stood the imposingly ornate Annabella apartment building with its bourgeois neoclassical interiors. In this high season the full-time residents would cash in on the Arabic influx and lease out their dwellings to the highest bidder, knowing that their prized sticks of furniture could be replaced if damaged by such wealthy tenants. Soon its balconies with unrivalled views overlooking the park were congested with gatherings of gossiping ladies dressed in the black hijab. The basement was given over to parking and a very large recording studio which was frequented by some of the most famous rock groups in the world including Queen who had recorded their last four albums in the basement of the Annabella. It wasn't uncommon for large groups of fans to congregate at the statue in the park and wait to get a sighting of one or other of their idols. The contrast couldn't have been more extreme in such a confined space where the brash collided with the designer labels and that in turn with the religious code of strict personal modesty but an accommodation had been found between the three and it worked.

It was while cleaning the triple glazed windows of each suite on the fourth floor of the Bayerischer Hof overlooking the park that Liam had easily got distracted. Each panelled window had to be opened carefully and cleaned inside and out alternately with a wet and a dry chamois cloth. A bucket of warm water mixed with vinegar made the panes smell but left them gleaming. On a hot sunny day the dazzle from so much glass was, after a while, disorientating so Liam opened the adjoining French doors and stepped out onto the balcony for a sneaky smoke. Below him the green canopy of trees, a tram lazily snaking its way to the Hauptbahnhof, a clutch of hopeful rock fans spread out on the lawn and there on one of the many park benches was Yaffat Laminieri chatting animatedly with a woman in a black abaya with matching hijab. Liam's first thought, the raw Dublinesque in him, was to take out his todger and see if he could piss down and maybe spray some on his boss. He didn't of course, but the thought made him smile. There was Yaffat out in the sunshine charming one of the many Arab women who had come to town. Was this the reason why he had been acting so pleased with himself for the past few days? Liam rubbed his hands as if he had just watched a winner in the last race at Chepstow and took one last draw on his rolled cigarette before flicking the butt over the balcony. He closed the French doors just in time as the Portuguese couple who were staying in the room had returned early from a visit to the King Ludwig castles in southern Bavaria. Liam was done anyhow so he nodded as they flaked out on the two chairs near the television. Taking his usual big strides he collected his bucket and chamois and closed their door behind him.

That fucking Moroccan knacker, he couldn't help thinking, as he let himself in with the electronic master key to the next suite down the hall. Sitting there with his white coat on and his arm on the bench beside her. Sure as shite he could charm the birds out of the trees and no mistake. He went into the en suite bathroom and poured the dirty water from his bucket down the toilet and flushed it. Just then he thought he heard a moan, he definitely heard the second one. He dropped the bucket and leaned against the shaving mirror on the party wall which conjoined the suite he had just been in. The Portuguese couple must have gotten their second wind because he could distinctly hear the plaintive and the affirmative cries of the two of them in there and they sounded like they were at it like knives. Their moans were the same in any language and Liam smiled and shook his head. Was everyone including Yaffat getting some except him? He saw the funny side of it though because the noise they made was the most hilarious thing he had heard that wasn't actually laughter. He began to fill up his bucket with fresh hot water and added some of the white vinegar when nearly full. The couple next door were reaching a crescendo so Liam backed out of the en suite and closed the door behind him as he did. Presently the Portuguese man opened his French doors dressed in one of the complimentary dressing gowns and was drawing deeply on a cigarette. Liam was finishing off the outside glazing panels and the two men nodded to one another. Liam couldn't help but just make out a shapely bronzed leg being towelled down fresh out the shower beyond the Portuguese man. He was staring, so he adjusted himself and peered over the balcony instead. Yaffat and the Arab lady had both gone.

Later that evening Liam cut across the main foyer and saw Andreas hard at work on the reception desk. The Boston Symphony Orchestra's arrival had been delayed by several hours due to bad weather and now Andreas was heading up the skeleton crew to check them in. It was interesting for Liam to see this side of Andreas; the consummate professional, delegating slickly, ushering confidently and perfectly at ease with the cultivated stampede at his reception desk. At the back of Andreas's mind was the knowledge that the Boston Symphony Orchestra were in town to perform highlights from his favourite composer Brahms at the Kleine Komoedie theatre. Andreas caught sight of Liam and scolded him for having both arms the same length and told him to help the concierge with the luggage. Liam didn't quite cut a sartorial front of house figure in his boiler suit and monkey boots, but he got stuck in and soon the tour bus out front had been cleared of all instruments and luggage. This made a welcome change from spending most of his days with his hands immersed in warm water. It got him into hot water of a different kind with the manager of the Alte Bayern Stube restaurant. Liam had been AWOL for the last hour helping to take the luggage up to each room on the floor allocated to the orchestra. Andreas stepped in on his behalf to cancel the riot act that was about to be read to Liam.

They met again at seven a.m. in the refectory, Andreas with his usual yeast beer with white sausage and Liam with his improvised German fry on a tray. Liam asked if he could join Andreas.

'Thanks for your help earlier Liam. We were being overrun and I had to look in control, that's why I called you over.'

'No bother. I was on my way to the jacks when you caught me. Some good-looking birds in that yank orchestra. Did you see them? Fuckin' gorgeous!'

'I missed that. Too busy trying to organize the room allocations and the luggage. I will keep a close eye out for them in future though.'

Liam tore into his piled breakfast with his usual gusto, adding lashings of brown sauce. He began to speak with a mouth half full of food.

'That Yaffat is in love I think. I mean he's as giddy as a schoolgirl this weather. Fucking sad if you ask me. A grown man reduced to that.'

'What are you on about Liam?' Andreas asked drily.

'I've seen him fawning over one of those Arab women in the park. Animated he was, in full swing and him being married and all that.'

'Yaffat's many things, but he is no ladies' man and if you ever saw his wife you would hold your tongue as she could tear strips off you and no mistake.'

'That's as maybe but I'm only telling you what I saw with my own eyes from a balcony on the fourth floor.'

Andreas thought it wise not to say anything further about Yaffat lest their discussion be overheard by any one of the growing number now seated at their table. They both finished breakfast in silence. This was only broken when they were both scraping their dirty plates and leaving them over at the collection counter to be washed. Liam asked Andreas if he wouldn't mind him sharing the U-bahn trip back to Virchow Strasse. They had only walked as far as the steps that led up to the lemon drizzle cake edifice of the Theatinerkirche when, out of curiosity, Liam prompted Andreas to enter. Andreas shrugged, looked at his watch and Liam followed him in. He was a lapsed Lutheran who hadn't thought about religion in ages but he could tell faith still meant something to Liam. It wouldn't have crossed his mind to go in there previously, it being a Catholic place of worship even though he had to pass it every day on the way to work. Perhaps it was the scale of the place. Or was it the juxtaposition between the freneticism of the street outside and the euphoria of calm that prevailed inside such an ancient space. Maybe it was the time of day affecting the light which literally appeared to come from heaven pervading the cut glass lantern and bouncing off the icing sugar ornamentation. Whatever it was, broad sections of the interior were bathed in tapering sunlight creating the most tangible atmosphere where this light fell to meet the vaulted shadows forming around the bases of the pillars. Liam dipped his fingers into the holy water just beyond the entrance door and crossed himself. It was still too early for tourists, the stalls were peppered with the faithful and the side aisles were already being frequented by those devoting themselves to the stations of the cross. Andreas made for the last stall but one and sat strategically behind a pillar well away from any religious activity. Liam soon joined him after genuflecting towards the altar which looked miles away.

'Why did you want to come in here?' whispered Andreas.

'I suddenly remembered that today was the fifth anniversary of what happened to the lads, my mates.'

'You mean back in the Lebanon?'

'Yeah. The pair of knackers would laugh at me for doing this. It just hit me that's all. Five years and what have I got to show for living and them dead all that time?'

'Don't look at it that way. You can't, if you do then eventually you will go nuts. Take it from me, I've been there too,' replied Andreas in a low voice whilst looking around to see if anyone was bothered by his talking. No one was near.

'I would go to confession but I can't speak any German. You are the only person I have been able to talk to about this,' said Liam.

'You have nothing to confess. Nothing that a stranger need know about.

Believe me you paid for your sins a long time ago. It's written on the frown you wear all the time. I no longer consider myself to be a stranger to you and what you experienced has parallels with what I went through too. But what happened then has no bearing on your life now. I mean that with no disrespect to your mates. By talking about them you are still celebrating their lives, remembering them and by doing so you reinvigorate your own. Up until recently you let the opposite be the case. The weight of what you experienced held you back from really enjoying your life. You have changed your future by opening up and talking about it. Something, I might add, that men of your calibre and background just don't normally do. You have been carrying this burden in your head, that you survived and they didn't. Part of that guilt stems from the things you were taught in places not too dissimilar from this when you were a child. Try thinking another way. You came through a trauma, decipher what it told you about yourself. That you have got this far, five years on, still trying, still interested, still have something to share and to give. So you have the basics intact to move forward with your life.'

'Where did that come from? I was about to head up there and light some candles for Lar and Gerry, but now you've turned me into an atheist!'

'Light two and then light another one for the person you used to be. I will still be here when you get back, it looks a long way to the altar rail and get a move on because the place is beginning to fill up and I have a sneaking suspicion that a mass is soon to take place.'

Andreas slumped back into his stall as Liam rose and walked deferentially up the central aisle until he was out of sight. Maybe he should have asked Liam to light some candles for his own loss. A row of candles perhaps. Did it really help to do such a thing? It was enough for him to let his gaze drift up into the stucco plaster ceiling far above his head and reconcile the myriad of emotions now forming in his mind. He knew up until this moment that he too had cheated death's silent roll call. This contemplative space gave him the time without interruption to formulate the faces in his mind of the people still close to him that he had lost. Those people who had nurtured him, protected and loved him. It didn't matter that it all took place forty-five years before, as with Liam these things had chiselled away at his character affecting his demeanour, his choices and his outlook on the way the world operated. Previously he had thought it a weakness to dwell on what had happened to his own family. But that notion had always been fuelled by immoderate amounts of Jägermeister which provided temporary insulation from naturally coming to terms with the finality of it. He was always depressed and angry with himself come first light. This place asked nothing of him, but instead wore the legacy of residual peace invested over generations by those seeking answers without prejudice. He didn't have to bend at the knee, or light any matches, no bells and smells or jiggery-pokery, it offered him a place to think about what had befallen him. He name-checked his close family members in his mind's eye. The protective unbroken human chain they had formed around him before he left them for that last time back in Strekerau. He had it always in his mind that he would meet them again, but certainly not in this life. He didn't contemplate it being in heaven either. Just a place where the good matriculate to and that one day he would enrol there as well depending on his own behaviour in this existence. In that place there would be study periods and free time. He would get to meet his relatives during the recreational periods as they were, by now, many grades above his own class. They could impart their wisdom to him and he would in turn rise up through the classes depending on what he had learnt. This ideology had been of comfort to him and was he knew too far-fetched to confide to any other living soul.

Liam arrived back and sat beside him once more. He looked relaxed, but tired.

Andreas left it a decent interval before suggesting that they should head back to Virchow Strasse.

'When I was a boy I attended mass quite regularly. I got it into my head that come the day of judgement I would hide in the spire of our church.'

'What good would that have done?' asked Andreas puzzled.

'I had a theory back then that church spires were actually cleverly disguised rockets that would somehow detach from the body of the church and launch into space with those on board who had been chosen by God. So if I went to mass often enough, then there was a good chance I would be saved. I would sit as close as possible to the spire just in case, but I soon got bored as my name was never called out and judgement day seemed always to be put on hold.'

For once Andreas was speechless, it was a charming nugget of juvenilia recounted without any saccharine from the viewpoint of an older man. Liam was able to express thoughts and emotions from childhood readily, something Andreas was only recently able to do by recounting his own wartime experiences. How long had he shut away the image of himself as a sixteen-year-old boy caught up in the trauma of the east? The idea of church steeples disguised as medieval rocket launchers was fanciful but it was full of imagination and made him realize just how much of his own boyhood persona he had closed himself off from. He had relinquished any thoughts of childish things on the day he left Strekerau. If he hadn't he would have just become another one of Stalin's statistics lost in the miasma of the great patriotic war. He had lost his family, his home, his inheritance and his childhood but visiting the Theatinerkirche had given him the space to contemplate that and not feel under any pressure to take part in the proceedings. He was still lapsed but no less spiritual than the regulars to these surroundings. It was also Liam's uncomplicated approach to life that had influenced him.

The two of them shared the same shift pattern that week so invariably they met up in the kitchen later after much needed sleep. Liam had prepared some bacon sandwiches and two big mugs of tea for them both. Andreas was getting used to Liam's limited, if well intentioned, cuisine.

'Liam, you mentioned Yaffat earlier on.'

'The Arab ganch, what about him?'

'The lady he was with. It wasn't his girlfriend,' said Andreas.

'Who is she then? He seemed very intimate with her.'

'It is his daughter, Jameela. She lives in the Gulf States and Yaffat only gets to see her when she visits here after Ramadan. She was an au pair for a rich family and even though you can't see from the hijab, she is very attractive and she snared a rich husband much to Yaffat's delight. So I wanted to let you know here in private before you go saying something to him about having a lady friend.'

'So she doesn't take after her dad in the looks department. Or the mum for that matter?' asked Liam.

'Yaffat doesn't bring her into the hotel, her new husband is very strict and doesn't want it known widely that he married beneath his station. Status is just about everything in Arab families and in their eyes Yaffat is only a hotel janitor. So he meets her in the park when she can steal away from her husband's family.'

'I almost feel pity for the old git. The pride he must feel mixed with emptiness of losing a daughter to such a closed bunch of people,' said Liam.

'She married well and had to turn her back on her cash-poor family. She has everything she could ever wish for except the freedom to mix with her parents. She makes sure that her new family stay at the Annabella apartments every summer so that she can be near to her father. From what I gather she is pregnant and that is why you have seen Yaffat so pleased with himself. He is going to be a grandfather. He is delighted with the prospect of his family bettering themselves as he is descended from Bedouin tribal stock.

Yaffat would remain a bastard in Liam's eyes but one who had just wanted the best for his daughter at the expense of his own involvement with her future. Yaffat had got as far as he ever would but his grandchildren would want for nothing and what father wouldn't trade for that? Liam's resentment of Yaffat was now diluted by the knowledge of why the Moroccan behaved the way he did. First of all there was the whole 'them and us' thing about foreigners working in West Germany. They were tolerated if they were white and couldn't speak the language and resented if they were of colour and could manage to speak some German. More often than not they did the most thankless, dirtiest, unskilled manual jobs. Then there appeared to be a hierarchy within the ranks of migrant workers themselves, in which the Turks, the Kurds and Irish appeared along with Romanian gypsies ignominiously at the bottom rung of the ladder. There were exceptions to the rule of course, especially among the Irish who had bothered to learn German, but as Liam hadn't, then he would always be viewed as pigheaded and inefficient. Any lingering feelings of resentment he might have harboured would always be nullified by the hashish he had become partial to. He purchased it from another Moroccan called Nami who was a boiler engineer in the hotel. He would buy an ounce of black resin each month and the price would fluctuate but Nami never got the arm in as Liam was just too imposing a character to mess with. Liam was careful where he smoked it. He had recently bought a bicycle and took advantage of the paths along the great expanse of the river which circumnavigated Munich.

The river Isar brought fresh alpine water through the city and had been untamed until relatively recently, when a system of weirs had been constructed to prevent further bank erosion by the torrent. Liam had noticed that within Andreas's collection he had a number of books written in English and he got his consent to borrow them. It didn't matter what the subject was, he just found himself wanting to read. His days off now became structured around the river. He packed four bottles of beer, bratwurst, bread and pickle with cheese all wrapped in paper from the Kaufhof delicatessen. A book, some Rizla skins, a pouch of tobacco, his black resin, his newly acquired swimming trunks and a towel. The duffle bag and the bicycle gave him freedom. The Isar still retained the charm of a mountain river and Liam took time to cycle through the many leafy districts until he found a particularly dappled and isolated area within Bogenhausen. It wasn't long before people became less frequent. It wasn't much further that he noticed those he met were also naked. This was a real shock while cycling and for those minutes he didn't know quite where to look. He was used to the scrotum shrinking climes of Dublin Bay in wet jeans, nudity just didn't happen in Ireland. But without noticing, he was becoming liberated.

He soon found a perfect spar of shingle jutting out near a weir under which he could deposit his beers to keep them cool all afternoon. The canopy of trees embraced overhead allowing dappled sunlight to pour through as he stretched out the towel and retrieved his book. He remained topless until he was confident that he was totally alone and then he stood up, kicked off his trainers, unzipped his jeans and peeled off his underpants. He allowed the warm breeze to cool his thighs before putting on the swimming trunks. He folded his jeans and placed them over the duffle bag to make a pillow for his head. The sound of the river rippling over the weir was proving to be therapeutic, washing at the drudgery of his hotel shifts. The latest book he had borrowed was a biography of the Duke of Marlborough by his descendant Winston Churchill, an intimidatingly large tome made accessible by Churchill's authoritatively frank terminology. The author's enthusiasm was all too apparent, which helped bring what was a dusty subject to life. Liam was a slow reader, often reading the same page more than once to properly understand. But he was reading, something he never did at home or in the army. He was taking in information, learning about events which happened to take place not very far from were he lay, how such a great commander kept the morale of his men high by resupplying them successfully deep into enemy territory and then turning the tactics of the day on their heads to steal a great victory.

Liam would alternate from reading to rolling a joint and then wading out into the river to retrieve one of his beers. The freedom to just enjoy this outdoors was so new to him. He had enough food to see him through the day and the black resin tempered his appetite so he didn't eat it all at once. Sometimes he would just sit and take it in, the beauty of the place and how unspoilt it was considering it was so close to the heart of the city. He got into the habit of heading there in any free moments after work, swimming in the river on his back watching herons take flight without a care in the world. The bicycle had opened this up for him, giving him the option to get out from underneath Andreas's feet back in the apartment. In time he got used to seeing the nudity as there was no avoiding what was normal for everyone else. If his trunks were still drying out back home from the day before then he would just have to get used to being naked when he swam in the river.

10

1942

By now you could not tell from my clothing what side I was on, German or Russian. I was somewhere in between. I think to the untrained eye I had the appearance of an unkempt poacher with the rifle slung over my shoulder or perhaps a chimney-sweep as I was covered in dirt. My uniform was reduced to rags that had congealed in the mud and rain to a waterproof consistency that began to reek in bright sunlight but kept me warm. I had fashioned a belt from cord unto which I had knotted together around my waist as many dried fish as I could stand the smell of, thus enabling me to eat as I walked. I still had the waterproof smock they had given me and I was able to carry the knapsack which contained my rubles, the scrolled-up title deeds along with a spare can of water, ammunition and the sight for my sniper rifle.

The compass proved vital, as much of the terrain folded into undulating hills with no clear horizon of the kind that reminded me of the sweep down to the Volga river. This was no man's land, the space between two protagonists, a disputed wasteland offering little if any shelter, only a brooding sense of foreboding. Rain slated skies had given way to smoke-filled pyres at night. The earth was taking a pounding somewhere close and resonated beneath where I lay. It could only be Stalingrad. I had devised a way of making a small tent out of my smock by propping it up with a stick thereby giving me a respite so I could try and rest under it after a days walking. But there was little chance of sleep as I was frozen to the spot listening to the growing cacophony being played out above and around me. Soon, wave after wave of Junkers JU88s and Dornier Do17z bombers blotted out the sky and began to concentrate on a single target intent obliterating it. Surely nothing could withstand such a battering, nothing could crawl out alive from under such devastation.

I had to see for myself. I soon cowered over the greasy grass bluffs that fed down to the river Volga. It was a crimson landscape painting reflected in the burning pools of oil now raging on the surface of the river. It was a vision of hell that I was allowed to interpret and it has never left me. I must have been three kilometres from the epicentre but I was still choking from the brick dust and oil vapour that hung in the air. From this distance people were just matchsticks being lit and tossed into the atmosphere by consecutive blasts that were too far away for me to even hear. Some fell without a mark on them other than blood trickling from their eardrums after succumbing to massive internal injuries. Others were horribly mutilated by the splinter shards from direct hits on the wooden stakes that had been driven in to protect the far shoreline.

The Stuka dive-bombers were acting with impunity, choosing targets at will, harvesting the ferry boats which were packed to the gills with terrified conscripts. They ploughed down almost vertically, sirens wailing at the unmissable targets prone beneath them. The Red Army commissars put no value on any individual and acted as drovers on the far bank, herding more poor souls at gunpoint into the meat grinder, certain in the credo that their sheer weight of numbers would prevail in the end. It was an unravelling theatre of the macabre in breadth and scale, mesmerizing in its intensity.

I needed to keep my wits about me as the Russians did have a foothold on my side of the river, albeit a tenuous one. They had scratched slit trenches into the sandbanks and chillingly had used the stockpile of their own dead to shore up their makeshift defences. What is more, scouts were sporadically moving up the shoreline in my direction. First individually then as pairs, using hand signals to pass on information as to any vulnerable spots in the German flanks. I reached for my knapsack and unwrapped the sniper sight from a protective cloth and cleaned the lens with it. It made so much more sense now; I could see that these scouts were elite Soviet marines and that they were intent on taking advantage of the German preoccupation with a large building within a factory complex. The German lines were just over two kilometres from me, they had numerous tanks to the front which were making hard work of negotiating the building rubble thrown up by the Luftwaffe previously. If anything, the defenders appeared to have the advantage as the tanks were being funnelled into a killing zone making ripe targets for the Russian tank destroyers secreted within the factory district. The German infantry was spread out behind the tanks or taking advantage of improvised cover and not making much headway. I could make out the supply trucks like the ones I used to sleep in at the rear and on the flanks of the wedge that made up the German attack army. These supply vehicles were not heavily guarded and I could see that the Soviet marines were intent on attacking them.

I counted the amount of ammunition I had left. I reckoned that I had enough to make a nuisance of myself and to draw attention to the fact that the Germans were in danger of being outflanked. I attached my rifle sight and loaded the weapon. There was enough going on all around me so as not to attract attention to myself. I had stalked enough game with my father back in the woods near Strekerau to have learnt a little about concealment. The dunes would muffle the sound from my rifle making it hard to tell where the shot came from. Most importantly the Marines thought that they still had the element of surprise and wouldn't have remotely considered a counter-strike. I watched them come on deliberately slow, using the terrain to their advantage, wholly unaware that my rifle was trained on them. Who could have begrudged their own tenacity and skill at stalking? I had to put this to the back of my mind immediately and concentrate on them being my unwitting targets. I followed every move their leader made, his athletic prowess dressed in a black naval fatigue uniform. He signalled with a pistol clenched in his fist and he had a commanding presence. I waited for him to isolate himself from the pack sufficiently before taking my shot with any confidence of not being discovered. He took so many risks and I'm sure his men looked up to him, but he stood between me and the rest of my division so he had to fall. I waited until he had just signalled another advance and was beginning to break from the cover of the dunes and then I squeezed the trigger.

The two black ribbons attached to the back of his beret were now dipped in red where he fell. His lifeless body lay face down in the rippling sand as I watched, rooted to the spot in mawkishness. His men had covered the ground in the interim and were now only metres from where he lay but couldn't see his condition without revealing themselves. Seconds turned into minutes in a breathless silence with the battle raging in the distance. One of them finally broke the cover of the long grass, only to fall when my second bullet grazed his shoulder. The others now knew they were dealing with a sniper. I had counted six of them before they had concealed themselves on the reverse slopes of the dunes. I had the advantage of the high ground on a bluff overlooking them with a clear field of fire. Their only hope was to rush me in a concerted attack which would have led to many casualties. I could hear the moans of the marine I had winged. His comrades were powerless to help him while I was at large. They couldn't lob grenades from that distance. I was sure they were weighing up their options. If they waited until darkness fell to overpower me, then their comrade might die. The stalemate was broken when the fallen marine began to cry out in delirious pain. I had to take a chance so I trained my sight onto one of the supply vehicles just close enough to one of the German sentries. It was easily within range so I fired into one of the tyres which immediately got his attention. The sentry raised the alarm and soon more joined him and they sheepishly began to search the perimeter, roughly in the direction of where my shot had been fired. It wasn't long until they stumbled on the body of the officer and found the injured marine nearby. The sentry prodded at the scarlet wound on his shoulder with the point of his rifle before taking aim and dispatching the defenceless soul into the next world without a second thought.

The six remaining marines had witnessed this and knew they were trapped without hope. I decided to try and intervene and called down to them in Russian to surrender. If they did, then I guaranteed them that they wouldn't be shot out of hand. This provoked a very rude response from them. I then shouted over to the sentries in German. I told them to get down and stay down as I was trying to negotiate with some Russian marines. One of the sentries shouted who the hell was I to tell them what to do? I told him my name and my division and they relented and stayed hidden. I spoke again to the Russians, telling them that this was futile and to give themselves up, avoiding a bloodbath. The one who had earlier insulted me now dared me to show myself, goading me that I didn't have the balls to come out from behind the tall grass. All the while the Germans were growing in strength, others now being attracted to the commotion on this flank. I took a risk, but I had to, to save face with these Russians. I stood up and they all could see me for the first time. The Russian who had provoked me cried out that he was surrendering his men to what looked like a Mamluk slave boy. He wasn't far wrong as my appearance was other-worldly and my story almost too incredible to be believed. I told them to lay down their weapons and led them down out of the cover of the dunes. The German escort that had formed up didn't know what to make of me and some tried to harass, provoke and disarm me until I remonstrated with them in perfect German. I led the six Russians to the nearest officer in command. I recognised him immediately, which was more than I could say for him. I saluted Oberleutnant Werner and presented my prisoners. He didn't know what to make of me and took me for a partisan. He began giving orders to those around him with his usual aplomb, mixed with a sternness I hadn't seen before.

'Keep these six separated until we can get all we can use from them. Take the bodies of the other two over to that collapsed building and cover them with rubble before the flies begin to light on them.'

'I promised them that they would get fair treatment from you Oberleutnant. One of their men was killed in cold blood and they are seething about it and won't give you any information lightly,' I said without being given permission to speak.

The Oberleutnant paused as I wondered what his next move would be. He still hadn't recognized me but he had taken in my remark. He ordered whoever it was had shot the marine to step forward. The sentry stood gingerly with his head bowed and his rifle slung over his left shoulder. Oberleutnant Werner squared up to him and punched him in the face whilst the Russian prisoners looked on. The sentry fell to his knees and the Oberleutnant kicked him in the stomach and cursed him at the same time. His actions had jeopardized the chances of any information and had rendered these prisoners useless to us. I had never seen the Oberleutnant so animated before now. A hardness had set in his character to fill the void of witnessing the loss of so many good men. He felt the strain of responsibility more keenly than most as we were all being funnelled into this quagmire of death. The sentry was dragged out of his sight as the Oberleutnant regained his composure and turned to me.

'You climb down out of the dunes with six prisoners, that's very impressive. They look a tough lot too, those marines. How did you come by them? You also happen to speak and understand German very well for a partisan?'

'Oberleutnant Werner. Do you still have my rubles?' was all I could reply. He was silent and then I could see warmth return to his complexion with the recognition.

'Boris? I mean, Mensche. Is it really you? You survived the attack?'

Everyone moved in closer to get a better look and the Oberleutnant put his arm around my shoulder.

'We had sent a number of scouts to search for any news of your Cossack friends and they came across the bodies which by then were unrecognisable. We just assumed that everyone was dead. My God Mensche what are you made of?' He patted me on the back. 'You really smell bad Mensche. What's this dried fish tied around your waist? Quite the Volga boatman now aren't you. You haven't gone native quite yet?'

He led me to the makeshift quarters of the 168th infantry division which was only remarkable in the sense that it was one of the few collections of buildings still relatively intact in this vicinity. He sat me down beside a washstand in his quarters and poured me some water to drink which I badly needed.

'Oberleutnant can I speak freely?'

He nodded and sat opposite along with a Feldwebel who began taking short-hand notes of what I said.

'I don't know what reports you are getting from air reconnaissance but you are very vulnerable down the right flank hard by the river shore. These fellows were intent on attacking your fuel supplies and service vehicles. It was only that I stumbled upon them that I was able to stop them in their tracks. They are ferrying men and supplies in vast quantities to at least four major industrial complexes within the city. I think they are trying to create strongholds so as to slow down the progress of our tanks and trap our men in a killing zone. Our bombing of the city only appears to have played into their hands.'

'We have been pouring men into the areas you mentioned without success for the last ten days losing many experienced people for little gain in the process. The 168th has been decimated and we are now attached to the 94th infantry division. For three days we tried to get the Russians to withdraw from the large building you can just see from this broken window over there, the grain elevator. It dominates the surrounding area so had to be taken. But the Russkis just don't know when to give in. We sent in an envoy in a tank under a flag of truce offering honourable terms for the defenders holed up there to surrender. They mocked us and kept the tank! They even set fire to the grain inside where they lay so that we might not have any of it. They are barbarians and when we finally broke through and took the place we found only forty dead sailors not unlike the marines you captured. Forty men had held back our division for three days!'

I could see the dust-worn frustration etched on his expression as it had in so many others. The realization that this fatal gamble was now bearing fruit. This army had bitten off more than it could chew.

'I am taking three men off sentry duty and they are going to man a machine-gun nest roughly where you had hidden on the bluff overlooking us. That should deter the Russians from making any further incursions.'

'It will only slow them down. They will keep throwing people at us like waves against a shore. You forget that this is their country and they see it as a patriotic duty to die for the motherland. We created this perfect environment for them to slow us down to a crawl. We pour our best men into this situation to die, for what? A few metres of rubble in a city already reduced to rubble. This place is slowly turning into a tomb, it's sapping away at our morale the longer it goes on.'

'You have been doing a lot of growing up while you were lost out there in the steppe, Private Mensche.'

'You grow up quick when you see that you have nothing left to call your home. I have learned to live off my wits and my rifle does the rest.'

Oberleutnant Werner instructed me to make use of his quarters and ordered a jug of hot water and soap of any description to be brought for me so that I might see my features once more. He had something he wanted to discuss with his superior officers and might be some time. I took advantage of the washstand as I wasn't sure just when I would next have a chance to wash in such relative comfort. I could tell that Oberleutnant Werner hadn't occupied this space for long as his fold-out sleeping cot hadn't been used. I constructed it and then stripped to wash myself. When done, I threw the dirty towel and the rags of my uniform into the corner of the room before wrapping myself up in a blanket and falling fast asleep on the cot. No barrage, not even Katyusha rockets were going to wake me.

Outside, some hours later, a fire was set and my clothes had been bundled up and were consigned to the flames without my knowledge. It was only when the wind changed direction and blew the smoke through the broken window into the space were I slept catching in my throat that I woke. I wasn't sure how long I had been asleep, but I felt better. On the chair opposite there was a clean pair of long johns, a folded pristine uniform with belt and a new pair of boots which looked my size. For the first time in months I felt as if I was the sole occupant of my hair and skin. I rose and got dressed then folded away the sleeping cot. The door swung open and there standing with a plate of white sausage with black bread was Obergefreiter Hauser.

'Now Mensche, be careful not to spill this plate over me like you did last time, I know how clumsy you can be!'

I was actually pleased to see him, the sour-faced old shit that he was. What was going on here? I walked up to him and touched the nearest sleeve of his to me. I wasn't dreaming, Hauser really had brought me my breakfast!

'Obergefreiter Hauser I'm glad you are not dead!' was all I could muster. Behind him came the Oberleutnant with a pot of coffee and some cups. There was no formality and I couldn't think why, it was just as I had experienced amongst the Cossacks. Presently the Oberleutnant drew up three chairs and invited myself and Hauser to sit with him. For a little while the incessant muffled barrage outside took a back seat as the Oberleutnant poured three coffees and offered them to each of us. Where did he get such coffee around here? It is the little things that mean so much. At length he spoke:

'Private Mensche I know this all seems unconventional and it is, but then so are you. I can tell that I am confusing you, so let me try and get to the point. Something you said earlier on hit home with me and planted an idea in my head that I had to take to the high command. I have convinced them to promote you to Feldwebel and to present you with the Iron Cross second class. How does that sound?'

'I'm not sure what to say.'

'Try thank you Oberleutnant,' said Hauser drily.

'Of course, thank you Oberleutnant. I meant to say that, only this comes as quite a surprise. Just getting back through the lines to the division was enough for me.'

'Something had to be made of this Mensche. Hauser and I both have come to know that you are different, you never set out to be different but you are. We didn't give you a prayer of a chance of making it back here in one piece and then you come strolling in with six prisoners in tow. They tell me that you killed their leader and wounded his second in command, now this is the sort of good news we have to try and circulate to lift the air of despondency that has settled over the front line. You mentioned morale earlier and that got me thinking. It would boost the division's confidence to know that somewhere hidden out there and yet in amongst them they had one of their own. The Volga German sharpshooter taking on the Soviets at their own game. They consider it a sport to employ snipers and the Russkis hold them in high esteem. Well, it's time to pay them back. You would have complete freedom to move anywhere you wanted within the city, choosing your own targets and high command would make sure that you had all the resources you need to exploit the Russian weak spots. What do you think of this Mensche?'

'I want to remain on the 168th muster roll even though I will be roaming elsewhere. I will only be answerable to you and, God forbid, your successor should the worst ever happen, Oberleutnant. There just isn't enough time to think this through but my instincts tell me to give it a try. Should the worst befall me, Oberleutnant, at least you won't have to write home to my family!'

This was symptomatic of the black humour that was increasingly developing on both sides caught in this fatal embrace within the city. Territorial gains had previously been marked out with pins on campaign maps stretching ever eastward until that late September when gains had to be re-evaluated instead and measured first by street and then by building and subsequently by rooms within that building. So it was not uncommon for the Soviets to control the upper floors and the Germans the downstairs living and dining areas within one block. Only when bloody hand-to-hand fighting had resolved the outcome, could any gain be evaluated. There was a new found 'intimacy' in all this. A morbidly successful technique deployed by the Russians, whereby they tried to locate and ensconce themselves as close as possible to the Germans. It was called 'hugging' and it proved very successful in ensuring no air or ground artillery fire could be brought to bear on the protagonists as they were almost on top of one another all the time. They made use of the extensive sewage and rain water tunnels that still operated below street level, introducing a darkly sinister subterranean encounter where no side really knew where their front lines began or ended. It came as quite a shock for both sets of combatants to encounter the troglodytical existence of so many civilians still scratching about amid the ruins of Stalingrad.

A little while later, Oberleutnant Werner had lined up the remnants of the 168th division who were not dead, captured or lost. They all had earned campaign medals since last Andreas had been amongst their ranks. Campaign medals never seemed to be in short supply unlike warm winter clothing which was already becoming a valued commodity, so much so that insulated apparel was being liberally taken from dead Russians and being worn beneath their Wehrmacht uniforms. Obergefreiter Hauser called them to attention and Andreas's name and citation was read out. Andreas stepped out from their midst and then Oberleutnant Werner approached and saluted him before pinning the Iron Cross 2nd Class to his new tunic. Werner then congratulated Andreas, shaking his hand before addressing the men.

'You all remember newly promoted Feldwebel Mensche as a Freiwillig volunteer. He has proved himself worthy of the 168th. He will always be one of us, but he is a specialist too and his skills with the rifle have been recognised and he has now been attached to the sniper division. I'm sure that you all will want to wish him well so you may fall out and do so.'

These men had all aged since I was last with them but their enthusiasm for me was genuine and untainted by the many hardships they had gone through. If I was to be held up as some kind of pawn in the renewed propaganda war then I would rather be seen as a protector of sorts for the 168th than as a cold calculating sniper, for they were now the only family I had. It was an all too fleeting reunion as my division was soon recalled to the front line to relieve thinly stretched and exhausted units that had only recently started out as divisions.

I wasn't going with them just yet. For me, it was all about preparation. I was surprised at just how well I was adapting to this new role. I attached myself to the reconnaissance section and began devouring information given by reliable Russian informants as to enemy troop strengths and formations. I knew which shock troop or army group to expect only metres from our frontline. I listened in as these informants spilt information and I slowly began to sieve through their disinformation and latch onto any nuggets of truth. They would invariably through nervousness spill some half-truth that could be utilized. I memorized the grid patterns of Stalingrad's streets even though no grids actually existed anymore. I flew low over the city at great risk both to me and my pilot in a Fieseler Storch and took photographs of all the strategic places that could be of use to a sniper. I flew only once as it was far too risky and we caught shrapnel in our tail fin and only just made it back to Gumrak airfield. I got familiar with the calling-cards of my unseen rivals over there where the naked eye is of no use. I saw the results of their handiwork, their traits, their modus operandi. Their arrogance had got the better of them I thought, for too long they have had it their own way. It wasn't just good enough to kill a German, they just couldn't resist leaving some kind of signature of their work in the style they executed.

Previously I had killed only two people, both of whom I had done out of what I termed necessity. If I hadn't have shot them then invariably my own future would have been in doubt. Two people isn't much of a credential for a much sought-after sniper hero but you only have to kill once to set you apart from everyone else. War is a cloak that hides men's actions from the clear light of peace. War throws up contradictions, black ironies and dark opportunities that would never normally exist. War produces leaders out of ranch hands and murderers out of scene painters. It takes a special kind of person to become a sniper. Firstly you don't always require something to live for. This might sound morbid but it's not meant to. Just because you are alone doesn't necessarily mean you are lonely. Just because you are German doesn't mean you are a Nazi. I followed this war on my radio back in Strekerau and back then it was a game to me, until it reached my front door. War had painted all the ethnic Germans into a corner until we were the one colour. Nazi coloured. It was easy for the Russian on the other side of the partition wall holding his breath before throwing in a grenade to think that the unwitting German on the receiving end is a raving Nazi. But more than likely, he wasn't. So to be a sniper you have to carry an inner detachment from real events. It doesn't mean that you don't care, it's just that you might not live long enough to be able to show it. It is really that you live your life for every day as if you already know when your number's up. Soldiers would never volunteer if they thought that they would have to walk about with targets on their backs, but without knowing it they do in the eyes of a sniper. I brought qualities that only recently had been recognised by my superiors. I had no attachments, family or loved ones. I was of dual nationality and I could hunt with a rifle. I also had motivation. This was probably the deciding factor for me, I wanted to kill those whom I saw as guilty of destroying my life so far. If things had been different, then this side of my character would have made do with hunting venison for the family table, but events overtook my family and made me what I am now.

I was embedded with the 168th ten days after being made a Feldwebel. They were entangled in the factory district and the division was being bled white with mounting casualties. The only safe way to join them was through the sewage tunnels and often where these tunnels conjoined, medical teams operated under the most perilous conditions performing minor miracles or dispatching the hopeless to a better world. On rare occasions a chase or fire fight would flare up around those poor wretches lying there helplessly. The sewage system could be a respite from the shelling and the men would alternate rest periods down there. I now wore a one-piece camouflaged flying suit and using what little influence I could, I stuffed every pocket with packets of cigarettes and chocolate which had recently been airlifted behind our lines. I distributed these to my comrades equally and in doing so I was able to decipher from them the enemies strong points and possible intentions. I would sit with them and break apart the stock of my rifle, employ a pipe cleaner to the barrelling, wipe it clean and put it back together.

I had taught myself to do this without needing to look as I would have to do it in the dark and often under fire. I'm sure I had many half-finished discussions and it was never my intention to be rude or cut conversations short but I would spontaneously absent myself from them without notice so as never to form a routine, often disappearing into the myriad of tunnels or climb down a manhole to take a look for myself. I wore thermal underwear and sheepskin gloves with my thermal flying suit. I always brought a pair of wire-cutters, a torch, matches, boot polish, a bottle of water, chocolate and a bandolier of ammunition. This, combined with the weight of my rifle, was more than enough to trail around the ruins of Stalingrad. I had modified what I carried from seeing what my quarry took with him into the fray. Like him I couldn't help but take trophies. The wire-cutters and the pen-thin torch came from Russian snipers I had bested. I always tried to conduct a clean kill and I didn't leave a signature if I was fortunate enough to encounter the scene afterwards, which nearly always wasn't possible for me to do as it would be crawling with furious Soviets.

I found myself forming a sneaking admiration for their resilience and their resolve. They had a feral tenacity to cling to a position that defied overwhelming odds, gnawing at our manpower and undermining our efficiency. The division had suffered greatly in overcoming their blocking techniques. It was no triumph to capture one of their citadels after a fire fight lasting twelve hours only to discover that three men had managed to pin down fifteen of ours for that length of time and then to witness their three chalk dust signatures on the parapet and the date of their glorious death for the motherland. This stubbornness only elevates the reputation of your opponent, giving them a psychological advantage. They become the bogey men of myth and legend much at odds to the subservient Slav so often heralded by the German media. You cannot subdue what you just can't see and they had a knack of blending into the debris. You might be able to hear an opponent occasionally, but you cannot be sure to take that shot just in case it is only one of your own comrades following up behind. The doubt that fills those seconds compounds the dryness in your throat as by now you are always thirsty and often disorientated by the cold air and the shorter days. If you take a chance and call to them, then you only give yourself away and you could be a dead man. This was no terrain for rule books or parade-ground tactics, it was a choking cauldron of brimstone where shots rang out continuously, echoing, without giving directions. If anything it was our own predictable efficiency that made it so easy for our enemies to anticipate our next move, allowing them to be pre-emptive and therefore create traps for us. For some considerable time we persisted in coming on to them in the same manner, making easy targets for their sharp-shooters. They had the local knowledge and they were drawing us in to a kill zone of their making.

The Russians had learnt much from the campaigns of the previous year and it was all too apparent that our own high command hadn't. I had long since realized that Stalingrad was a trap set to capture a whole German army group. But everyone around me was either sleepwalking to oblivion, selfishly grumbling about their lot or just too afraid to face up to the reality. It was by now very apparent that the Red Army was conducting this struggle with one hand tied behind its back. They were reinforcing the city with just enough men to maintain the stalemate, creating the illusion that they were on their knees. Quietly, fresh troops had been trained in from the far east and arms, tanks and supplies including ample warm winter clothing had been stockpiled for two massive shock armies. All of this was taking place just beyond the horizon of German reconnaissance. The Soviets had been taking enough prisoners of their own to be fully aware of the formation and strengths of the units that opposed them. These 'mouths' had informed them that the German achilles heel was in actual fact Romanian. The extremities of the German frontline were manned by two circumspect allies, Italian and Romanian. They had inferior equipment and had next to no experience of a winter war of this calibre. They did possess some capable officers, but not enough to maintain discipline. German troops carried a growing resentment for their allies borne out of their lack of campaign experience. Communications between this fragile alliance was shakey and tenuous and the Russians strove to hit them hard at their weakest points and in doing so achieve the unthinkable. Surround the entire German 6th army and cut them off from any hope of salvation.

This is historical legacy and nothing I could do would alter the result. I had my own small theatre of concern to occupy my time and I was determined to affect the outcome there to no small degree. So I took it upon myself to be a sentinel protecting my men as best I could. I would shadow them, knowing full well what easy targets they made in the tangled wasteland of the tractor factory. The weather was by now closing in and drifting snow was changing the debris scape markedly, making things easier, making tracks harder to conceal, making targets easier to see. Another example of the kind of people we were up against was all too apparent at the tractor factory. For one thing it was still operating, but not making tractors, they were making tanks. For another, the majority of people still working in there were women! These amazons were constructing T34 tanks and driving them straight out of the construction yard and into the raging battle just yards away from where they worked. It just made no sense when German women weren't under the same pressures to help with the war effort. I could never bring myself to aim at one of them even though I had many occasions to take shot. Red Army snipers soon thought twice about using the tractor factory for safe refuge after I had successfully staked out the overhead gantries and flushed out one of their number. I managed to wing him and he fell from a height into their protective custody, leading to a tirade of abuse in my direction. They would have torn me apart for sure but the incident had served its purpose and production work ceased as my men took control below and set fuses in the machinery. These formidable women had left their mark on me though, we couldn't hope to defeat people with spirit such as this.

11

1987

Liam was careful not to smoke the Lebanese black resin in his bedroom, restricting himself instead to lighting up on the balcony where the frost was now his only companion, serving notice each evening by laying siege to the window panes. The pungent red glow from the tip of the joint could just be made out from street level if anyone cared to notice as he reclined on a lounger with a beer on the third floor. He realised that as the effects of the resin subsided, his calm reflection could often be hijacked by an exaggerated paranoia about a number of things. Firstly Dublin. He knew he just didn't fit in there anymore, if he ever did. Its hold had diminished to the extent that he would only go back there for a specific reason. He wasn't misguided enough in himself to believe that he had outgrown it but he had shed some of the threads that had bound him to it. His new circumstances hadn't made him blasé, just more introspective. Dublin represented his formative self, it had set him on the path to somewhere aimless until Andreas's timely intervention. Dublin had offered him little in the way of opportunity that wasn't unlawful. From where he lay he couldn't understand why more people didn't just leave. Those that couldn't got ground down by the same drudgery day in, day out. He had nothing there to be grateful for other than his mother.

Dublin was a backdrop to her fragile household, propped up with good intentions, beset by reminders, missed payments and final demands on the doorstep. It had always been like this, his mother had hidden many of them from him, her way of coping but they still kept coming along with the bailiffs who would trample on the toys where he once played. Part of Liam's motivation to join the army had been to help her pay some of the bills. He wired a percentage of his army pay home to her along with a short letter telling her he was fine every month, even if he wasn't. His pay was often of little use to him in any case, depending on where he was billeted. He did gamble some of it away with the other men out of boredom. He didn't pursue whores or catch the clap with it as he was awkward around women and was uninitiated until he arrived in Germany. He did drink it but often that was hard to come by in some of the strictly Muslim places he served in. He saw himself as the absentee head of her household, having never known his own biological father. This money would continue to arrive as long as it was put to good use paying bills such as the telephone or partly alleviating the rent and rates. He would often dial her telephone number in the middle of the night allowing it to ring just twice to let her know that he was thinking of her and to reassure himself that it hadn't been cut off and that she had paid the bill. The Irish Army didn't legislate for notable diary dates such as Easter and Christmas and Liam was too affable to press his case for leave at those times and as a result he hadn't been home to Dublin since the funerals of his two army friends. This was his third Christmas in Germany and it would be very different from the previous ones which had been pointedly uncelebrated within the confines of the hotel accommodation block.

His time in the army had given him a template to live by, a discipline with a routine pattern which he liked and now adhered to in civilian life despite the distraction of the black resin. He only smoked when he was done with other things or had fulfilled the chores that needed doing and even then it was just becoming something to fill a gap. Previously it had been a crutch to take away the cruel images of what he had witnessed in the Lebanon, but now it was just a way to relax after an interminable shift washing pots and dishes for eight hours. His life was plain and he certainly didn't add colour to it by smoking, it didn't make him any wiser or cleverer but it did help him make sense of the fact that there was nothing he could have done to change what happened back then.

The street below his balcony was empty of people, perhaps it was a European football night, Liam didn't follow it that closely enough to know. Two rows of neatly parked cars occupied either side of Virchow Strasse, encased by conifer trees, illuminated by pools of light from the energy efficient street lamps. These tidy postwar dwellings with their advent calendar windows and storm shutters propped open, revealed warm interiors, the light from each was now laced in frost as the temperatures began to plummet. The alpine microclimate was closing in on the city which nestled in its foothills. There were fresh footprints on the ice-stricken pavement leading to Andreas's apartment block. Liam had missed that, lulled into other-worldly thoughts where he had travelled among unknown men in lands beyond the sea. The unknown visitor had accessed the main door by pressing Frau Kaltenbrunner's doorbell and asking for Andreas by name. She had let him in, it wouldn't have been polite to do otherwise considering the freezing temperature outside. Footsteps echoed in the hallway that Liam could not hear, then a pause before his doorbell chimed. Liam definitely heard that. Andreas never got visitors. Liam roused himself out of the lounger on the balcony, annoyed at the intrusion, he began cursing in the old brogue, stubbing out his joint before sending it tapering over the balcony into the beckoning darkness. He looked through the spyhole in the front door which only magnified the ruddy face of a man he had never seen before, in a hat wearing a raincoat in the communal hallway. He opened the door with the safety latch bolted and chain still attached and waited for the visitor to speak so that he might try and decipher what it was he wanted.

'Is this the residence of Andreas Mensche?' The man asked in faltering German. There was a pause as Liam tried to decipher, slowly picking out words he understood and lining them up in sequence. There was no way he was going to try and respond in German of which his grasp was still pitiful.

'What's it to you pal?' Liam replied defensively in English.

'May I speak with him?' the stranger slurred in broken English.

'He's not here right now, so I guess not.'

'Do you know when to expect his return?'

'I couldn't say, he doesn't keep regular hours.'

'Can I come in and wait for him? I would rather speak to him here than at the hotel,' the man appeared unstable on his feet as his question tailed off.

'I told you that he doesn't keep regular hours and I don't know you from Adam!'

Frustrated at having to hold a conversation in a door jar and conscious that his voice would carry throughout the hallway, Liam unhooked the door chain and opened the door wider to get a look at the stranger. He was greeted by the muzzle of a Tokarev TT-30 semi–automatic pistol being pressed into his face. Stoned as he was, Liam could still smell traces of alcohol on the man's breath. He withdrew the pistol and gestured with it for Liam to raise his hands up and to move backwards slowly into the living area. The gunman then closed the front door behind him with his free hand and moved out of the vestibule, his weapon continually trained on Liam. He switched on the TV and selected the station showing the football match, making sure the volume was loud enough for them not to be overheard. He then told Liam to draw up two chairs opposite each other in the centre of the room and bid him to sit down so they both could 'watch' the football. He wore the archetypal hat and raincoat so often preferred by nefarious film noir hit men of the 1940s. No one had thought to mention this in the intervening years and judging by the gun no one ever would. It was a standard issue Soviet firearm which had proved very reliable from 1930 until the present time. It was only now under the glare of the overhead light that Liam could get a good look at him as he navigated the room and helped himself to Andreas's brandy decanter with one hand, pistol in the other. He must have been at least sixty-five, he didn't move like an old man, but he certainly dressed like one. Liam was coming back down from the resin and the drug-subdued soldier instinct in him began to wonder if he could overpower him. Best leave it until his senses had hit the earth again. But last thing he needed now was to come out with some smart remark, so why he said what he did next remains a mystery.

'Not from around these parts are you Bogey?'

What was it in Liam's character that sailed in the face of adversity and compelled him to stick both fingers up at it both bravely and foolishly? He didn't have a death-wish, he just had the balls to say what he felt and to hell with the consequences. But if his mother ever had cause to worry for her son it was now. The stranger sat grim faced nursing a half empty glass of Jäegermeister in one hand and his TT-30 in the other resting on his lap but always trained on Liam. He looked as if he had been waiting for some time already for this moment to arrive. He looked as if he had rehearsed what he wanted to say and that Liam wasn't included in that rehearsal. Liam decided to quit while behind and go easy with the one-liners. This character was different, he had a bit of the Slav in him judging by his knitted brow and thickset features. He looked stoical, slightly glazed but maybe that was the alcohol in his veins, he also looked easily provoked and eager to get a move on.

Liam's system had definitely flattened out and again he pondered the idea of struggling for the gun. The intruder's stare bored deeper into him as if he had read his thoughts already:

'If you want to see your family again on this side of the grave then just sit quietly.'

His voice wavered between Russian and English but answered any doubts in Liam's mind as to his intentions. All the while the TV blasted out frantic commentaries, goal kicks, near misses and feigned injuries. Players dropping like a sack of potatoes inside the penalty area and getting no sympathy whatsoever from the referee. They sat opposite each other until extra time came around and tiredness had begun to sap at both sets of players, having used up all their available substitutes. Liam looked at the man's shoes. You could tell a lot from a man's shoes. The soles were worn at the heel and they hadn't been polished for some time, leading Liam to believe that this character had covered a significant distance to get here this evening. Previously as the dope wore off a deep hunger would set in that Liam called the munchies, but one look at the gun had put paid to any appetite.

The man hadn't taken his hat off in the ninety minutes since he had sat down opposite Liam; it cast a shadow onto the floor exaggerated by the shape of the light shade within the ceiling rose above them. He just stared right through Liam with it seemed, years of experience in doing so, gleaned somewhere foul and unfeeling. The big Irishman now froze his own expression when, just beyond his assailant, Andreas crept into the hallway amid frantic pleas for yet another penalty on the television. Andreas's entrance was smothered by the fracas and he was primed and ready having just put his key in the latch to be greeted by the TV set nearly at full blast. Neither of them watched television ordinarily. Andreas grabbed the nearest thing to hand which might render the gunman useless. It could only be the Meissen vase displayed on a stand in the vestibule. It had reminded him of the one his mother placed cut flowers in to grace the Bechstein piano back in Strekerau. He started to run clutching it above his head like a trophy but then slipped on a highly polished door saddle and lunged, striking the back of the gunman's head. It splintered in his hands as his assailant half turned to confront the disturbance and then fell backwards off the chair, dropping his drink with a loud groan before collapsing unconscious on the floor. Liam bolted over to his prone body and took possession of the TT-30 pistol. He instinctively counted how many rounds were left in the magazine clip, checked the safety catch was on and put the pistol in his pocket.

'Just who the fuck do we have here Andreas?' cried Liam.

Andreas was kneeling over the gunman, he was by now very pale and visibly shaken. He began picking out the shards from a fresh cut in the palm of his hand. Liam went into the kitchen and ran cold water over a kitchen towel before twisting it around Andreas's open palm and knotting it tightly.

'Turn him over onto his back for me Liam, I want to see his face.'

Liam removed the chair that the gunman had previously sat on and then rolled him over onto his back. His thick mop of grey curly hair was now enriched with blood that had drained down from his scalp. His raincoat was spattered and his belly heaved slowly, his breath labouring through much alcohol. His wound had already begun to congeal, helped no doubt by the thick strands of hair that had silted up the flow of blood. Liam then frisked his coat and inside the jacket he wore underneath he found a wallet and he gave that over to Andreas. He unbuttoned the wallet and found a Russian driving licence, CPSU Communist party membership card and an MVD Soviet internal affairs identity card along with assorted East German and Soviet banknotes. His name was Sergei Ivanov and Andreas knew instantly why he was here. Andreas sat on the floor while Liam looked on.

'I'm sorry that you had to go through that ordeal just now Liam.'

'Who is this guy Andreas? What does he want?'

The intruder moaned on the floor as he began to regain consciousness and as the pain began to register in his head once more.

'We don't have much time, go into the kitchen again and in the second drawer down you will find a roll of gaffer tape. Bring it and a pair of scissors here and we will bind this fellow good and tight and then we will hear his side of the story when he wakes up. You remember asking me how come my hands were so badly frostbitten back when we first met?'

Liam nodded as he struggled to remove Sergei's raincoat and began to apply the tape to the man's wrists.

'I took exception with you asking me in front of all the others and I left the table soon after,' Liam bowed his head at the recollection, he knew his big mouth had often got him into trouble in the past. 'Well, this man here is the reason why my hands are so raw-looking to this day. We have quite a history, we go back further even than Stalingrad. He was once my prisoner and then I was also once his. He was captured at Belgorod, I saw he got fair treatment even though he provided us with very little information that was of use and some of the men I was with wanted to string him up from the nearest tree after he had spat at me and verbally abused me whilst under interrogation. He was bullish and aggressive and took real exception to me coming from an ethnic minority background and throwing my lot in with the Germans. He squared up to me and threatened me with what he would do if the shoe was ever on the other foot. There was no negotiating with him and it comes as no surprise to me that he carries an MVD internal security identity card.'

As Andreas's words began to fade, so Sergei opened his eyes and slowly adjusted to his surroundings.

'Liam, may I introduce you to Sergei Ivanov, formerly of the 220th rifle division, a card-carrying apparatchik whose job it is to make people, whole groups of people, disappear. Sergei, this is Liam Broy, late of the Irish army and presently chief bottle washer at the Bayerischer Hof hotel.'

Liam smiled wryly.

'Mensche, you fucking traitor, untie me now or there will be hell to pay.'

'Do you believe this guy? Doesn't he know when he is done for?' Liam asked.

The Russian was in obvious discomfort but that took nothing away from his anger at being restrained in parcel tape. Liam heard Andreas begin to speak in Russian for the first time. In slow deliberate terms, accentuating his words, lingering on them as Sergei wasn't going anywhere sometime soon.

'You haven't changed a bit in all this time Sergei. How long has it been? Over forty-five years and you still have all your own hair. The red colour suits you, I mean the bloody rinse I gave you really works. We had to tie you up as you brought a gun into my home and that was very naughty of you. You bring all this crap to my door after so many years have gone by. No one cares any more except you. If you keep on swearing at me and my friend here we will seal up your mouth too while we decide what to do with you next, so be a good fellow and calm the fuck down.'

Even though he couldn't understand a single word, Liam felt sure that the animated gravitas of what Andreas had just said had hit home. It was as if a whole other nature in Andreas was slowly revealing itself. Liam had been getting comfortable with the phlegmatically private man who only ever seemed to get passionate about Brahms, but that mask had slipped revealing a hitherto unseen quality. Andreas had a dry persona which grew more arid in his dealings with Sergei. His opponent scoured Andreas's face for any sign of weakness in resolve and found none forthcoming. Sergei had never let go of the fact that he had once been bested by a German farm boy as he had always scathingly regarded Andreas. This humiliation had been compounded by the fact that even though he had managed to escape back to the Russian defence lines, he was punished for doing so. The western allies viewed escaping as almost a sport, but the Soviets saw it quite differently. Escapees were treated with suspicion, cowardice and even as spies. Sergei was charged with a lesser offence on his return, seen as an agitator, tainted by being captured instead of dying for the motherland and he was consigned to a penal battalion. It was here that Sergei honed his bitterness, fine-tuning his resentment amongst the rabble and the thieves and minority groups who were seen as fodder for the German machine-guns. His penal battalion was corralled in with guns pointed at their own backs should they try and retreat from the front. They suicidally threw themselves time and again against the Germans like waves on a shoreline, unnerving their opponents with their fierce and foolhardy bravery. Their dead and broken bodies filled the breach between the two, their sacrifice leaving just the merest possibility of their surviving comrades reintegration back into Soviet society.

Andreas, albeit unwittingly, was again to play no small role in Sergei's rehabilitation. Both sides knew this was a fight without compromise like no other struggle in German history perhaps since the destruction of the three Roman legions in the Teutoburg forest in AD 9. The tactics and the methods were reflected in the monolithic struggle to oust the advantage away from the other side. Propaganda was a crucial tool in stirring up fear and hatred between the two protagonists. Propaganda twisted your opponent's resolve, depending on how it was handled. Terror had been struck into the hearts of ordinary German soldiers by way of the Russian school of sniping. The Soviets had become proficient in the art of sniping, masters of the art of concealment and camouflage. German casualties had mounted steadily, especially amongst officers, specialist troops and engineers, the decision-makers and the risk takers. So emasculated by dread of a sniper were the Germans that lines of communication once severed were almost impossible to re-establish without taking up the efforts of six soldiers when ordinarily it should have taken just one. To counter this growing fear and at great personal risk, a leaflet-drop had been flown over the Russian lines warning them of an embedded Volga German, raised on their native soil and only too familiar with Soviet tactics, use of the terrain and troop formations. This sniper was an enemy from within and would strike fear into the hearts of ordinary Russian soldiers. After catching and reading one of the leaflets Sergei knew straight away that the sniper could only be Andreas Mensche. He had seen Andreas's handiwork with a rifle in Belgorod firsthand and it just had to be him. The boy sniper. He made it his patriotic duty to personally deal with him.

'At least you are on your knees in front of me now Andreas,' Sergei spat out defiantly.

Andreas untied the towel from his palm as it had stopped bleeding and he instead applied it to Sergei's head wound and mopped up the blood on his scalp. Sergei flinched and cursed him but there was nothing he could do to stop Andreas.

'I'm just worried that you will ruin my carpet. Only you would use bombast to try and overcome what is clearly a humiliating situation to be in, Sergei. Only you could hold a grudge that long. Only you remember what the grudge was even about. Everyone else has moved on with their lives. When did you convince yourself that you could really get away with killing me on my own doorstep? Was it after plying the Czech border guards with vodka all evening so that they would relent and give you permission to drive your Trabant into West Germany? That is your glorified lawnmower parked down the street, isn't it? Hardly subtle for a Soviet official. I'm amazed that you weren't stopped before now. As for your pistol, when was the last time you even fired that thing? It belongs in the Deutsches Museum. Would you really have used it on Liam there? Not that he would have felt anything, being stoned as he was when he let you in. By the way, didn't I say that smoking on my balcony wasn't allowed Liam?'

'Yeah, but that fucker pointed it right in my cheek, stoned or not!' said

Liam meekly.

'Sergei you brought this all to my door and I now only have to lift the receiver and dial to have you carted off, creating a very sensitive diplomatic incident. This is free West Germany and you can be sure that I would drag your ugly face across every newspaper editor's desk from Lake Geneva to the Finland Station. You also threatened my friend who has done nothing to you to warrant a pistol in the face. You are fortunate that Liam is not the sensitive type and is likely to get over this quickly. You are lucky too that I am so forgiving because I know that Liam could make short work of you if I asked him to. I'm lost as to why you came here this evening. Forgive me but didn't your side win the war? Oh that's it! You can't handle the peace. It's still raging on in your head, is that the problem? You hold me responsible for all the things that went wrong for you after Belgorod? Did you lose everything? Did you lose all your family? Your home? Possessions? Entitlements? No? Because I did! You look at me as if I was something you just scraped off your shoe, something beneath you, but that is just as fascist in attitude as that other bunch who I paid the price by throwing my lot in with back then when I had no choice in the matter. You are no different, sure you can dress it up as socialist and fair-minded, when in reality it is just as elitist and discriminating. A different coloured flag that's all, just as dark and just as nefarious and under the auspices of your former boss Lavrentiy Beria, just as capable of committing heinous crimes. There are too many to quote, but Katyn Wood is a good example of what your people were prepared to do to impress your boss. Fifteen thousand unarmed Polish officers shot in the back of the head to purge any chance of a leadership elite in that country. You consider any ethnic group or minority within the Soviet sphere of influence to be a threat to Communism, forgetting in the process its broad appeal that spans all nationalities. You took an innate hatred of a minority such as my own and abused your own position to make whole communities simply disappear. People are reduced to statistics in your eyes, counters on a gaming board to be hoarded or dispensed with. Did you thrive in that atmosphere of intimidation and suspicion when you joined the MVD? Imagine the fates of so many innocents dependent on your fluctuating mood-swings for their own existence. I took your identity card from your wallet. Not a good likeness. You see I couldn't for the life of me understand why you held onto this grudge for so many years. That got me thinking about your line of work within the Ministry of the Interior. You act out of bitterness and resentment because of the way you were treated by the Red Army. This fear of not fitting in drives you and led you to become a specialist within the ministry, isn't that so? You get to move swathes of people across the gaming board of the Soviet Union. You decide if they are a malleable asset and as such can be put to work as slave labour or if they are politically undesirable and can be exiled to the remotest gulag to die as ignominiously as possible away from influence. So if your role is to make whole groups of people disappear, then you will know where they have gone to and presumably those decisions are backed up by reams of paperwork typed up and gathered in by diligent Communist party officials over the intervening decades and shared between the various departments responsible'

'I finally get to speak? You denounce me, threaten to drag my name through the papers? You? A Volga blow-in who has no country to call his own since we kicked you out. You presume that you have the upper hand? Do you think I work alone, that I came here on my own?'

'You did Sergei and that's where this gets quite sad. There is no accomplice out there keeping the lawnmower ticking over. That Trabant is no getaway car. If this was an authorized 'hit', then I would have been abducted and taken out sooner, cleaner, somewhere neutral. In the street behind the Bayerischer Hof perhaps, apprehended without any fuss and bundled into a car with a powerful engine. Vodka convinced you that you could get away with it on my doorstep. How many quarts do you pour down your neck on a nightly basis by the way? How many nights has it seen you through with no family around to urge you to stop drinking. I'm just a tick on an ass and of no consequence to anyone. But you resent me all the same and you have fed off this resentment for over forty-five years. It would have served you better if I had died back then, or at least if you thought I had. Because your job allows you to probe into other people's lives at will, you found out that I had survived the war and managed to settle in the west.'

'I tracked you down because you were the Volga sniper. Because you killed so many of my comrades, your fellow countrymen. You never paid the ultimate price for their sacrifice. You got away with your life and now live in comfort in the west. How could you kill your brother Russians? But that's it, you weren't Russian: you are a German mongrel whose ancestors stole all the best land along the Volga and kept the harvests among themselves.'

'That could also be interpreted as having been a resourceful hardworking minority who reaped what they sowed and ploughed all profits back into their own small community. It's my reality against your supposition.'

'The reality is that your people no longer exist along the Volga basin. We saw to that. They were all resettled successfully,' said Sergei coldly.

'If you want to see the light of another day then you had better help me find out exactly what befell my family. You do this and then all bets are off and we call it quits between us. You help me find out this information and by doing so you prove that this vendetta of yours is finally over. You are not leaving Munich until I have your word on this.'

'Much good it will do you to know what happened to your family. Do you really care that much? After all, you have had forty-five years of your own to try and find out what their fate was. Better to let the past remain where it is.'

'I have been punished enough, Sergei. You know I can't return to the Soviet Union and search for them. You are so full of shit when you talk about avenging your fallen comrades. You don't speak for them. You focused on me because I lived to tell the tale. Truth is, I have never spoken of my war to anyone until I let Liam stay here. I have come to terms with what I did, but you haven't because you are still destroying people's lives and inside you hate yourself. I am a constant reminder of the creature you allowed yourself to become. I was there, just across the wasteland, just as afraid as you. I was captured and spent ten years making amends for joining the wrong side. But I had no choice, I belonged to an ethnic minority that had no voice in Russia. You took advantage of your position after the war and vented all your spleen on the other minorities whose only crime was that they got in the way of the reclassification of the modern map of Europe. I am a silent witness of this forgotten history and you sought to erase me. The real truth died long ago with so many innocents and subsequent generations have too much to contend with in their daily struggle to find the time to reflect on things that didn't affect them. They get a flavour of it every so often when aged relatives gather together for weddings and funerals and perhaps they sup too much washing sherry and embroider tales to yawning grandchildren. The truth is Sergei, no one cares anymore. That torch you carry is very heavy and you appear to me to have no one else to pass it on to. We both cut sad figures in a modern setting, but I do need the answer before I too die.'

12

1942

The lucky ones are the dogs for at least they get the option to escape from the ruins by running across the ice mantle that has sealed over the mighty Volga. Nothing really lives here anymore. Things just exist until throttled out of that existence by another's bare hands. We live for the fight. Fighting hand-to-hand lends reason to our being here. Fighting this close, unable to fire off a round for fear that the ricochet might in turn hit you. You can smell your opponent's foul breath as you struggle and this fatal embrace wakes up the lice colonies on you both as they begin to heat up and then you can watch them flee from the corpse as one of you begins to freeze after death.

That is your only reward. That and maybe his boots and if they pinch a bit so what? What shapes we make when we die in this place. Corpses become perverse gun-embrasures or macabre signposts to destinations we will never get to see again. The ground is so hard it would break a shovel so the snow embalms the horror with a deep covering until next spring when we will all be dead anyway. I am now a shepherd to my flock. I keep watch over this ever dwindling bunch of men with whom I would gladly give up my life. I had heard tales from Obergefreiter Hauser of their valour in the days of victories, how they marched down the Champs-Élysées with their chests beating with pride after the fall of France. Whether it was the Fourth or the Sixth army, they were once the cream of the Reich and had overrun the low countries and Scandinavia sweeping all before them until reaching this place. Now there is nowhere to march to even if they could, for this is 'The Kessel' the cauldron and we are the captive prey inside the cooking pot. On the 19th November the Soviets unleashed a barrage that would have stopped the armies of Satan in their tracks. Panic has set in, draining our morale, leading to a fatalistic realism in our ultimate defeat that is endemic. Men write last wills and testaments and sew them into the collars of their uniforms, sending fond farewells to loved ones so at least their remains may be identified after the spring thaw. By the 23rd we heard news that the Russians had taken the bridge at Kalach on the Don river intact. This location was the artery that pumped life into the Sixth army and with its capture we are now completely surrounded.

There are now just eight men left in my unit that I remember from the 168th division last summer. The rest are irregulars, volunteers, specialist pioneers, Romanians, volunteer Ukrainians and the flotsam of other divisions. We are threaded together by a fear of the unknown. It's difficult to tell anyone apart in these conditions. We are reduced to pillaging Russian clothing from their corpses and their living compatriots shoot us out of hand if we are captured wearing any vestige of Soviet uniform. Since the encirclement I have heard our military aircraft struggling to re-supply our ever-decreasing lines and often taking severe losses from accurate soviet anti-aircraft fire in the process. The Luftwaffe no longer controls the skies, we endure in the fruits of their labour, the ruins they created which turned our war on its head. Even the rats have a better time of it as there is always plenty for them to scrounge from. We now pool our own rations, ammunition and anything else to make this existence more bearable. The Soviets know we are in severe difficulty and they rub it in by using loud-speakers and Tannoys to dishearten us. They goad us, cajole and make light of the fact that we are suffering inexorably from hunger and frost-bite. They offer a reward to anyone who gives up any information as to the whereabouts of the Volga

German sniper in their midst. The eight men I know would do anything to protect me from anyone stupid enough to try and take up the Russians' offer.

It would be difficult to even point me out amongst this group as we all look the same. Our boots are swathed in bandages as the leather has worn out leading to foot-rot closely followed by the onset of frostbite. Some have resorted to wearing wicker clogs which restrict movement but still allow you to trample over drifting snow. We no longer resemble a fighting unit. We look like scavengers in a quarry where it snows all the time. Our priorities have diversified, nothing is strategic any more, there are no tactics, only ways to survive. Things we took for granted are now prized commodities to be fought over if need be amongst our own men. Firewood, kindling, candle wax, axle-grease, cigarettes, alcohol and lice-free thermal clothing are all valuable and out of reach to many. The most basic of bodily functions is an ordeal in these temperatures as piss can freeze before it even hits the ground. Our diet has narrowed down to a thin soup and black rye bread with hardly any meat since all the horses were butchered. Many faces are wrapped in bandages as we have the most appalling cases of frostbite, so rank and recognition are almost impossible to discern until someone has the energy to speak or salute. We are glued to the radio for any hope of relief. The radio crackles into life but feeds us bullshit bulletins that purport to come from our front, making light of our predicament so as to sugar the pill for those worried about us back home. It is better that any loved one doesn't know the truth yet. How many of the young officers are unable to cope with the stress of having to rally men at the end of their tether, when they themselves have endured just about all they can and then stagger out into a blizzard never to return.

How the littlest thing can become a symbol of hope within a dwindling company of men. A hand-carved wooden Christmas tree appeared from nowhere in a hollow niche above a parapet within a covered trench. It reminded us of a time of innocence beyond hostilities and gave hope that maybe we would live to see another festive season. When hope is lost there are other choices. A bullet through the foot was a ticket home until recently, but the increasing occurrence of such a wound now only leads to a court martial and even worse; being left on a stretcher unattended until you froze to death in the open air at one of the two remaining airfields still operational in German hands. Pitomnik and Gumrak play host to the most harrowing scenes of mass inhumanity. They are crucibles of increasing panic leading to needless deaths and fatal decisions exacerbated by the military police who guard the vicinity and shoot anyone who dares to stray onto the airfield without prior authorization. The Russians shell both airfields, constantly trying to destroy the runways and often hitting the already haemorrhaging field hospitals. They can't help but hit something that will cause bloody mayhem and stoke up tensions.

Rumours are rife and often exaggerated of an imminent breakthrough by our comrades from Hoth's 4th Panzer army overseen by the brilliant Field Marshal Erich Von Manstein. These rumours act as fuel for our faltering hopes. Each day we listen for the sound of our Panzer engines on every horizon and instead we are greeted by the whooshing scream of their Katyusha rockets accurately finding their targets. Men get so disheartened that they just shoot themselves, even in mid conversation which is crippling to witness and saps at all our morale. I am increasingly conscious of being given up by one of the many desperate faces I see when I'm patrolling our ever-decreasing area of engagement. I don't stand out with my captured grubby thermal winter clothing, but my sniper rifle gives me away and the fact that I carry very little other equipment. I do understand their motivation to survive but at what cost to themselves? The Soviets treat their own prisoners with contempt and disdain and few, if any, German ones have ever made it back to tell of how they were treated. I think nothing now of picking off one of our own men if I believe they have strayed too close to the Russian lines for any good it could be doing for our division. A 'mouth' would be invaluable to our enemy and put us all in jeopardy. I have refused the offer of one of the 'eight' alternating to act as my shadow as I go out hunting with my rifle. I try to break up any routine that I might have been guilty of forming. I eat apart from them more often than not, I think it boosts their confidence to know that I could be there for them at any time when they patrol. I have seen our methods of attack adapt and change to try and compete with the tactics used by the Soviets. They don't fight fair and either do we. I always try and kill one of their officers or anyone who shows leadership qualities, singling them out and tracking them down. I am as careful as I can be that my location will not be discernible to those who mop up after I have felled the one giving the orders. The confusion I create can often be just seconds and my men need to harness this confusion and kill as many of them as they can, causing panic in their ranks and for them to retreat in some disarray so that we might even capture one of their 'mouths' and glean some all too depressing information as to their troop strengths and formations. I always go for a clean kill, he is no use just wounded as he will only draw more attention to my location with his screams. Whenever practicable I try and kill the next person who comes to his aid if I can because he is usually a subordinate who would assume command. If I get him then I break up the chain of control, allowing my boys get the upper hand for a while at least.

Oberleutnant Werner and Obergefreiter Hauser are complete opposites, but of the same coin and they work well as a team. Previously Hauser was a bit dismissive of Werner, often grumbling that he didn't get his hands dirty enough and took too much of a back seat. But attrition has seen off any soft-centered individuals, long since leaving only the core who watch out for one another's backs. The Oberleutnant is careful to listen as well as mete out orders. He is all too aware of the predicament we face and measures his responses to the orders he receives. Importantly he is a calming influence on the raw young recruits that they kept sending us. You grow up quickly out here, or else you freeze to death. Hauser takes many risks and I swear he does it to get my blood to boil, knowing that I have his back covered from a well hidden vantage point.

We take our cue from the radio which is ominously dedicating sombre martial music in our honour and which to us sounds as if they are already preparing to close the lid on our casket. Our own High Command appears to be sleepwalking to capitulation. From what I can tell and this is just second-hand, General Paulus is of the view that we should hold tight here in the ruined city, turning it into a bastion and wait for relief. His opinion hardened by a vile Nazi lap-dog on his staff called Schmidt who appears to have some Mephistophelian hold over him. I heard from one who was there that a senior officer on Manstein's staff was flown into the cauldron to plead with General Paulus to rally his men and to try and punch a hole through the Soviet cordon before it was too strong to penetrate. Paulus seemed more preoccupied with what could be rustled up for the lunch menu that afternoon and when pressed, he kept procrastinating that we had not enough fuel for our trucks or any horses left to make such a break-out and hope to reach Manstein's men. I think Paulus may be unwell and that illness has clouded his judgement; but he is also a weak and unimaginative general who, unlike Hoth, isn't prepared to take any risks and who is willing to consign us to a wintry tomb in the name of the Fatherland.

Manstein's envoy managed to fly out of Stalingrad and safely convey General Paulus's bleak summary of our chances. This in turn filtered down to the individual groups arming the strong points within the ruined citadel, eventually reaching our pocket of defiance where it percolated in our minds continually. By this time our lines of communication were tenuous at best so we were practically autonomous and free to act as we please in our area of influence. Strong points and key positions that could alter the outcome of a fire fight now change hands with worrying frequency, up to eight times a day at great personal cost and for very little gain. Our losses could not be replenished and our casualties, those with whom we had formed close bonds, more often than not we had to leave behind, as it was a drain on our attacking momentum. This was harsh and the only comfort we could give them now when they were beyond our help were the ampules of morphine we had left to help ease their entry into the afterlife. It was just as well the snow fell continually as it hid so many vile and cruel necessities. You tried valiantly to block out the images in your mind of the people you had trained with, ate with, argued and laughed with. Think only that they are gone and that at any moment you might join them. Truth is, in the deafening lulls between exchanges, we are more angry with our own leadership than with the Russians. After all, this is their land and they have every right to defend it to the last man.

There is an overwhelming atmosphere of blinding negativity pervading the tomb we inhabit. The stark realisation that you might never see a loved one again. Some of the boys were talking last night of their home towns and villages, of how rich and fertile they were and that there was more than enough land to go around. So just why did we think we needed all this foreign territory? No one could think of a reason to defend the view of 'Lebensraum', it didn't hold water, it just froze in the bucket and with it our hopes of any lasting victory. We all just wanted to live and to go home so we independently decided to make our own bid to break out of the cauldron. As far as the remnants of our divisional headquarters were concerned, we were just statistics to be withdrawn from an ever shrinking map of influence. We wouldn't be missed, such was the mesmeric hold that the ever tightening ring of steel being developed by the Soviets had on our own high command. It wasn't in our instincts to just sit tight and wait for the best. Oberleutnant Werner addressed the company that morning after we had brewed up:

'Men, we all have mixed emotions about what we have to do next. But I simply want to put it to you like this. We are surrounded and we are running low on food and ammunition. The information we receive from what is left of our division is at best spurious and at worst defeatist. There are enough of us left to make a fist of trying to punch a hole in the Soviet encirclement. I would rather fall trying than to crouch cowering. There is no advantage to our being here anymore. We have to cut our losses and make for our own lines or face a grave certainty. Let's try for home boys, home is where we belong, we have proved our worth to each other if not to those who ordered us here in the first place. I realise that I am contravening existing orders, but these orders are only going to hand us on a plate to the Russians. There are those amongst you who have perhaps more to lose than the rest of us by staying here, those members of Russian ethnic groups whom the Soviets will not take kindly to repatriating. I put it to you to come with us and bolster our chances of a break out. I need your support, I need your bravery, I need the loyalty you have shown to help us get this far. Let's get back to Hoth's army group and have a tale to tell. Are you with me boys?'

All fifty-five of them rallied, infused with fresh hope as his question hung in the air invitingly. It was agreed that we would try for a break out after sunset which fell around 15.50 p.m. German time. Oberleutnant Werner and Obergefreiter Hauser were huddled around the communications wireless for the better part of that morning anxiously devouring any grains of information as to where Von Manstein's thrust into the Soviet encirclement might be expected. We had a rough idea that it was south and west of where we now sat and that the distance in between was about thirty kilometres. It was all speculation, as in reality the radio traffic consisted of vague often misleading disinformation that was perhaps meant to confuse Soviet eavesdroppers and in the process only succeeded in disheartening our own men.

Just over thirty kilometres away Hoth's tanks had indeed made progress, but only because the Soviets wanted to draw them into a killing zone of their own devising and on their terms. The leading convoy advanced and made steady uninterrupted progress over terrain that had frozen solid and was flat for most of the first twenty kilometres. But the next horizon they encountered brought with it the undulating snowdrifts so similar in outlook, if not content, to the sand dunes of the north African deserts over which Rommel had tried to negotiate that very summer before El Alamein. These steep snowdrifts had reverse slopes which allowed for dismounted Russian cavalrymen to hide their sturdy mounts and lie in wait with tank destroyer rifles and pick off the panzers as they struggled to negotiate through the terrain at a snail's pace. It was a turkey shoot and Hoth's tanks and trucks suffered greatly in the white desolation. Georgy Zhukov's iron determination had prevailed and nothing was to be allowed to prevent his stranglehold over the city so that he would be able to present the 6th German army as a trophy to his boss.

We were determined not to hang around to witness that eventuality. For the better part of the afternoon our men had been actively acquiring as much light armament as we could feasibly carry. Enemy mortars, Russian tommy-guns and as much ammunition and thermal clothing as we dared take from the dead in no man's land. We did this as best we could without drawing too much attention to our efforts. I was exempted from the task as I could prove more of a distraction by taking pot luck shots at any Soviet who dared move from the cover of the ruins to get a better look at what we were up to. There was now a pungent sense of purpose and urgency that had long since absented itself. It was contained in strict silence and gave the men a renewed sense of value that had previously been dissolved within the marrow-sapping cauldron. For my part I had negotiated the ruins on my own for so long now that I knew the best rat runs that led out into the suburbs and beyond Stalingrad. I had watched the Russians move troops from one location to another to deliberately mislead and appear to strengthen their weaker positions with fresh troops. What is more they had got sloppy, confident that we would never do the unthinkable and try and make a break out. It was left to me to lead the men out when the time came to do so.

I took my last shot with my sniper rifle at 2.15 that afternoon. A Soviet Commissar was rumoured to have been seen bolstering morale within a blocking brigade behind a penal unit. A peach of a target if it was true. My area of influence was about two kilometres square, I patrolled it very stealthily and I had my 'hides' well disguised from the attentions of the ordinary Russian soldier. Footprints in the snow could be your best friend or your worst enemy. On many occasions I would have to double back or abandon any attempt to make it to one of my 'hides' because of strange footprints. Fresh snowfalls always helped discover new places to conceal, but the downside was you couldn't use your scope in poor visibility. The rumours of a new Commissar were well-founded. This character must have been fast tracked in because he had no sense of his own dwindling mortality. He took risks but I think he did so more out of bravado than bravery. He was too busy trying to show who was boss to have any real concern for his own personal safety. I was able to watch him from the relative seclusion of an elevated gantry within the grain elevator. All that manpower, time and energy expended on progressing through the ruins of this city and here I was in the grain elevator near the cusp of where it had all begun for me in Stalingrad.

I had him in my sights for nearly thirty minutes before I was comfortable enough to allow a shot. He never strayed far from the penal unit and continually kept admonishing and provoking them. I could see him brandishing his pistol and walking down the line behind the men. He would stop behind every third man and put the pistol to the back of their head and pretend to fire. I watched this through my scope and then I began to wonder if, in actual fact, I was doing these men a service by taking him off their hands. I let him progress to the end of the column of men which stretched beyond fifty metres. It was beginning to flurry lightly from the sky which ordinarily did magical things, dulling the sound, insulating the atmosphere but it only helped me hone in on my target. I squeezed lightly and released the bullet which traversed through the flakes of snow before slicing open the back of his head like a melon. He collapsed bleeding profusely causing much consternation in the ranks of the raw recruits. Every time this happens I swear time stands still for me. I'm transfixed and I can't help being so. A legacy from the deer hunt I suppose but it also leaves me very vulnerable to a counter-attack. I always tell myself later to react quicker after taking the shot but I can't help but linger in the moment. Now they will react, seek revenge and soon one of their own indomitable snipers will strike back at us and the game goes on. I just have to make sure that it is not me on the receiving end and that I can help lead the men out of this frozen hell.

By twilight I had taken up the point position within our group. Obergefreiter Hauser had done a headcount before we entered the network of sewage tunnels that once served the city. Each one of us was encumbered with as much ammunition and supplies as we could carry. We had to crawl through streams of effluent and rat's piss on our hands and knees as the sewers weren't originally designed to accommodate humans. We couldn't help but breathe in the acrid stench and just hope that our stomachs wouldn't react badly to the fumes in such a confined space. I was conscious of my responsibility in leading these men through tunnels that I had only ever negotiated alone before. We were crawling below our own front line positions now and could hear the muffled shouts and conversations of our former comrades as we silently took our leave of them. Oberleutnant Werner was at my shoulder, the weight of the world on his own shoulders now that he had ordered us to abandon our post.

The sewer pipe ran out sooner than many expected and we could breathe freely again and took our chances in the open within the mangled wasteland of the ruined worker's apartment blocks that stretched out into the suburbs. We emerged into an unfamiliar district draped in an uneasy silence. Not a pane of glass remained intact within these ruins. Behind every pitch-black hollow window frame there could be an enemy gun lying in wait with your name on the bullet. This area had been captured, lost and retaken at great cost for very little and now belonged to no one. Russian flares cast pale light down upon our awkward shapes as we nervously paced through the debris field. Flares weren't an uncommon sight previously but that was when we had plenty of cover to watch them fall and extinguish. Each man now scanned his horizon nervously for any sign of a muzzle flash. We began to trip over fallen masonry and look for any crater large enough to dive into at short notice. We had lost our symmetry in the growing tension. It was as if we knew that we were being stalked. When I was back in the forests near Strekerau hunting with my father, I often came across the quarry we had stalked and shot. I always remarked about the composure on a hunted animal's face after death. It was unaware of the lengths we had gone to make its demise as humane as possible. One minute it was sampling an unrestricted life and the next it had been cleanly dispatched. It didn't even know that it was being hunted and therefore died a sudden and natural death. Whereas we were exposed to the grim certainty that at any minute a fire fight might erupt and we were living on our wits. The men around me had already been tested to the limits of endurance. We had come to view our enemy as a faceless gangster who made the rules up as he went along. He was a street fighter, ever resourceful and worst of all, so full of resentment that you had better make sure you kill everyone you come across because they weren't ever going to give up trying to kill you.

Some of us slipped as we lost a foothold, dropping rifles as we reached out to regain balance on the brick piles, much to the consternation of Obergefreiter Hauser. He was ever watchful over his charges, slow to praise, quick to admonish, but always unequivocal. It was perhaps because of his powerful presence that he stood out and when the silence was finally broken it was him who fell first. Whoever squeezed the trigger had released a high velocity round which instilled terror mixed with apprehension as the echo of the shot ricocheted off the buildings. They could have had their pick of us but chose him as I would have done in their place. Hauser wavered from the initial punch on impact but characteristically summoned the strength to keep his balance and managed to continue waving his men forward silently with a mauser pistol in his hand. But he was now clutching his shoulder with his free hand and the blood from the wound began to form a large red clot on his white winter smock. He collapsed just as the tail of our column scattered past him and into the relative safety of the abandoned apartment blocks. He lay crumpled in the hollow of a crater in the middle of what was once a street, now strewn with fallen masonry. He didn't moan or make a sound that could be overheard, but I knew that I had to get to him somehow. Shots now rang out overhead as the enemy began to get our range in their sights. Hauser was safe where he lay for now but was increasingly vulnerable to grenade attack if the enemy encroached any further on foot. I could tell by the way he dropped that the wound was serious. More flares began to rise into the night sky, marking out our position, drawing attention to the certainty that the Soviets would now concentrate all their efforts to finish us off. Without thinking I dropped my knapsack and rifle and sprinted over to where Hauser had fallen and dived into his crater to join him, bullets snapping at my heels.

'You did that with a bit more panache than the last time you fell over me back in Belgorod, Feldwebel Mensche! But you shouldn't have bothered as I'm done for. I couldn't get up now even if they weren't trying to shoot our heads off. The bullet has shattered my spine. It's strange that I'm not in more discomfort. Must be the adrenalin at work. You really didn't have to come over here and keep me company you know. Do me a favour though. Keep the boys together. You are a veteran now...bet you never thought that you would hear me say that.'

I was no orator and I was lost for anything of value to say that would suit the moment. But maybe by my seeing to him in his last moments he would realise what an influence he had been on my perilous experience. I hated him once for no other reason than that he blindly hated me. I could see that he hated what he didn't understand. He had been conditioned to question anything that strayed from his nationalism. I was foreign to him and my background was literally a thousand miles from anything he was familiar with. Yet he had encroached into my world, bringing his own brand of nationalism to bear on different castes of people who had already suffered greatly under Stalin. I also saw the change in him, how this vast country wore at him, no matter how many easy victories fell into his lap, the final victory always lay just over the next horizon. I soon saw what a leader he was, totally brusque and unpolished, but a soldier's soldier none the less. I caught myself forming epitaphs in my head for a man beside me who wasn't dead yet. I think he might have read my mind because he asked me to retrieve his Mauser from the crater floor so that he might have something to say if a Russki happened to drop by. I gave it to him and he wiped it clean of snow on his blood clotted smock. The fire fight played out over our heads. It made a weirdly beautiful sight, the green flashes from our own weapons mixing with the orange flashes from Russian automatic weapons. I lay back beside him and saw that he was beginning to shiver vigorously, so I reached into my pocket for Fyodor's hip-flask. I unscrewed the lid and offered him a swig. I held it over his open mouth and poured a measure of schnapps down his throat. This quelled his shaking for now, so I then took a swig and we both returned to watching the fire fight above our heads and below the star-pocked canopy. I couldn't have let him just die out here alone. I did selfishly wonder if anyone else would have done the same for me, then I realised that Hauser would have without any hesitation. I didn't know or care how I was going to get out of this trench, it didn't matter. Hauser began to breathe heavily next to me and then he tried to speak and instead blood began to pour from his mouth and I knew that it wouldn't be long in coming.

Some muted constellation I couldn't name appeared above my head between the intermittent bands of snow flurries and beyond reach of the madness being played out here below. Why should the elements think to draw breath and wait for our paltry efforts to kill one another to cease? The rules don't apply to nature. The night canopy had enough shooting stars of its own to occupy itself with to have recourse to be concerned with our petty earthbound squabbles. Nature will in due course break down our dead flesh, bleach our bones and fertilize the soil until disturbed by the plough or the excavator on some distant date that we will not witness. Nature's elements were slowly extracting our very essence from where we lay. The plummeting temperatures were leaching at the heat from within our core. If I stayed here too much longer I would succumb to hypothermia and drift into a fatal slumber forming one of the myriad misshapen human sculptures who, although unmarked, make brittle shapes that terrify unseasoned conscripts when stumbled upon. Obergefreiter Hauser didn't die alone. Before he did pass on he asked me to take his army pay book that still bore my handwriting from the interrogation back in Belgorod. Inside he had a picture of his wife and son, Irmgard and Lothar Hauser. I held it up to his face as his breathing laboured and the death-rattle began to take hold. It was enough for him to see their image for a final moment and his last breath hung in the night air and he was gone from me. I lay beside him for a little while longer, clutching his pay book and photograph. Then I felt drowsy, the cold air was beginning to sap at me, lull me into that false sleep that you cannot ever wake from. I took another swig from the hip-flask and revived myself. I could hear muffled calls from the ruins I had previously been hiding in.

'Mensche, can you hear me? Mensche, are you wounded? Mensche, answer me,' it was Oberleutnant Werner.

He had gathered up my rifle and my knapsack and was poised to give me covering fire when I was ready to leave the crater. I closed Obergefreiter Hauser's eyes for the last time and took his Mauser pistol before scrambling up the loose shingle of the crater. There was an interval between the firing that had now lasted seven minutes. I wasn't sure just how long I had been lying there beside his body but it was long enough to convince the Russians that I might have succumbed as well. I scanned each ruined building for any tracer fire and found none. Some were reloading, some were applying bandages, some were changing places with fresh reserves. None were firing in my direction at present.

'Mensche, now's your time,' whispered the Oberleutnant just audibly enough for me to hear.

There was no moon but plenty of starlight to both distract and attract attention to my actions. Fresh snow had hidden the footprints I had previously made and I now had no idea from which direction I had originally come.

'Over here Mensche...' is all I could make out coming from the abandoned worker's apartment blocks. The Oberleutnant had gauged it safe enough for him to keep whispering to me. I crawled flat on my stomach over the lip of the crater and was now at my most vulnerable but luckily some clouds had dulled the glow from the unknown constellation above. His muffled voice crucially guided me across the vulnerable terrain until at last I was able to raise myself and flee into the malty blackness of the ruined buildings.

'I'm sure you did what you could, Mensche. You were with him when it mattered. We couldn't very well leave you behind as none of us except you have been in this district before.'

I caught my breath as the Oberleutnant patted me on the back in consolation for what I had just gone through. Before long a fresh covering of snow would obscure Obergefreiter Hauser and placate his toughness with an altogether different winter coat that he would never be able to shrug off. I gave his pay book to the Oberleutnant. If we survived this then he would surely want to write to Hauser's people and let them know he died urging his men forward. I picked up my rifle and placed his Mauser into my knapsack and made my way to the head of our column. We couldn't afford to use torches to light our way through the mangled spaces, so progress was onerously slow before reaching the path that I had seen the Soviets use as an artery into the smouldering city. It was a symbol of just how confident the enemy was in our hopeless situation that they hadn't bothered to post sentries along this important route. It was no less nerve-racking to tread through the rubble and debris with the knowledge that at any given moment we would be sitting ducks to accurate rifle fire from any of the surrounding buildings. I decided to stagger our approach and took half the column ahead while the Oberleutnant waited for my signal to follow.

Each step led us away from the centre of the cauldron and out into the immolated suburbs where the ruined buildings began to thin out and were constructed of wood as apposed to concrete. Snow had been permitted to drift here smothering the desolation wreaked previously from the fire-storms. Snow piled so high that it met and distorted the horizon. I wondered where all the civilians were? Had they gathered their things with enough time to avoid the bombings? I doubted it. Were we now trampling on their graves? This morbidity was gnawing at me, leading to confusion through tiredness. We urgently needed a place to re-group and rest up in as the wind had begun to gather in strength, making the snow flurries blisteringly painful to try and walk through. I could see a torn up railway line on a raised embankment and decided to try and follow it using the reverse slope as shelter from the biting wind and to give us cover from the prying eyes of our enemy, still lurking within the debris of the ruined city. Soon we approached the remnants of a marshalling yard, which must have been targeted early in the Luftwaffe attacks. Some of the outbuildings were just about habitable and the Oberleutnant had read my mind and gave orders for us to seek shelter there for the remainder of the snow-storm. The manager's office still had a roof and more importantly a stove that looked functional. We barricaded the broken windows and broke up wood from the floorboards to light a fire in the stove. Soon it glowed and we all congregated as close as possible to the heat. Outside the storm hid our actions, dissipating the smoke from our stove as soon as it appeared, giving us a respite and a cloak of invisibility for a few hours at least and allowing the men to rest.

13

1987

'You were snoring loudly for quite a while Sergei which is a good sign I suppose. That knock on the head won't need stitches after all but it has caused a mild concussion. It gave us some time to make you more comfortable. Liam has gone in to work but don't worry you haven't hurt his feelings by not saying goodbye. You will see him again soon enough. We have some unfinished business, you and I. I have leave due to me and I have decided to take a few days off to help you convalesce. I know you think I'm all heart. But there is method in this too as I want you to help me find out what befell my family.'

'Why should I help you? I came here to harm you, not help you.'

'You came here inebriated, do you still intend to shoot me now?'

'I…don't know. Maybe. Where is my pistol?'

'Liam has it hidden safe somewhere. Don't make jokes when you are in no position to.'

'I'm in no position to do anything else, you saw to that when you smashed that vase over my head.'

'Forgive me for overreacting when I arrived home to find you pointing a pistol at Liam. Shall I put it down to high spirits?'

'Okay so I was careless to get drunk in the first place and then brandish my pistol in your friend's face, but I wasn't intending to use it, I swear to you.'

'I'm still trying to work out just why you are here in the first place and after all this time did you go to such lengths to seek me out? I am no threat to you, we don't even live in the same country. I was forced out long ago, they dressed it up as repatriation but I was an embarrassment, the last of my kind from Strekerau, the model village on the Volga that Stalin tore to pieces. Is it because we both don't fit in? As far as I can gather you hold a grudging resentment against your employers for how you were treated during the war. I may speak the language fluently but I know that my presence here in West Germany is more tolerated than welcomed. It was very hard for me to get a foothold in this new country after so many lost years in the Begavat gulag. The stigma of being some kind of half-breed German. Just as everyone else is getting back on their own two feet, I hobble into Munich with the look and pallor of a plague victim. Have you had to beg or heat up stolen dog food to eat from the tin? And yet you seem to resent me all the same. How can you resent what you don't know or think to understand?'

'I just did. It used to be so black and white. You knew your enemy back then. You committed treason by taking up arms with the invaders. You betrayed the place of your birth. Your kind, the minorities, the troublemakers intent on destroying the system from within.'

'My kind wanted nothing of the sort from your system but paid our taxes all the same. We shared our crops and ploughed everything back into the collective. We offered no threat to the state and there was no organised revolt following the German invasion. Comrade Stalin just used the German attack as an excuse to take all the rich and fertile land we held and drive off a million ethnic Germans into the gulags to be worked to death in Siberia. We were never the troublemakers or the agitators, we were just different. Being different doesn't sit well with totalitarianism does it? Being critical, intellectual, being Jewish or Muslim or even homosexual, just didn't fit the party mould did it? You hated me because I was a Russian dressed in German uniform. You may not want to hear it but I had no other choice than to seek out the Germans. My own father set me on this course because he knew if I stayed with my family then only death lay in wait for me further down the rail tracks. I saw what the NKVD did to my home. It was wiped clean off the map, as if it never existed.'

'You joined up with the invaders. You committed treason.'

'You are as cracked and played out as any of my old vinyl records. I paid my debt to mother Russia a long time ago, Sergei. I was among the one hundred and seventy thousand axis troops captured alive within the cauldron at Stalingrad. I am one of only five thousand survivors released by the Soviets in 1953. An appalling statistic that even you must acknowledge.'

Sergei shrugged but he knew that by the end of January 1943 the Sixth German Army had ceased to be a threat as a fighting force. It was a bedraggled assortment of frozen men in foxholes and cellars clinging on to life by a thread. Ammunition had all but run out and supplies from the Luftwaffe had trickled down to nothing as the airfields had been overrun. The outside world had read our own obituary and left the grave side long since and we were now just ghosts going through the motions, slipping down the gears to malnutrition, illness and death. This universe of cold smothered lives and emotions and a fresh blanket of snow covered our crimes and misdemeanours. We were matchstick figures bathed in white light, moving targets shuffling through over rubble with no other thought than that of something to eat. Always the preoccupation of something to eat until you cried with the memory of what real food tasted like. Only it was too cold even to do that and your tears froze to your face before they had a chance to fall.

'My dwindling unit opted to make a break for it before it was too late to try and ultimately that's when I ran into you again, Sergei. Who else but you and your gangster penal division would entertain the idea of attacking in a snow storm?'

'I searched for you among the dead German wretches I came across. I lost count of how many were stacked like fence posts on top of one another, shoring up the snow banks by the side of the road. Always the same forlorn expression, they probably froze while crying for their mummy and too cold to even piss themselves. They sent boys to do a man's job. Is that all you had left in reserve? Farm boys? It was becoming very one-sided,' replied Sergei.

'All the men had fallen earlier. The brave ones had given their lives for us and for nothing. I can see that clearly now. We were duped, then betrayed, so my comrades struck out and then that's when I came across you again, wasn't it? You had still something to prove and your belief that you had to get revenge on me helped spur you on. Thoughts of revenge kept you alive Sergei, kept you warm, didn't they?

'You had stylized yourself as the Volga sniper, I had firsthand experience of you, so it was personal.'

'It was pure propaganda, I didn't invent the term. I started out as a mascot for my division and then when there was no more division I was singled out as a marksman who just happened to be from the Volga.'

'Well it backfired on you, Mensche. It made you a target to me and gave me plenty of motivation. I should have killed you when I had the chance instead of letting that Mongol Commissar take you as a trophy.'

'He intervened when he saw that you were paying me more than enough attention with your rifle butt, you cracked my jaw with it, smashed the bones of my fingers with it and he could see that you intended to stove my head in even though I was unarmed.'

'I smashed your fingers on both hands so that you might not ever take pot-shots at Russian soldiers again, Mensche.'

1943

Sergei's penal battalion had come across our hiding-place purely by chance in the morning after the snowstorm on the outskirts of Stalingrad. We didn't know it but we were still fifteen kilometres away from Manstein's panzers and had no realistic hope of ever reaching them on foot in the prevailing weather conditions. Sergei and his men had been sweeping the area for stragglers, deserters and pockets of resistance. Violence ensued in the confusion caused over wrongly answered passwords being exchanged between both sides in the blindness of the blizzard. By mid morning the depot at the marshalling yard where we had sought shelter was now surrounded. The Oberleutnant had deployed his men as best he could, they had plenty of cover but were running dangerously low in ammunition. The manager's office and the surrounding outbuildings were now being perforated by small arms and mortar shells sending splinters wildly into the air and causing severe cuts and grazes. I was only able to fire back intermittently through the broken windows with the Mauser pistol as vantage points to stretch out with a rifle were hard to come by. The casualties began to mount up on the floor around the stove, their moans went unheeded and soon they slumped back on one another to become unwitting embrasures for the living to hide behind and reload. I counted only six able-bodied men including myself and the Oberleutnant cowering behind the wall of our own dead. When the mortar barrage suddenly stopped we braced ourselves for what we knew would come next. Their charge, when it came, had a heathen quality about it. A shrill cry went up, breaking the insulated silence as they effortlessly traversed over the drifts in lattice-framed snowshoes. These were then expertly extricated once they had reached our location. Their cry was so psychologically debilitating that it should be adequately covered in the military textbooks. It was loud and primal and the six of us left braced ourselves behind the human rampart of our fallen comrades.

Sergei had been one of the first to enter the manager's office through a hail of bullets where the door had disintegrated. He was a brave bastard, it must be said, he sprayed his tommy-gun with one hand and threw a grenade in with the other before being felled by one of the defenders alongside me. Oberleutnant Werner followed the flight of the grenade and selflessly flung himself over to where it landed and thus took the full impact of the blast and was a crumpled mess in the corner as his blood sprayed out and over us. There was no time to dwell on his characteristic sacrifice or wipe his blood from my face. Just begin the grim trade of hand-to-hand fighting on the floor, grabbing, stabbing at anything to try and kill your opponent. Sergei was wounded in the thigh but the lividity of his injury was matched by his virulent hatred on recognizing me. He singled me out even though the flue from the stove pipe was broken and smoke began to fill up the room. My pistol jammed as he charged me, I was pointing it directly at him as he jumped me, I cleaved him with it gashing his forehead open, but he felt nothing. He just kept on until our eyes met the sniper rifle lying on the floor and he was first to grab it and began pummelling me with it. One of my comrades stabbed him in the calf muscle and that was the last thing I remembered.

Sergei would no doubt have finished me off but for the Mongol Commissar who prevented him from caving in my head. He had witnessed enough barbarism and could see that I was already very close to joining the fallen. Sergei protested that I was the Volga sniper and as such had to be punished, whereupon the Mongol Commissar said that if I was, then I would be of more value alive than dead. I slumped back onto the bodies of my brave friends, while they talked over me, forgetting momentarily that I understood their every word. I was the last of my division, I lay amongst them for a little while longer until the stove smoke and cordite cleared and the light from the snowscape outside was once again permitted to permeate through the carnage. They had died well. They had died for nothing but they had died bravely. They weren't to be lined up and humiliated, paraded through the streets of Moscow as a lesson to others. No, they had fallen with their weapons in their hands, far from home and for nothing other than for each other.

Thirty days later, Paulus was confirmed as a Field Marshal over the telephone by Hitler. This was an ever so cynical attempt to entreat Paulus not to give in. No Field Marshal in German service had ever surrendered whilst in the field. Paulus, weakened by dysentery and crippled by self-doubt in his own abilities from the onset, capitulated and surrendered the remnants of the once mighty Sixth army. They had held one fist of the Russian host in check in the city since the preceding August, they had been bled white by forces beyond their control. They had been abandoned and had even heard their own epitaph being read over the wireless back in Berlin by the grossly overweight Herman Goering. He compared the struggle of the Sixth army to that of the last stand by the Spartans at Thermopylae. The German Generals and leading staff officers who were thought to be compliant now automatically rose to the top of the food chain in Soviet captivity as the Russians still recognised hierarchy, a legacy from the days of serfdom. The enlisted men fared somewhat worse and many were to die in the forced marches into captivity. The ragged band of survivors who crawled out from the cellars and sewers of the fractured city were unrecognisable from the sure-footed grenadiers who had marched so confidently to the sound of gunfire just six months earlier.

How different was my fate to be and and perhaps it would have been better if I had joined my fallen comrades. While others died of neglect and calorific starvation, I was hospitalized, my wounds were bandaged and I was given half-rations. I was to be kept alive as a reminder of just how close the enemy had come to crippling Soviet morale from within. I was to be held up for the world to see an example of how benevolent the the Russians were, even to their sworn enemies. I made for excellent propaganda. Their newsreels used up acres of film on how the Volga sniper was now out of commission, out of harm behind the front. It didn't last of course, the pace of the war was picking up all the time and soon new fronts were opening up, new tales of Soviet mastery would soon overshadow the captivity of a teenage sniper from the Volga delta. Sergei didn't forget me though. He recovered from his wounds and whilst still on sick-leave he did seek me out at the Begavat gulag where I languished in the infirmary. He rounded on the medics for what he took as being convivial with me, reminding them of just how many of their comrades I had killed with my sniper rifle. I was to be shown no leniency just because I had the appearance of a vulnerable teenager who had misguidedly joined forces with the Germans. He wasn't about to bury the past any time soon even though he had taken his pound of my own flesh.

At length I was deemed fit enough to resume light tasks of labour with other German prisoners in the construction of the Syr Darya dam. I was given remedial repetitive chores until the bones in my hands began to knit together once more. They would always be staved in appearance and marbled with the after-effects of severe frostbite making them vulnerable to the early onset of arthritis. It was an ironic legacy that those Germans who survived the dysentery, the malnutrition, the severe weather conditions and the sheer horror of such confinement, actually managed to help construct some of the most outstanding building projects within the Soviet Union. While the war raged all around, these German work units were engaged in raising housing developments that were to become the envy of ordinary Russians who knew all too well the fallibility and corruption that went on within the Soviet building model. The reputation of craftsmanship and the high standards of competency among the German labourers was growing and widespread, as were the waiting lists among ordinary citizens for German-built apartment blocks which could be anything up to two years.

This information fell as pearls before swine in the eyes of his former tormentor. How belittling it must be for Sergei, his crumpled form lying prostrate on Andreas's living room sofa, years away from having any influence over his own existence. Andreas still had a use for him though and for that reason he would persist with getting him back to health. He must have fallen asleep again while he recounted his gulag experiences after managing to stay awake right up to the bit where he heard how he captured Andreas. How typically selfish of him to want to hear about himself as observed from his enemies viewpoint and then fall into slumber when his back was turned, leaving Andreas to talk with himself without knowing it.

The two protagonists now faced each other across the floor of Andreas's apartment after a gap of forty-five years. Each had their own way of interpreting and remembering it. Each had undiminished memories of what had taken place and of the resulting fallout which influenced the intervening years from which they were both still recovering. Andreas only had to look down at his brittle fingers to see the damage Sergei had inflicted on him in the struggle back then. Every time he struck a piano key the rheumatoid arthritis curtailed his playing and his enjoyment. Now here he was in his own place of safety confronting the man who had striven to ruin his life and most likely had something to do with the fate of his own family. Sergei was on the winning side after all, but that was never enough for him. He wore a haunted malevolence which was never far from the surface and which had never been disarmed by love. It therefore went unchecked, given free licence by the department he operated in to mete out punishment to those considered undesirable. He hadn't set out to be this way and circumstances hadn't conspired against him, like they had against Andreas. But unlike Andreas, he was a hollow man, lacking goodness or empathy. Was it hopeless then for Andreas even to try and converse with him?

It suddenly struck Andreas that Sergei had served a kind of life sentence too. His role at the ministry had desensitized him at safe distance from the feelings of the faceless people whose lives he had interfered with. He had low self-esteem and believed that whatever he did was not appreciated or sufficiently rewarded, which stoked his own bitterness, making him singularly callous. War had crafted him, embittered him, marked him as suitable for recruitment to the Ministry of Internal Affairs. But then maybe he was just born to be a monster like so many others. He would be nothing without the role, he lived it, he had no other talent or reason to engage with society, other than being the furtive apparatchik. This was the material Andreas now had to try and work with, steeped in a longevity of hate towards him and the minority he represented in Sergei's eyes. Did he really come here to rub Andreas out? Was he just drunk the other night or was it something deeper? Could he not live with the fact that someone knew the unwritten truth about what happened to his people? The irony is that Andreas had kept silent about the matter for the last forty-five years until Liam showed up. Talking to him had helped him finally come to terms with the loss and the finality of it all. Liam had disarmed his own bitterness to the extent he felt no malice towards Sergei, just pity and right now he had the high ground which is everything in a personal duel.

'I trust you slept well, Sergei.'

'Well enough to forget I was here when I woke,' he answered.

'Good, we both know what it means to get proper rest as opposed to stolen respites.'

'How long was I sleeping for?'

'You fell asleep during our last conversation over four hours ago.'

Sergei motioned to try and sit up and succeeded in managing a leaning position that was a compromise to himself. Andreas offered him coffee and Sergei took a steaming cup and nursed it with his free hand while still leaning with the other.

He stared impassively at every feature in the room until he settled his gaze on some point of his own reference on the far wall. His head was no longer pounding and Andreas had taken away the bandage to let some air at the wound on his head. He appeared to like the flavour as he took regular sips whilst still taking in every aspect of Andreas's dwelling.

'So this is what you have to show for all those years?' Sergei chortled.

'This place is really not that dissimilar to the apartment I used to live in back in Nevsky Prospect. It's German prisoner built by the way!' He added.

'Maybe you were listening to me after all. I thought you dozed off after the highlights that included you.'

'Really, Mensche? You might be boring but not enough to drive even me to fall asleep. I caught most of your little testimony, how you escaped my clutches and fell back in with your German friends at the Begavat camp. That place was a holiday camp compared with some of the places I could have sent you to if I had any say in the matter. But it was beyond my control back then before I had even joined the Ministry. You were seen as some kind of trophy prisoner and given special status, better rations and your compatriots latched onto you as they realised that they stood a better chance of survival around you. The west has turned you soft, Mensche. I much prefer the Volga version, for at least he was a worthy opponent.'

'Perhaps time has mellowed me. Time has done its work and allowed me to distance myself from what happened back then but time has weathered me too. Weathered, not softened. I can be objective about the past, which hasn't been easy. You wallow in the past Sergei, you soak it up believing that we are just as we were when we last met. You don't account for the intervening years and the bumps and scrapes that influence us, mould us, leaving tyre marks along the road we follow to the present. That road led you here. It's probably the most unwittingly constructive thing you have done since the war's end. You can mock and be as taciturn as you want but I don't think that the underlying reason you sought me out was so that you could kill me. Is it that you are seeking a way out? If not, then how many unplanned excursions do you normally make into the free west on a yearly basis and at great risk? You got intoxicated to numb any doubt so that you could see it through but you must have been planning this move for some time? Where do I fit in with this venture? What you need is a safe house and a new identity, both of which I can't help you with.'

'You presume to know the answers even as you are still asking me the questions Mensche. You are cocooned in a smug belief of just how right you are, aided and abetted no doubt by the rich collection of tomes in this room that have only bolstered your opinions. You have completed your own education here I don't doubt. This is your den where you recharge and make sense of the world from a safe vantage point. You probably thought that way up until the moment I knocked on your door. Events have a terrible knack of catching up with people throughout history and I would vouch that most of these books were written years after the actual facts and as such are cloudy in their accuracy and truthfulness. But in your naïvety you hold onto their every word as if they were forged in the fires of what they are trying to recount. Your views are hardened by loss and that has stifled your judgement. Even though I don't empathize, I can understand how you have allowed personal events to impair your outlook and sway your judgement. We are both diametrically poles apart, but we are both survivors too. You have painted me into a darkly nefarious corner and ironically you are right to because I am in one. You pull out all the stops to survive, we both learnt that in Russia, so you know I am here for a reason but you have come to the wrong conclusion. I take it that you don't follow events that closely in the Soviet Union? I know you wouldn't recognise it, not that you would ever have time for it given what happened to your family. I hardly recognise it myself today and I have to admit that it caught me completely off guard. Maybe some of what you said about me being insulated by the past has a ring of truth about it. I am from your past, just as you are part of mine and I wouldn't be here without due cause. Of course it is out of selfishness, every action I take is borne out of my innate survival instinct. I need to elaborate it better for you.

The rate of change being meted out by the new regime at the head of the Politburo is out of control. In a nod to the west, this perestroika is being heralded as the road map to a new all inclusive Soviet Union. The old ways and the symbols of the old ways, of which I most definitely am one, are under the utmost scrutiny. Gorbachev wants plaudits, he wants to help distance himself from the Stalinist legacy by empowering the many nationalities that go to make up the Soviet Union. I'm not surprised personally, given that he is half Ukrainian, but these reforms are beginning to get a head of steam and I want an insurance policy, should I need one. I have read the tea leaves so to speak and I know that the Volga German community is being given special attention because of its obvious connections with the greatest economic powerhouse in western Europe.'

'So that's what it is. You want to hide your dirty washing, better still you want me to launder it for you! This really is rich coming from you,' cried Andreas.

'I have a bargaining chip. You want to know the fate of your own family and I want a share in the riches that will no doubt flow from your people's reinstatement to the confiscated lands along the river Volga. I am sure to be ousted from the Ministry as part of its face-saving operation. They will no doubt try and palm me off with a modest pension, whatever it is they offer will be a pittance for all the dirty jobs I have carried out for them over the years. I can see it coming and then I remembered that I have a further ace in the hole. I have safely under lock and key the title deeds of property in that ghost town that you were brought up in. I found them in your knapsack when I took your sniper rifle as a prize back in Stalingrad. I found rubles too which I spent, of course. The deeds I once or twice came very close to wiping my bum with as they were useless to me. But I kept them as officious people tend to do and now in this new political climate I have come to help you achieve your rightful inheritance.'

'If only it were true. If even some of this is true, then nothing could stop me exposing you for what you are, which is a vile miscreant who would sell his grandmother for a bag of rubles.'

'No doubt if I knew who she ever was, then that would be true. But don't forget my other insurance policy. I know what befell your family and you can't afford to let me disappear into captivity without knowing the truth.'

14

1943

I spent my seventeenth birthday kneeling on the floor of a guards wagon coupled to a goods train, my face pressed against an open slat to enable me to breathe. We were heading for an undisclosed location further east than could be imagined. Further east than had ever previously been pointed out by my tutors on any of the wall maps back in my classroom in Strekerau. My homeland had been insular in its naïvety as we had never been taught about the vastness of Russia. Ours was an inward looking and fully autonomous region, given concessions and special privileges that had long been upheld by the Tzars and the Communists. We had been insulated from the purges and pogroms that had been committed outside our territory. We had been spared because we had been successful, diligent and resourceful. My community preferred to adopt a form of splendid isolation that was to be its own undoing. Events ignore boundaries and offer up opportunities that might not normally arise in peacetime. Events forced my family to choose sides, leading me to take up arms with an invader whose language I shared even if their politics were abhorrent to me. A chain of events had now delivered me into purgatory within this rapid transit charnel-house whose weak and dying cargo we continually stacked like fence posts along the length of the carriage. There was not enough space for sentiment, just the necessity to avoid contamination and where practicable they could perhaps act as draught excluders so that the dead might insulate the living.

My seventeenth birthday, languishing among a base congregation of foul depravity, who stooped just beyond your face to defecate. A band of disparate strangers who would unhesitatingly prize out a gold filling in your mouth while you slept if they could in exchange for food. You clung to your great coat for fear that it might be torn from you should they sense any sign that your body might be giving in to the elements. All vestiges of military protocol had broken down in here. The officers were either dead or corralled in another carriage, leaving a new hierarchy based on predatory strength and brutal tenacity. Maybe it was my age that was in my favour in such a setting. My constitution was strong and I began to prove my worth to the others on each occasion the train came to a halt, which was every four hours. On reaching one of these scheduled stops I would fight my way to the head of the queue so as to be allowed down to forage for firewood to feed the ravenous stove in the middle of the carriage. I would often stray over to where some guards were smoking and gossiping. They would cajole and mock me in Russian, little knowing that I understood their every word. They would unwittingly divulge nuggets of information regarding the progress of the war or the proximity of some village that might provide physical comfort for them.

We had previously halted on the outskirts of Astrakhan, whose fertile plains swept down to the Caspian Sea. Astrakhan was on the very periphery of my collective knowledge. With its passing, the last recognizable point in my small universe gave in to darkness and uncharted continents. We skirted around the vast body of fresh water contained within the Caspian Sea in pitch darkness with no reflection given from its surface. I could make out lights every so often from what must have been fishermen's hovels along the shore line. I was parched from the prospect of so much fresh water within touching distance of our train. We curved around its northernmost tip, ignorant of any landmarks as the territory slowly opened up to swallow us whole.

Every railway sleeper which groaned beneath the weight of our carriage took me farther away from the landscape of my memory. My boyhood had been stolen along with my freedom but until now I could still recognize places that had formed the basis of my character. We had travelled so far that the local Communist Party officials had confidently chosen not to hide the signposts that identified the towns and villages we came across. We were out of range of any long-distance German bomber and as far as I could tell there was nothing of any strategic importance along the route to arouse their interest. With each mile, the arrogant hubris of my former employer became more evident. How could the German 6th Army have ever hoped to conquer this amount of territory? The dregs of that army now slouched around me, once proud soldiers reduced to peasantry two thousand miles from Hamburg, Bremen, Dortmund, Kiel, Mannheim, Passau, Lech, Andechs, Bad Tolz, Bayreuth, Garmisch, Bonn, Koln and Berlin. The map just got bigger and the new names didn't roll off the tongue quite so easily. Atyrau, Oktyabrsk, Emba, Shalkar, Aralsk, Baikonuv, Kyzlorda, Turkestan, Bugun, Shymkent, Chirchik, Tashkent and Begavat. We travelled through two regions to get to our gulag. Kazakhstan and Uzbekistan, we were closer geographically to Tehran and Beijing than to Strekerau or Moscow. The terrain sapped at the eyes when viewed from the opening in the guards wagon. This country had been created by nature to overawe the senses inexorably, it undulated gradually, was barren, then fertile, arid, then lush. It was alien and daunting and endless. Perhaps it was with this intent that our captors sought to nullify our spirits and take away the prospect of escape and survival. Perhaps I gave them too much credit for intending this. The mind has free reign to speculate, coming up with unanswered scenarios in this vast expanse of unknown territory. Reason goes errant when confined to a festering guards wagon for days on end. Reason flies away and hope takes its place. Hope is the beacon, the lighthouse, the respite, the spark that keeps your spirit alive. They can't possibly steal that from you too… can they?

Ullman was a scrounger, he always seemed to have a morsel of black rye bread to eat and the strength to defend himself when he bartered food for cigarettes and clothing. I gravitated into his service because he knew how to handle himself in the way that Hauser had done. He was an NCO, a signalman and capable of drawing maps from memory. So far he had outlined our journey according to the major rivers we had crossed or the outskirts of villages we had passed. He diligently chalked up a name I fed him onto the ever increasing map of the Soviet Union stretching down one side of the guards carriage. The map became an obsession with me, a distraction from the harrowing circumstances I now found myself part of. So it was for any other survivor, they could see just how far they had come from Germany and they could ruminate on the lives they probably had left behind forever.

'Pass me the chalk kid, what was the name of that last village we came through?'

'Tashkent,' I answered.

'Congratulations. I believe that we have extended the Reich immeasurably by taking this new territory peaceably and with the full cooperation of the Soviet authorities. There will be plaudits and medals cast in diamonds on our safe return to Berlin, I have no doubt.'

Ullman had turned everything on its head and suggested that we were the first Europeans since Alexander the Great to conquer Kazakhstan. That we had done it with the connivance of the Russians was a bonus as very little blood had been shed. He wasn't quite mad but you could be forgiven for thinking so. What did it matter if the spearhead of Germany had managed to strike into the heart of central Asia, albeit within the confines of a prisoner of war carriage. In his eyes we had advanced the Reich to the foothills of the Himalayas. It was strangely comforting amidst the appalling conditions, to still have the strength to be able to laugh at our precarious predicament. Who says Germans don't have a sense of humour now? A gallows humour took hold of the German army after the victories had begun to dry up, long before our ignominious defeat at Stalingrad.

'Tashkent! How much more exotic can you get? Kneel, young Mensche.'

I knew where this was going so I relented and played along with Ullman's musings. I kneeled before him with my head bowed.

'In the name of the Fuhrer and for services to the greater German nation I have the honour to bestow the title of Emir of Tashkent on Feldwebel Andreas Mensche.'

He touched me on each shoulder with a soup ladle and then asked me to rise like a knight of yore. Those still lucid enough to notice in our immediate vicinity tried to summon a smile but gave up out of hunger and passivity. I knew that my chances of survival grew stronger if I allied myself to this joker who had boundless energy to spare from some quarter. As far as Ullman was concerned this was to be my initiation into his circle. Darwinism encapsulated within the confines of a train carriage, where the strongest really did survive. Some of those around me were already spent from the long march after Stalingrad. I could see it in their eyes, the spark had long since disappeared from their inner vitality. Ullman had rivals to his authority in the early stages of the journey east but he had prevailed through subterfuge and tenacity and many now looked to him for leadership. Humour was important to him, it broke the omnipresent atmosphere of boredom, defeat and drudgery. He used humour to sound people out and if that didn't work he could fall back on his strength. Ullman had the ability to anticipate friction and rivalry before the matter even arose, giving him enough time to come up with a solution that suited him. Like many leaders before and since, he played people off each other, those that sought his favour and contention within his group. I think he knew that I was different from the rest. I was the youngest for a start and I was Russian born, which proved my usefulness as a linguist. He may have observed a steely resolve within my character, an unspoken strength that had got me out of so many scrapes in the past.

There had been three more casualties who had succumbed on the morning we arrived at Begavat. The guards carriage doors were swung open wide for the first time since we had left Stalingrad. The relief we felt was tangible as some began to think that we would never arrive alive at our mystery destination. Fresh air and sunlight now poured in and over this festering rabble of humanity. Those deemed strong enough by the sentries were tasked with lifting out the bodies from the rear of the carriage. I counted twenty and then I stopped counting as it was truly awful to witness. The sentries then ordered us all to get down from the carriage and fall in for inspection. These soldiers were Eurasian in appearance; stocky and weather-beaten, different from the guards back at the front line. They spoke a regional dialect which was beyond me and they almost appeared like tribal horsemen in uniform. The bodies had been piled on top of one another between us and the perimeter of the camp which stretched out along the road in front of us. It struck me that although the prison camp had a series of watch towers, it hadn't resorted to barbed wire fencing but instead was enclosed in a wooden stockade which was palpably climbable. Perhaps it didn't require barbed wire this far from civilisation. Did they seriously not expect anyone to mount an escape attempt? It was the duty of any captive soldier to divert as much attention behind the lines as possible by attempting mass escapes. But here? It was daunting, we had already witnessed the ever changing character of the landscape. The terrain would just swallow you up without help from someone knowledgeable and none of the indigenous people would dare risk all for a German escapee.

Whilst I pondered the poor prospects, a subaltern poured gasoline over the pyre of our dead and set a light to it, which though shocking was sensible given the pestilent vapours and rancid smells that had begun to emanate from it under the influence of the mid morning sun. I looked down the line of the train which snaked for the better part of one hundred metres and counted four more pyres being lit in front of the line of prisoners. A roll call was taken and out of the seventy-five men who had originally been herded into the guards carriage along with me, twenty-five had perished. The subaltern then gestured for us to strip naked and we soon formed a pitiful sight of impoverished manhood, smelling to high heaven. Our clothes were then thrown onto the funeral pyre and then three men in civilian clothing appeared from the direction of the camp, one pushed a wheelbarrow with three tea chests in it and the other two wore backpacks which looked like large water canisters and both held on to a hosepipe attached to a nozzle. They began walking in and around us, spraying liberally with what must have been some kind of disinfectant. I closed my eyes when they reached me as I had witnessed others get stung full in the face by the liquid. Ullman was beside me and didn't flinch as they hosed down his body, he winked at me and whispered that they had better get a move on as he had a dinner date that evening. When I opened my eyes again I could get a better look at the three men and could tell that they were Japanese. It turned out that over half of the camp's two thousand inmates were Japanese prisoners of war. This place was so far east that it had prisoners taken from the campaigns in Manchuria. The Japanese, I soon learnt, were treated differently from the German prisoners. There wasn't the same animosity between the Russians and the Japanese. It was as if their war was a more honourable affair than the bitter struggle to the death that we had grown accustomed to.

One of them lifted the tea chests off the wheelbarrow and proceeded to prize them open with a crowbar. Inside, neatly folded, were assorted pairs of black boiler suits. He gestured for us to come forward and take a pair each, there was a scramble as we exchanged different sizes. Each pair was emblazoned on the back with the words 'Farhadstroy' written large in yellow. Farhadstroy, we were to subsequently learn, was the title of the building firm given the contract to construct the Syr Darya dam which would eventually control the flow of water into the Aral Sea. Farhadstroy took advantage of the ever growing supply of free labour resulting from the swelling number of German prisoners being taken. The remaining tea chests contained boots of different sizes, which the men compared and fought over. Some of us hadn't touched shoe leather since the preceding October when so many pairs had been worn out. We quite forgot where we were such was the distraction of something clean and new. During this forgetfulness a contingent of armed troops had arrived escorting a senior officer and a smartly dressed man in a civilian suit. They watched us barter and bicker like fishwives over the boots and boiler suits until their patience at last ran out. The officer nodded to an enlisted man and he fired a shot into the air instantly grabbing everyone's attention. The officer then took a step forward and waited another moment before speaking.

'There is no need to fight like heathens, we have ensured that there is an adequate amount of clothing to go around. In fact, there is more than enough as we didn't budget for the attritional number of casualties, which,' he consulted the list, 'appears to be twenty-five. No matter, now we have clothed you, we expect something in return.'

The officer was a Colonel, battle-seasoned from what I could tell, as he walked with a limp, a shrapnel wound perhaps. I wondered what he had done to end up spending his recoupment here. He had presence and didn't slouch because of his injury as he walked down our ragged line, noting each one of us individually.

'Is there anyone amongst you who understands Russian?' he asked.

I looked at Ullman and the officer noticed me doing so and walked up to me.

'Perhaps you can understand what I say? It will go better for you if you cooperate from the off. If I find out later that you can translate, then you are finished. Understand?'

I nodded and said in Russian that I understood. He ushered me out of the line of men and stood me beside him. I was close enough to have tried to overpower him and take his side arm but to what end? He told me to translate his words verbatim and not to try and water anything down that he said:

'My name is Colonel Rokkosovsky, your names no longer matter, perhaps they will on some distant date but until hell freezes over, your names won't matter to me. You gave up the right to a name the moment you set foot on Russian soil. You gave up all privileges when you took up arms against the Motherland. You signed up for whatever I will throw your way a long time ago when in your own arrogance you thought that you were going to win this conflict. The notion that you are still able to think for yourself is a common misconception to any new arrival. You are no more in charge of your destiny now than you were before you were born. Your life means nothing so forget everything that came before as you enter the gates behind me. Read the inscription over the gate, take note of the message of welcome from comrade Stalin. The only thing that matters now is how you perform. Time and work are the two things that you have in abundance. You will repay my country for the death and violation you have wreaked. You will do this every day from now on because you made the decision to invade my country. You can ponder on every single decision since until you arrived at this destination. This is your one luxury as the days stretch out like the endless steppe you crossed to get here. Your performance will be monitored and any shirkers will soon fall by the wayside which matters little to me. Every week we are taking more of your countrymen prisoner, replenishing those that we don't have to shoot first because they are fascist fanatics. Learn to work harder than you ever thought possible and you might just survive this. Learn to work as a team and by so doing help increase your performance rate. Learn this fast and then you will begin to make amends for the misery you have poured over so many Russian lives. To my left is the distinguished architect, Joseph Karakis who has been given the task of designing the dam you are to construct. I know that he wishes to say a few words to you.'

I later learned that Joseph Karakis was born in 1902 in the Ukraine, was from humble Jewish stock. He had risen by stealth and talent to become one of Stalin's most proficient architects. He was a strong proponent of the monolithic structures being thrown up within the Soviet Union to dwarf the idealism and the individualistic notions of dissidents and dissenters. I discovered that architecture throughout millennia was a vehicle of expression for tyrants of any flavour and Karakis had thrived under Stalin's patronage. Architecture could overwhelm the individual and so convert the masses to the message the dictator was endeavouring to convey. Architecture and infrastructure such as the lavish Moscow underground railway system belied the oppressive nature of the Soviet regime and was intended as an opulent public backdrop of pure theatre to lift the spirits of the workers as they were shuttled efficiently around the city on their daily grind. Karakis had secured the contract with Farhadstroy by winning a competition with his ambitious design for the Syr Darya dam and we had fallen into his lap as free labour providing the means of realizing his landmark legacy. He now stood beside me and nodded to the Colonel in appreciation before speaking.

'You are to be tasked with one of the signature constructions of this or any other era. We have clothed you which is more than you deserve, we will house you and feed you adequately so that deadlines are met and that your work is completed to the highest standard. You have to prove your worth to us, look around and see that you are just a number here. The work comes first and we will get it out of you. There are no political prisoners here, no dissidents or troublemakers, just you imperious Germans and our Japanese guests. Forget everything you were seduced by in Germany and produce work that you can be proud of. Nothing less than your best work will be tolerated. We will inspect your due diligence and if we suspect any sabotage, you will be shot in front of your co-workers. No debate, no trial, no delay. We expect you to give your best to us in repayment for the devastation you brought in your wake. Let your skills come to the fore and you will reap dividends. We reward loyalty and commitment, when targets are met, rations will improve, this is a project that must be completed on time and under budget. Do this and prove to yourselves that you can still take pride in work that is unpaid and of benefit to your sworn enemy. There is no war out here, ideology pales when confronted by the need to survive. We are beyond your dwindling conflict, the fences at this camp are not designed to confine you, they are designed to remind you that even if you did escape, there is nowhere for you to go. Focus on the work, it will keep you alive that bit longer if you do and we will all be the better for it.'

Karakis didn't wait for any reaction and was soon engulfed by aides and flunkies all too eager for his signature on some draft or requisition as he made his way back to his purpose-built work/accommodation block. We were escorted from the railway siding, across the dust track road and on under the sign with a large political slogan by Stalin that drily welcomed us into the Begavat camp. We were to sleep twenty-four men per hut and we were expected to form two working groups of twelve, a night shift and a day shift, twelve hour shifts and our bunk beds would be shared and so never get cold which led to a lice fest. I was given relatively light work to begin with as my wounds received at the hands of Sergei had yet to fully heal. I was fortunate to be on the same shift as Ullman and it wasn't long before his gifts as a scrounger became apparent.

Any morsel of food was eaten with our hands as we had no utensils and very few pieces of cutlery. Ullman was always on the make and when exercising he had noticed six large wooden spools of rubber insulated aluminium cable earmarked for telegraph communication posts at the dam site but being kept in storage at one end of the camp. Farhadstroy had decided to store raw materials within the prison compound instead of stockpiling it on site or in warehouses near the dam. They supposed, quite naturally, that the raw materials would be safe behind a fence with an armed guard patrolling both day and night. They didn't reckon on Ullman's business acumen. He asked me to accompany him on his daily rambles to the far end of the camp where the spools had been stored. He was forever taking notes, making an inventory of the things he could make money from and he wanted to use me as an interpreter to ingratiate himself to the guards. I was useful teaching him cursory Russian and he was able to barter items that were in very short supply in this region. He took me into his confidence and only I was entrusted with the knowledge of where he cached all his sequestered goods. Two others were his runners, they bribed and supplied the guards who we knew could be persuaded to help us. These two answered to me. I was in charge of the float and I kept Ullman's accounts, if the money was short I knew he trusted me to get it from one or other of the runners. The money always balanced as they could be trusted and the guards knew that they were on to a good thing. The money always balanced as the runners knew only too well what it was like to be on the wrong side of Ullman's temperament.

Within a few short days of arriving he was on the most convivial terms with the guards near the Farhadstroy consignment, playing at cards and losing on purpose. Their drudgery he had alleviated with schnapps and cigarettes. His losses I bankrolled from the endless supply of Russian banknotes sewn into the lining of his long coat which I wore when he gambled. The coat swamped me to begin with, being so heavy with currency and getting lighter every day that he lost. By losing he was able to show them his humour and humility, thus breaking down any residue of animosity that they might have harboured towards Germans. Ullman was no ordinary German, he was efficacious and planned every transaction he did with an end product in mind. That he did so with a modicum of charm was also in his favour. He sweetened future transactions with the guards by losing regularly at cards because he saw an end product. He focused on the Japanese, not as fellow prisoners, but as a market place for him to prosper from. The Japanese were given special privileges that we couldn't ever hope to have. He needed a bargaining chip to begin with to give him leverage and mark him out as someone to be taken seriously.

Soon he had purloined chisels, wood files and fire-bricks and had fashioned a rudimentary brick oven kiln in the crawl space under the floorboards of the latrine attached to our hut. He managed to seal up the bricks with wet clay which hardened as the temperatures rose dramatically when the fire was lit. The vent pipe for the fumes was made of soup tins soldered together and the flue was convincingly hidden in the gap between our hut and the latrine. He now had a working kiln and was thus able to melt down lengths of aluminium cable and turn the molten aluminium into knives, forks, cups and plates using crude clay moulds which could withstand high temperatures. He got so proficient that he was able to hammer on each piece a personalised stamp, a hallmark bearing his moniker and limited edition numbering. Ullman arranged a meeting with the aide de camp to the most senior Japanese officer, this aide just happened to be the boss of the long established Japanese black market within Begavat. His name was Nagia Taramachi. I accompanied Ullman to the guards hut after roll call one morning. I carried one of the tea chests which had previously been used to provide us with uniforms earlier in the month. It now contained samples of the best aluminium tableware that Ullman had been able to smelt. The guards hut had been taken over by a delegation of the Japanese and the Soviet guards who were off duty had absented themselves through bribery. It was quite disconcerting to be among so many healthy looking individuals chatting animatedly in a vociferously foreign language. Nagia was sitting on the most comfortable chair with his back to the door and his muted conversation ceased on seeing us enter. It wasn't until I lowered the tea chest and stood in front of one of his junior officers that I really got a good look at him. What struck me first was that they wore civilian clothing albeit ethnic garb which was clean, laundered even. Taramachi stood and bowed to us, he was heavy lidded and swarthy but not without presence even though he was about five feet in height. Ullman preferred to shake rather than to salute and reached for his hand enthusiastically.

'You must be Herr Oldman the scrounger that everyone is talking about?' he said in heavily accented German.

'It's Ullman sir. May I say your German pronunciation is impeccable.'

'Thank you very much Oldman, my father was once an engineer with BMW and I speak some German having lived in Bavaria when very small. Please to sit with us and perhaps you would like some rice wine?'

'I would love some, thank you.'

A bottle wrapped in cord was produced from somewhere and a measure was poured into a crude wooden tumbler for Ullman.

'My colleague is only seventeen but has enough experience of life to take a measure too.' Another rustic tumbler was produced from God knows where and a drink was poured for me.

'This is where I can be of some use to you if you don't mind me talking out of turn,' Ullman raised his tumbler in unison with myself and we toasted our Japanese hosts, 'I have samples of my wares for you to see and taste from. Perhaps you would care to pour another measure into the aluminium cups I have made and see if it enhances your enjoyment of the Saki.'

Ullman rose and began unpacking the tea chest. He laid out the glittering cups and plates alongside the knives and forks he had so diligently smelted.

He had brought his best work, his apprentice pieces were on show and impressed his hosts. The Japanese black market delegation craned over the desk in the guards room and poured more rice wine into Ullman's aluminium cups before clinking them together in appreciation of his workmanship.

'You won't find better quality this side of the Urals. You have my word on that, if you choose to purchase from me you are guaranteed quality and bespoke items that you can sell in Begavat for a profit.'

'And what do you want from us, Herr Oldman?' Taramachi asked.

'I want fresh produce, something to help put the flesh back on our bones. I want to taste bacon rind, coffee instead of chicory, I want soap and a shaving mirror, I want what you have, what you might take for granted. I want to know just what is going on in the world, I want to talk to a woman and to breathe her in and perhaps even be with her. I want to know that I am still alive and not just existing.'

'Not much then!' Taramachi's circle began laughing until his stare interrupted their servile outbursts. He looked around the room and saw them for the sycophants they had turned into since their incarceration. This confinement had rid them of any individuality and he was heartened by Ullman's frankness.

'If you can provide me with further examples we may be in business Herr Oldman. There is a market I can help you with and I haven't seen work of this quality in this region. If you don't mind I will take this exhibition work as a token of your esteem. Until then let us help you by sharing our good fortune with you. We will put the flesh back on your bones, we will help you and those close to you, but that's all. Your people are here to work for Farhadstroy and I have no sway with Karakis, you have shown remarkable individuality by getting this far, but your fellow soldiers are beyond my help. I can help you to sell your wares and I can make sure you get the best price for them, I can get you fresh produce from the markets in Begavat and I can even get you physical sustenance from the many cooperative womenfolk in the village. That's all I can do. This I will do for you and your young friend here who you must rate highly to place such trust in. What does he want?'

The barrack room closed in on me as all eyes turned in my direction. His question hung in the air for what seemed an eternity and even though Taramachi had been incarcerated for close to three and a half years, his authority had been undiminished and he expected a response from me.

'I want to know what became of my family, somehow I know that they are still alive, I just know that they are.'

'Then maybe we can help you find out something to put your mind at rest.'

It was tenuous but it was the first time assistance had been offered from people on the inside who had influence over the Soviet authorities.

Taramachi told me to give as much background as I could to his next in command and they would take it from there.

15

1987

Political events began to gather speed and prove Sergei's assumptions correct. History was unfolding dramatically whilst Andreas and Sergei watched television over the following days. Erich Honecker, the German communist leader of the DDR, the portion of Germany ceded to the Soviets as a buffer state in 1945, was paying a visit to the West German capital in Bonn. It wasn't given the trimmings of a state visit as West Germany had never formally recognised East Germany's sovereignty. It was everything else but in name, the communist head of a neighbouring country was being invited to speak to the West German parliament. This was outwardly viewed as a thaw in the almost negligible relations between the two countries since the construction of the Berlin wall in 1961. For Honecker who was just turning seventy-five, it was a signature moment; the pinnacle of his career and it helped usher in fresh negotiations as to reparations and repatriations as well as the measures to deal with the seismic convolutions of so many displaced people and broken families within the two states. Political largesse was at work behind the scenes, West Germany's economy had recovered magnificently in the post-war years, much to the chagrin of her eastern cousin and subsequently had an economic clout that left Honecker and his idealistic cronies moribund, languishing in its wake. To his credit Honecker realised that the severed entity of East Germany would also flourish in the rays that overspilled from her industrious neighbour. He wasn't one to let political dogma cloud his judgement and perhaps along the way it would allow him a more fitting epitaph as opposed to a footnote in European history.

'What did I tell you Mensche, the carpet has been lifted from beneath our own feet and we didn't even notice.'

'I for one didn't see this coming Sergei, expectations go out the window along with any dreams you might have once had. Imprisonment saw to that.'

'Time has moved on, Mensche. Your memories are outdated, they don't fit you anymore, I saw the writing on the wall a long time ago. I had to react first before I was jettisoned with all the dead wood. I embraced this so-called perestroika in the only way I know how, out of self-interest, out of necessity, or else it would have made a statistic out of me.'

'Statistics always did matter to you Sergei. People were just counters on a board-game to you.'

'If I hadn't been that way I wouldn't have made it this far. I know that I have outlived my usefulness, I know that I'm a throwback in their young eyes. But I'm still here aren't I?'

Andreas thought it wiser not to continue with this line of verbal jousting and decided to use a different tack on Sergei.

'You are a survivor Sergei. You read the wind before it changed and now you want to cash in and that could even benefit me. It makes you wonder what we were ever loyal to all this time, doesn't it?'

'I put myself before the ghost of a political ideal any day, Mensche. You are haunted by what happened to your family and that is to my benefit as I can reconcile you with what in actual fact did befall them to my own financial advantage. A transaction if you like, your peace of mind for my secure retirement.'

The television coverage infilled the lull in their conversation as each of them considered their next move. Andreas hadn't watched so much TV until Sergei's arrival, he despised it ordinarily and couldn't remember what necessity had brought him to possess one. It was black and white and had valves which heated up the wings and entrails of dead flies and any other insects unfortunate enough to disappear down the ventilation grilles. They both knew that they were watching a new era unfold, albeit it tentatively, grudgingly and slowly.

'Do you think you will be strong enough to leave soon?' asked Andreas.

'You don't have to dance around the subject with me Mensche. I will be out of your hair shortly and it will be to our mutual benefit.'

'I am anxious for you to get the information I need about my family, that's all.'

'I know and don't think I'm not grateful for your hospitality. It didn't get off to the best of starts but I think we understand one another better now.'

Sergei was able to sit up unaided and capable of moving freely within the apartment. Presently Liam returned from a shift at the hotel and Sergei greeted him as he came in through the door, 'So Irishman, how was your day? Did you cap anyone's ass with my starting pistol yet?'

'Christ are you still here? With that gob on ye! I have your pistol under safe keeping in my locker at work, comrade fuck!'

Sergei mused at Liam's cheek and laughed openly calming any atmosphere between the two men.

'You have a good bodyguard here Mensche, he's loyal to you and that's hard to find these days.'

'He's a tenant and a workmate, he's a friend as well and he could break you in two Sergei if I told him to,' retorted Andreas.

'Not to worry. What's on the menu tonight boys? More of the same vitriol and spite?' asked Liam.

'I think we have ironed out our differences both comrade Ivanov and I. He is going to furnish me with information as to what befell my family and I in return will give him entitlement to a parcel of land near Strekerau with the title deeds in my name, currently in his possession.'

'So he does okay out of all this, not bad comrade fuck! Well for some, innit?'

'You are still bitter with me about the other night Liam, I shouldn't have brandished my pistol in your face, I was drunk and I regret doing that. But you have landed on your feet too, Irishman. Andreas is soon to be reinstated, a wealthy landowner again and he will need your help to cultivate the land he will inherit.'

'That remains to be seen Sergei, when last I saw Strekerau it was a barren tinderbox where every building had been razed to the ground.'

'It didn't take but a few seasons to regenerate its soil. The tenants who toil there now will soon be paying their tithes to you as their landlord once more.'

'What a rosy picture you paint Sergei, do you really think that these existing tenants will take lightly to my reinstatement? They will resent my intrusion. I can't believe I'm even contemplating the prospect of this happening.'

'It will happen Mensche because opinion has changed in the Soviet Union. They need outside help and the Volga German resettlement is an issue that holds sway when it comes to doing business with West Germany. The Soviet Union is a house of cards settling on a foundation of former glories and pure bravado as I have witnessed from within. It will cave in one day soon and you shall inherit from its passing.'

Liam then tried to change the channel on the TV and was berated for his efforts by both Sergei and Andreas, the events being played out on the screen were lost on him. He sulked in the kitchen nursing an Erdinger weissbier as Andreas helped Sergei up from the sofa.

'Do you feel well enough to go now, Sergei?'

'I need to report back before someone actually notices my absence and they send out a search party. Anyway it's better that I get things in motion with the investigation into what happened to your family. It will all be contained in a file somewhere and I will make copies of them for you when I return to the MVD building back in Leningrad. There is an answer for everything within the filing cabinets at the ministry. That's how they like it, neatly labelled, conveniently forgotten and safely stored away. The sooner I go, the better it will be for both of us.'

Andreas helped him on with his raincoat and Sergei then took his leave in the silence of a mutual understanding. Liam watched from the balcony as Sergei gingerly made his way to the spot where he had parked his car on Virchow Strasse. He then began retracing his route back to the Eastern sector in his squalid Trabant which afforded him scant comfort as he had previously plied two crates of whiskey and six cartons of cigarettes under a travel blanket in the foot well on the passenger side which now strayed onto the seat with every bend he negotiated. He had to crane his head to avoid the protrusion of the driver's rear mirror which only rekindled the pain from his injury. He was prudent enough to ensure that he had a full tank of petrol as its engine spluttered to life and protested noisily through the tidy suburbs of Munich and on along the ring roads that led to an autobahn east. He had a high level pass of security clearance and his vehicle was only too familiar to the border guards even if his stints in the west had never lasted as long previous to this. He was careful to endear himself by providing western alcohol and cigarettes to those that manned the various checkpoints along his route as well as to the numerous department bosses who might have doubted his suitability for this task. His injury gave him much cause for discomfort and slowed his uneventful journey back to Bratislava and from there by charter flight with Aeroflot via Kaliningrad and on to Leningrad.

It was already snowing in Leningrad as his plane touched down. His remaining alcohol and cigarettes having been parcelled up with his hand luggage which had then been fast tracked through airport security. The taxi driver who took his fare knew better than to try and hoodwink him by taking the scenic route as his dishevelled condition only confirmed that he was no tourist. They sped along the Neva river where it flowed vociferously from its origins at Lake Ladoga, along the bog lands that began to drain as they approached the great city. Soon enough they crossed over the Griboyedov canal and past the church of the Saviour on Spilled Blood where his landlady was an impassioned member of the congregation. Not far now to Nevsky Prospekt, the grand thoroughfare of Leningrad where Sergei clung to an aspirational address, a door number too large for his shoe box of a domicile. He paid the driver and carried the remaining crate of whiskey and cigarettes through the ankle-high slush on the pavements and up to the imposing entrance door of his apartment building. He depressed any buzzer without studying them and the front door relented allowing him to move through the dimly lit foyer reaching in the dark with his free arm for the handrail of the worn stone staircase that led up to his floor. Sanctuary of a sorts greeted him. That and nothing else and in this he was more like Andreas than he had ever thought previously. For both men had up until recently been living alone and both had given up trying to make a place fit to ever entertain a prospective companion.

Sergei had gone through an ugly separation from his third wife after he was discovered having relations with a young internee, who it turned out was only using him as a stepping stone to further her own career. His much younger spouse, Svetlana had turfed him out of their three bedroom apartment on Winter Palace Square and his two young children, too vulnerable and easily swayed, viewed him through poisoned eyes that would take much groundwork to help reconcile. He now resided in the single men accommodation provided by the MVD for new incumbents. All in one room living with a bed that folded out from a wardrobe and a wall mirror that concealed a small meal table and an alcove door that opened out to provide a washstand with enough space to hide some extra chairs for that unexpected visitor who would never materialize. There was a communal toilet block and shower facilities further down the corridor from his room. This was his sanctuary of a sorts and it came to his aid just now as a place to finally collapse in after he had made his all too obligatory phone call to his department chief regarding his contact with the Volga German. He had gone to the west at their behest but they had no idea of his vested interest in Andreas, or any of the previous dealings between the two over the last forty-five years. Sergei had made sure he got the role over the heads of much younger more fastidious men. He had stayed sober just long enough before the interviews to impress his boss with valuable background knowledge and history of the Volga German community. He was viewed as the best candidate to help feather the caps back at the ministry in this new age that he was at odds with and which he had often very vocally disparaged in the numerous watering-holes within walking distance of his place of work.

Having outwardly done all that had been asked of him and for appearing to have no ulterior motive, Sergei even obtained a degree of sympathy for being injured in the line of duty so to speak. He was free once more to leaf unmolested through the plethora of displaced people files stored within the cellars of the Interior Ministry. This perfect environment for the maturation of fine wine was now perforated with bleak rows of locked storage cabinets housing the names of the millions of people who had 'disappeared' in the interests of state security. It was certain that for most, no marker, no footnote or headstone ever stood above their last resting place, but thanks to Soviet officialdom their names had been recorded in perpetuity and lay alphabetically somewhere within its vaulted arched recesses.

Sergei wouldn't try and sugar the pill for Andreas no matter what he found, it wasn't in his nature to hide the facts or dilute the reports of rough treatment no doubt meted out to Andreas's family at the hands of the NKVD. Rough treatment was widespread, expected and indiscriminate. Anything remotely seen as favouritism by the guards was reported and severely punished. The Soviet Ministry of Interior had inherited a blend of barbarism and officiousness from previous incarnations under the rule of the Tsars. Its apparatus moved at a pace which could be frustratingly slow for the individual, but it wasn't put in place to serve the individual, it was more concerned with the masses and particularly those troublesome minorities of which the rich tapestry of Russia was inherently formed. The MVD kept files on everybody, including himself, very probably. It was a state within the state, with its own internal police force which was a law unto itself.

It wasn't hard to find the file which contained the mass deportation of the Volga Germans from Strekerau and elsewhere. This dossier had been well thumbed recently as the profile of the plight of this particular ethnic group had been highlighted by questions recently raised by concerned members within the West German parliament in Bonn. Forty years and more after the events, the past had finally come back to haunt the Ministry of the Interior. It was time for the silent monolith to account for actions taken at a time of national crisis. The file was alphabetical by family surname and it didn't take long to find the Mensche family. Their fate had been catalogued long since using bleak typographical terminology to describe their transportation and ultimate destination. Kolyma gulag was about as far east as you could be dispatched within the Soviet penal system and the peninsula where it was situated was bounded on three sides by Arctic waters and was vulnerable to resultant winter temperatures that dropped below minus thirty-six degrees. If you survived the four thousand mile journey from Strekerau your life expectancy was just three weeks from the time of your arrival at the camp.

Huge deposits of gold and titanium had been discovered there as recently as the 1920s and Stalin was determined to harness this natural resource to fund his series of five year plans. Large numbers of political undesirables were drafted in as forced labour to dig in the unrelenting harshness of the Magadan (oblast) region where Kolyma was located. No prisoner up to this point, no matter what gender or age group was excused from the daily work quota expected at the mines. To make matters worse the camp was run by politically motivated prison guards many of whom were German communists who relished the prospect of welcoming the fifth columnist

Volga Germans. These German-speaking guards had free reign to run amok taking their pick of the new arrivals and it would appear that Andreas's sisters suffered from their particular brand of cruelty.

The official report is outwardly innocuous in its terminology and handling of the fates of Andreas's three older siblings. It offers tacit eyewitness accounts as to his sisters' relative good health and condition on reaching the gulag. That they survived the journey in the first place was symbolic of their tenacity and forbearance. Reading between the lines it became clear that Andreas's sisters were earmarked early on by the network of communist German guards trafficking girls for sex on board the gulag trains. They were pointed out and given sufficient rations along the route under the cloak of kindness from a cynically sympathetic quarter who spoke a common language. The sisters witnessed the deaths of so many other girls simply because they were deemed of having no physical value that could be cashed in once the Kolyma gulag had been reached. The two twins, Katja and Elena, along with their younger sister Rosa, shared these extra rations with their parents and all five of them reached the Kolyma gulag alive. Upon arrival they were separated from their parents and confined in an annexe hut attached to the barrack quarters. They were to be excused the daily roll-call and they would rarely if ever be seen again in the compound of the camp within daylight hours. Their existence relied on their usefulness, their own resourcefulness and their obituaries shed a little light on just how long they were able to stand the systematic sexual abuse by the guards. It was only a matter of time before they were finally dispensed with. Tossed aside with the same scant regard afforded to lemon peel on the grass.

Their parents would pass the barracks every day on their way out of the camp to the mines. Anguish soon replaced any lost shades of hopeful expectancy by glancing over at the huts for a face in the window or any sign that their girls might still be able to contact them. They shut out the screams and cries that they thought they might have heard and concentrated instead on becoming part of the hollowed-out myriad shapes growing fainter with each day that passed, quickly outliving their usefulness. It was as if their spirits had already departed their bodily husks and it would just be a matter of days before either one collapsed first. Patreous internalized his feelings and hardly ever spoke to his wife again as they were segregated until they joined the work details each day. The loss of his girls, the mine, the relentless ever-stretching days of hardship soon broke him completely and his health quickly deserted him.

Patreous Mensche, born March 17th 1904, Strekerau autonomous district within the Volga region. Age at transportation 38. Married. Occupation:bank manager. Transported to the Kolyma gulag in the Magadan oblast region of eastern Siberia. Age at death, 39. Cause of death: Malnutrition/hypothermia/dysentery.

Lottie Mensche, born July 14th 1905, Strekerau autonomous district within the Volga region. Age at transportation 37. Married. Occupation:housewife. Transported to the Kolyma gulag in the Magadan oblast region of eastern Siberia.Age at death, 37. Cause of death: Malnutrition/exhaustion/hypothermia.

Katja Mensche, born August 12th 1923, Strekerau autonomous district within the Volga region. Age at transportation 19. Single. Occupation: receptionist at Strekerau cooperative. Transported to the Kolyma gulag in the Magadan oblast region of eastern Siberia. Age at death, 20. Cause of death: Suicide.

Elena Mensche, born August 12th 1923, Strekerau autonomous district within the Volga region. Age at transportation 19. Single. Occupation: student teacher at Strekerau preparatory school. Transported to the Kolyma gulag in the Magadan oblast region of eastern Siberia. Age at death, 20. Cause of death: Suicide.

Rosa Mensche, born November 5th 1925, Strekerau autonomous district within the Volga region. Age at transportation 17. Single. Occupation: scholar at Strekerau college. Transported to the Kolyma gulag in the Magadan oblast region of eastern Siberia. Age at death, 17. Cause of death: double pneumonia.

There it was. Andreas would finally know the truth and Sergei would get the title deeds for a parcel of land within the Strekerau district to build his retirement home. But even he shuddered to think of the tragedy so coldly recorded here and the lack of humanity portrayed on this page. He could see that Andreas had twin sisters who very probably died together, in a pact perhaps to escape their ordeal. What they must have endured was beyond his comprehension. The parents probably didn't even hear about their daughters' deaths as the girls were hidden from them on entering the camp. What was it that struck him so hard on reading this account? He had read other files many times before, he had even instructed those who typed them to be as succinct as possible so as not to leak too much detail to prying eyes. Andreas had been right, previously people were just pawns in the game to be moved around the board by Sergei and the department. Faceless numbers of ethnic groups, troublemakers, dissidents and enemies of the motherland. But this family? What threat did they pose to the security of the Soviet Union when taken as a whole?

A new era even for him, required new thinking. Alcohol wasn't the answer this time to drown out the uncertainty of what he had played an active role in. He could tell himself that he was busy fighting the German invader when this particular family were uprooted and sent to hell, but how many other families did he consign to such a similar fate in his time at the ministry? He could try and convince himself that he was right in holding a grudge for forty-five years against Andreas up until this moment. He had considered him to be a traitor to the Soviet Union for daring to take up arms with the Germans. He could see now that Andreas's name would certainly have been included below the others but for the choice he had made and paid dearly for with his own incarceration which lasted until 1953. Sergei would never previously have lost a night's sleep over it before getting to know Andreas. Everything was different now that he could personalize the family with the man.

His own treatment at the hands of the Russian army, the NKVD and the penal battalion he had been consigned to had made him a bitter man. He could see now that the ministry had used his bitterness as a weapon against the vulnerable, the minority groups, moulding him into the callous being he knew himself to be. His failings were his own doing, if he had made more of an effort to stay sober and not to stray, then perhaps he would still have a family to go home to. Andreas didn't have that option and his life ever after was blighted with pain and remorse. Sergei was so wrapped up in himself that he blamed everyone else around him for his own failings and for the things that never went his way. The patriotism he blindly hid behind was his shield against change and uncertainty. The ideal he had believed in had been corrupted by the worms, the functionaries, long ago and millions of innocent lives that had been lost had no one left to speak for them. Yes, the new era was coming, the old guard were dropping away, the blood on their hands now shrouded where they lay in hollow accolades and false glory. Change was dripping down slowly in the Soviet Union as the wartime generation began to die and thin back sufficiently enough taking with them the silent regrets, daring feats and painful misdemeanours. Sergei knew he had been duped into thinking what he did at the ministry was for the benefit of the Soviet people. He was the station master of the death trains in everything but name, making sure that they had run on time and that everything had been correctly catalogued. He was guilty because he hadn't cared up until this moment. He would remain guilty but he, as far as he could make out, was still on the winning side and all dark deeds would for the present remain under the red carpet. He had shown that he was still capable of influential manipulation by attaining the Volga mission to seek out Andreas but this was because he had been motivated by greed and that had enabled him to focus and stay sober at least until that mission was completed. Strangely drink now was the last thing he craved, what he really wanted was a way to atone to Andreas for some of the hurt he had caused him.

The Honecker visit was indeed viewed as a thaw in East West relations, the fallout, pace and progression from which nobody could have foreseen. Some three hundred thousand exiled Volga Germans had found refuge within the severed entity that was the two Germanys and beyond. They were grudgingly tolerated but were viewed with suspicion as outsiders invariably are and many had found it hard to assimilate and sought travel permits to join the well established Volga communities both in north and south America. None of their descendants or dependents had expected to receive an open invitation from the Soviet government to take repossession of the tracts of lands that had been so harshly confiscated from them in 1941. It was only two weeks after Sergei had so bluntly intruded into their lives that Andreas received a letter of notification bearing a Soviet postage mark on his doormat. It contained an outline proposal for his reinstatement to the title deeds in Strekerau that had been previously confiscated from his family. It went into great detail acknowledging their subsequent unjustified and unlawful imprisonment and apologised unreservedly for the hardship and devastation that they had suffered before their untimely deaths. Andreas always knew that they had died in a gulag somewhere but to have it confirmed after forty-five years in this fashion was still painful. He poured fresh coffee for both himself and Liam and then made more toast as he wanted to digest everything in his midst. He then passed the letter over for Liam to read.

'Jeez that comrade fuck really came through for you after all, Andreas!'

'It says here that I will receive a formal invitation along with the title deeds in person from the agent who was dealing with my case,' remarked Andreas.

Sergei returned to Virchow Strasse two days later. On this final occasion he was fully in control of all his faculties. He presented Andreas with the formal letter of apology signed by the General Secretary of the Soviet Politburo. He also gave him a copy of the page from the Strekerau deportation file that concerned his family as well as the title deeds to the Strekerau land owned by the Mensche family. Sergei embellished the limited contents of the file by answering in-depth Andreas's many probing questions. Sergei was the best person to give this harrowing account as he now felt like a time-served opponent who had obtained an ever increasing modicum of respect for his adversary. Andreas sat by his piano as if it gave him sustenance to listen to what befell his parents and his sisters in full. Perhaps the piano was his alpha and omega, his full stop as every time he played it he had done so out of memory for a family member. A piece of music to sum up the fading characteristics of a much loved sibling. A soothing balm perchance for him and those others passing who might hear it from the hallway or even out in the street and who had also lost much in the past.

Liam knew the relevance of this closure and sat at the table listening to Sergei drily account for things that happened a long time ago. Liam looked around the room and for the first time realised that Andreas had no photographs of any family member on show. He had nothing but the resonance of his playing to help conjure their images to life. How much more important it was for music to transport a person to a formative place in their mind's eye. In that place they remain the same, forever full of love and vitality, accompanied by some of the most personal music. Andreas had never doubted that his family wouldn't return and he had closed off many avenues of pleasure in his life as a result of the stabbing hurt he had borne all these years, which to many made him appear miserable, but Liam knew better. Liam had come to know he was just someone from an older generation burdened by grief and moulded by hardship and up until recently that had obscured his outlook on life. It was never going to be easy to digest the facts about what befell his family and circumstances had moved on to such an extent that it was now impossible to imagine the torment they had suffered. But the Soviet proposal offered a new beginning if Andreas thought he was still up to it and Liam waited for his friend to come to a decision.

Andreas allowed for Sergei's last words to wane and then began playing the opening bars of Symphony No. 5 – 2nd Movement by Tchaikovsky. The slow build up performed beautifully on the Bechstein for all three to hear. He played it right the way through filling the apartment with an air of cultivated expectancy, before speaking as it began to die away.

'Liam, I want you to give him back his pistol. Mind that you make sure the magazine is empty before you hand it over to him. I know it sounds crazy, but just do it for me.'

Liam got up and went into his bedroom and retrieved the weapon from his rucksack that he took to work every day. He reluctantly handed it to Sergei who for once had nothing sarcastic to say to Liam. Andreas then approached his former tormentor.

'Sergei, this is all you will get from me. What you do with it is up to you.

You can try and kill us both but where would that get you? This is the only thing you are entitled to from me, the only thing that belongs to you. The deeds are mine by right and you know in that black heart of yours that you deserve absolutely nothing. Our duel is finally over and I would appreciate it if in your future dealings with me that you would do me the courtesy of conducting yourself in the manner of a dead person.'

It was all Sergei could manage to secrete the weapon in his overcoat, ashen-faced, in stunned silence. It was Liam who led him to the door and who ushered him out into the communal hallway.

Today there are 597,212 ethnic Germans and one particular Irishman living in the Volga region of southern Russia.

16

1943~1953

The completion of the the Syr Darya dam stole nearly ten years of my life. Years that should have been filled with the joy of familial milestones were instead pock-marked by infilled screed cement craters and bastions of riven steel supports diverting the waters of the Aral Sea. This involved outdoor work in an exposed location, within a region that can experience four seasons in one day and for most of us no provision for the elements and no respite from the rush to complete the work. Farhadstroy had budgeted for longer but, given the ever-swelling numbers of German prisoners passing through their hands, work on the dam reached saturation point in 1945 and was completed years ahead of schedule and just before Stalin's death. Events outside were anathema to us and the conflict we had once been so devoted to often seemed as remote as the crescent moon which lit our path to the dam. We had expunged the inevitable defeat and collapse of Germany from our thoughts. We had witnessed the resurgence of the Soviet Union firsthand as we were now a committed part of that recovery in constructing this colossus. The harsh manual work in such biting conditions took with it over two hundred lives, some fell, some were crushed, some drowned and some took their own lives out of sheer despair. To others the dam became their reason to live, the focus of their own existence and they would obsess about it constantly. They embellished, often exaggerating the importance of their role in constructing it beyond their waking hours. They had customised their own work tools and equipment and pointed out to others the parts they had proudly fashioned or worked on. It seeped into their daily lives, their conversations at mealtimes and before lights-out every evening. The dam gave them a reason to be as it grew ever bigger around us, enveloping our every thought. We left signatures on the drying cement as testament to our being alive and as proof that we had been part of something positive other than just existing. Daily quotas had been met and surpassed and pride had grown up in the work carried out.

Yet even in this austere and attritional environment a hierarchy of sorts had been formed and it was this that for the better part of the first four years had saved my life. I was assigned to a team of twelve men including Ullman, who by now was in an unassailable position of authority from which he could bribe the guards to ensure that our daily work targets were always met. It was gallingly obvious that we were being spared the harshest of chores and this began to provoke a great deal of resentment among the others and was especially apparent at mealtimes. The Japanese had been true to their word and we began to receive improved rations, fresh vegetables from the village market and on occasion, even butchered cuts of meat from the surrounding goat herds. We now ate apart and at different times from the rest of the men, as our improved menu would instil a riot. Soon the twelve of us stood out dramatically from the rest of the prisoners. Our skin conditions began to clear and we earned the sobriquet of 'cannibals' as some of the others were convinced that we could only have put on weight by eating human flesh.

It was without a shadow of doubt Ullman's enterprise and ingenuity that spared my life. Those few who were drawn to his circle and accepted by him were instantly better off than their fellow prisoners. He was a one-off and saw something in me, an unsullied honesty perhaps that he realised early on he could trust. He instinctively knew how to tailor for people's needs with what he could reasonably provide and still hope to make a profit from. Business was his religion and more often than not I wondered what set of circumstances must have occurred for him to have ended up here. With his profit-making credentials I was sure he could have been of more use to the country in the financial sector as opposed to soldiering. But then every one of these shockingly disparate band of souls once had reasons as to why they joined up. All sense of which now lost in this hostile place where we have been condemned to pay for making the wrong choices.

Colonel Rokkosovsky was a Russian rarity in that he couldn't be bought no matter what the price or enticement. He was a recuperating war hero who missed the frenetic excitement engendered at the front. Ullman had tried from the off to curry favour with the Colonel to no avail. He was marble man, cold and resentful to those of us whom he considered cowards for not having died fighting. The direction of the conflict was now going irrevocably in Russia's favour and Rokkosovsy knew that he was going to miss out on the big finale in Berlin. He had been an NCO and risen up through the ranks surviving the many purges on the officer corps within the army by Stalin. He was viewed as reliable if unremarkable which probably saved his skin and his subsequent wounding had earned him credibility as well as medals for heroism, plaudits and ultimately the hollow promotion to the command of this gulag in the place of exile he deeply resented. Rokkosovsky seethed at the bonhomie now being openly displayed between his prison guards and Ullman. He knew about the card schools, the bartering and the illicit trading between Ullman and the Japanese that the guards helped negotiate for a slice of the action. But what could he do? Corruption was expected within the Soviet military, it was how things got done, but a German was quietly running the show behind his back. Rokkosovsky decided to germinate the seeds of resentment that were manifest within the German ranks. He gathered the senior German officers who still held sway with what could only now be called the workforce as opposed to soldiers. He berated them for not taking charge of a growing situation which posed a threat to the hierarchy of brittle German command over their men. It was up to the Germans to put their house in order as he was powerless because Ullman held such sway over his own prison guards. A Luftwaffe Colonel, Stefan Ubrecht then stepped forward and suggested that a watch be put on Ullman and his cronies so that they might be intercepted whilst dealing in their black market activities. Ubrecht had previously never shown any vestige of a backbone especially proving ineffective when in charge of the flak air defences in and around Stalingrad. He like so many other Luftwaffe ground personnel had been stranded within the cauldron as the Soviets closed their ring of steel. Ubrecht had resented Ullman from the start as Ullman wasn't much given to taking orders now that all authority had broken down. It was resentment mixed with jealousy over Ullman's tactics for survival.

On the only occasion I was smuggled out of the gulag our judgement was so clouded at the prospect that we never once entertained the idea that we might have been followed. Rokkosovsky was impressed enough with Ubrecht's servility to let him take control of apprehending us using fair means or foul. Ubrecht's adjutant had infiltrated one of Ullman's many card schools and was now acting on a tip off from a disgruntled watch tower guard who had lost heavily to Ullman at cards the previous evening. Ullman and I had earlier been handed written instructions whilst on our daily perambulation by one of the more malleable guards. We were to leave our hut after curfew and our path would be unimpeded. We would be met at the perimeter gate at ten thirty p.m. by the Japanese. We then accompanied them into the Japanese compound without hindrance from the Soviet guards. The informality we found there was both tangible and conducive and in complete contrast to the squalor we had been accustomed to. Nagia Taramachi greeted us outside his quarters. He said how pleased he was with our trading partnership and that by way of thanks he wished to take us both to one of the designated brothels in the village of Begavat for the Japanese officers. Ullman's eyes lit up at the prospect, dropping his usual sanguine disposition at the thought of being with a woman. It was an unreal experience being able to walk out of the camp and on down the road to Begavat. I had seen the village many times on my marches to and from the dam, but never imagined that I would be able to visit there. A starlit evening guided our way through the outhouses and livestock pens and on to the dust track that led to the village. We had no idea that we were being watched. Rokkosovsky had given permission for Ubrecht and six others to leave the gulag by the main entrance and tail us from a discreet distance and Ubrecht was too bent on retribution to have notions of his own escape as he didn't have the imagination to contemplate such a daring thing.

The brothel was conveniently located in an outhouse at the rear of an undertakers where all nefarious activities could be assuredly transacted and transpire undisturbed. I vaguely remember the wicker basket coffin lids that were neatly stacked on the shelves above our heads upon entering. If only we hadn't been so distracted then we would have realised that it was the perfect spot for an ambush. But our groins had ruled our heads and soon our bellies were full of rice wine and we had our complement of native women to choose from. Ullman took the opportunity to smoke some opium with the girl of his choice to heighten the experience even more. I lost my virginity that same evening. I lost it in such haste to a girl whose face I will never forget as she smiled at me throughout. She chose me, I swear I was in her hands before I knew what was going on and she led me to the room she must have operated from and she seemed to take away the pains of the world with her kisses as she led me to her straw cot bed. She taught me how to kiss and I was a willing fool only too eager to do her bidding. Her hair smelled of crushed black cardamom seeds and her skin was resinous to touch. For those few hours I was transported to another place where I could lose myself in the folds of her skin and the musk she generated mixed with my own sweat until at last she let me fall asleep in her arms.

It was Ullman who woke us both. He had a slightly rouge complexion mixed with the self-satisfied grin on his face that I had come to know. He shook his head knowingly at me as if admonishing a kid brother and then offered us both a swig of his rice wine before saying that we had better make tracks soon back to the camp. The four Japanese companions were still occupied elsewhere as we said goodbye to the girls and their madam who by this time was smoking a long clay pipe by a large open fire, rocking contentedly, her pockets fatter with our coins. We made it out into the starlit alleyway and on for a few hundred metres before something disturbed Ullman and shook me from my waking reverie.

It was no fair contest, it was so stacked against us, but we put up a fight just the same. Ubrecht the coward looked on from the shadows where he belonged. Six against two. Two who were the worse for Saki and opiates and who had already had a surfeit of strenuous exercise that evening only now to be coldly confronted by these silent assailants. They concentrated their attack on Ullman and four of them had him on the ground only to be thrown off by him. He was up on his feet again brushing himself down and able to parry their blows with his own which accounted for two of them straight away. They stayed down moaning in the dust which now clouded them. It was so unnerving that this was all happening in silence as if our attackers were under strict instructions to remain quiet. I recognised the one who had singled me out, he was about my size and went by the name of Kupke, a mealy-mouthed Hitler Youth who I had never got on with. Kupke swung at me and hit the air where I had ducked and he was sent reeling by me as I managed to thump him in the stomach. I launched at him while he was winded and couldn't help but land blows onto his head and he too fell to the dust in submission. I waited for him to get up and then heard the moan which I knew was Ullman. Ubrecht had stealthily crept up on him and stabbed him in the back as he defended himself against the three others. Ubrecht had used a knife that Ullman had fashioned from his own kiln bearing his own hallmark. The other three now rushed him and he was soon under a barrage of their blows and I couldn't make him out any more. Ubrecht prized them off his body and coldly leaned over to wipe his knife down Ullman's overalls. I was transfixed until Kupke must have come up from behind me and rendered me unconscious.

I remained in the gulag infirmary for two months with a skull fracture and three broken ribs. I had plenty of time to reflect on why they hadn't murdered me too, along with everything else that had happened. I slumped into a lethargy of selfishness that I could not shake, knowing that my guardian was dead. My connections to him meant that I was now exposed and vulnerable but still alive. He was dead and now lay in a mass grave outside the camp. No ceremony, no witnesses, just a night burial into a pit of quicklime bulging with other crumpled corpses. How redolent this task was in reflecting the manner of his death and the cowards who had murdered him. I had lost yet another soul who had opened his life up to me and protected me, nurtured me and made this place that bit more palatable. From this point on I would have to watch my back and use some of the resolve and tenacity I had learnt from Ullman to survive.

Colonel Rokkosovsky was imperious after the slaying of Ullman. He took steps to ensure that there would be no further interactions between the Japanese and the German prisoners. The contraband economy had been extinguished and Ullman's kiln had been discovered and broken up. The corrupted soviet guards had been replaced with freshly untainted recruits who were warned of the penalties for fraternizing with the enemy in any way. The steady influx of new prisoners soon expunged any lingering memories about Ullman's black market operation. In time I was reintroduced to my fellow inmates. I was given a bunk in a different hut with a new work detail to grow attached to. I was resented of course at first, but even that gave way to apathy over time as reasons for resentment always do when they go unfed. Eventually my weight began to drop away pathetically and my flesh started to fold back over my bones once more. Some of my molars came loose and fell out as I ate the meagre rations and I began to notice how my lips were peeling raw and chapped from lack of vitamins. In a matter of months you couldn't point me out from the crowd of other undernourished specimens who just about existed this side of death's door. Memories fade but the scars still linger and hunger just made you forgetful, you focus on the minutiae of what you can eat, you fixate on anything that might ease the pain in your stomach.

By 1949 the dam was nearing completion and a fuss had to be seen to be made of it in the name of the comrade leader Stalin. By 1949 I had long since given my life over to the physical reparation of helping to complete this great project. I had almost forgotten my past until I was suddenly reminded of it at the opening ceremony. The regional communist party officials were fighting over the rights of ownership to the dam as it straddled both Uzbekistan and Kazakhstan. Duel ownership was agreed and this compromise would later prove to be a hindrance to the dam's efficiency. A rostrum had been purpose-built by us for foreign press, local dignitaries and party apparachiks. It was bedecked in reams of the soviet red material which followed Stalin ubiquitously wherever he went. We were given new boiler suits by the Farhadstroy corporation and would form an honour guard for the visit of the great leader. His team of bodyguards had vetted us beforehand and for some unknown reason I was chosen to be in the front row upon his arrival. I was emaciated but honed in such a way as to look the part for a parade that would be covered and relayed by newsreels throughout the Soviet Union and beyond. I remember thinking about Stalin's appearance upon arrival. He wore a drab, if freshly ironed, peasant outfit that was in stark contrast to the plumage of his entourage with their highly decorated uniforms. His appearance gave no hint as to why such a wearer could possibly be the focal point of a nation. He emerged from the back of a modestly unmarked black car. No fuss or theatricals, just him and two hefty NKVD protectors. A second car pulled up in quick succession and numerous officials and hangers-on decanted out to follow his progress down our line of welcome and on to the rostrum at the mouth of the dam. In an unscripted moment Stalin walked over to me. I was too dejected to react, too slow to acknowledge him as he stared at me for the longest time, or so it seemed. So this was his enemy, no, this was more. I was now his captive, subject to his every caprice, his slave and he wanted to get a look at me. I think he must have thought I couldn't speak Russian as he turned around and asked for an interpreter. Another flunky stood in front of me and I recognised him as instantly as he did me. He shook his head before speaking.

'Comrade Stalin if I may say, you have no use for me here. I can safely vouch that this prisoner speaks fluent Russian.'

His words tailed off as my interest began to reignite with the recognition of his voice. It was Sergei Ivanov.

'Really, Ivanov? Out of all these people, you know that this one speaks Russian?'

I looked into Stalin's eyes and saw my own mortality reflected back in the dark pools of infamy that have swallowed up the lives of countless others. I saw the eyes of a gambler, a street murderer, a thief and a survivor. He took ages to blink as he in turn studied me. He had smiling eyes that belied his true intentions and made the subject of that intention all the more vulnerable.

'This is someone you might remember comrade leader. This is none other than the Volga German sniper!'

Once more he took me in, this time even more intensely, he appeared to even smell me animatedly. He called for a photographer to be allowed through the throng of the cordon and asked for a picture of me to be taken with him. I stood at least a foot taller than him even though I crouched through malnutrition and the contrast to his girth and highly polished boots must have made the oddest picture. I was strangely reminded of the photographs I had seen back in the hunting lodges I had visited with my father. Those lifelessly defiant stags hung on a meat hook beside the innocuously proud hunter. I was the cornered game and he was the squire intent on capturing the moment.

'Take a picture Sukarov. Take one and print it in the next edition of Pravda along with the pictures of this mighty dam. Let everyone see my beneficence. Let them see how close I got to the very thing that wanted my death on a platter for the fascist monster to drool over! Let them see that I can forgive my enemies and that given time they can be rehabilitated and be of use to our motherland. Yes Surakov, send a message here to our people. We are an inclusive society, we forgive if you prove worthy of our forgiveness.'

With those emphatic remarks he stood beside me, close enough for my lice to have jumped onto his clean skin and to have infested his unruly moustache. Sergei Ivanov glared at me all the while as if he couldn't get over the fact that our paths had crossed yet again, only this time it was completely out of his control and it almost made me smile. Presently the comrade leader was whisked away to the rostrum and completed the formalities by opening the floodgates that held back the weight of the Aral Sea.

I was treated differently from that day forward. Colonel Rokkosovsky had been given strict instructions to increase my rations which he was very reluctant to act upon, no doubt, but which he was coerced into by the local party headquarters. The photograph that was circulated widely had done the trick, further enhancing Stalin's patriarchal image, a forgiving parent to an unruly nation made up of wayward minorities. He had created this propaganda opportunity and by doing so had inadvertently saved my life. The war had ended four years earlier but he was a master at injecting new blood into shelf-worn remedies. My currency within the gulag had risen to the extent that I became de facto leader of the German prisoners, their spokesman and their arbitrator. This lasted for the remainder of Stalin's time on earth which ended abruptly in 1953. It was now ten years after Stalingrad had fallen and over two hundred and fifty thousand axis men at arms had been captured in the fallen citadel. The forced march East, the lack of winter clothing, being shot out of hand, the want of anything to eat, the need for medicines of any kind, all these factors had played their part. Nine thousand German prisoners were left alive and were finally allowed to go home after the death of Stalin and at the behest and intervention of the new German Chancellor Willy Brandt.

I no longer had a home to return to in the Soviet Union. I had no community on the banks of the Volga left to welcome me back. I had no choice but to return to Germany with the other survivors and take my chances in a new country still coming to terms with its past, only to be reminded of it by the influx of these ghosts of the Reich.